Expo 58

Expo 58

JONATHAN COE

VIKING
an imprint of
PENGUIN BOOKS

VIKING

Published by the Penguin Group
Penguin Books Ltd, 80 Strand, London WC2R ORL, England
Penguin Group (USA) Inc., 375 Hudson Street, New York, New York 10014, USA
Penguin Group (Canada), 90 Eglinton Avenue East, Suite 700, Toronto, Ontario, Canada M4P 2Y3
(a division of Pearson Penguin Canada Inc.)
Penguin Ireland, 25 St Stephen's Green, Dublin 2, Ireland (a division of Penguin Books Ltd)
Penguin Group (Australia), 707 Collins Street, Melbourne, Victoria 3008, Australia
(a division of Pearson Australia Group Pty Ltd)
Penguin Books India Pvt Ltd, 11 Community Centre, Panchsheel Park, New Delhi – 110 017, India
Penguin Group (NZ), 67 Apollo Drive, Rosedale, Auckland 0632, New Zealand
(a division of Pearson New Zealand Ltd)
Penguin Books (South Africa) (Pty) Ltd, Block D, Rosebank Office Park,
181 Jan Smuts Avenue, Parktown North, Gauteng 2193, South Africa

Penguin Books Ltd, Registered Offices: 80 Strand, London WC2R ORL, England

www.penguin.com

First published 2013
001

Copyright © Jonathan Coe, 2013

The moral right of the author has been asserted

Typeset in 12/14.75 pt Dante by Palimpsest Book Production Ltd, Falkirk, Stirlingshire
Printed in Great Britain by Clays Ltd, St Ives plc

A CIP catalogue record for this book is available from the British Library

HARDBACK ISBN: 978–0–670–92371–7
TRADE PAPERBACK ISBN: 978–0–670–92372–4

www.greenpenguin.co.uk

Penguin Books is committed to a sustainable
future for our business, our readers and our planet.
This book is made from Forest Stewardship
Council™ certified paper.

ALWAYS LEARNING   **PEARSON**

To Dad
who never got to finish it

Contents

'You know, I'm half inclined to believe that there's some rational explanation to all this.'

Naunton Wayne to Basil Radford in *The Lady Vanishes* (1938)

'By opening day, the American pavilion had been molded into an espionage weapon against the Soviet Union and its allies.'

Robert W. Rydell, *World of Fairs: The Century-of-Progress Expositions*

We're all excited about Brussels

In a note dated 3 June 1954, the Belgian Ambassador in London conveyed an invitation to Her Majesty's Government of Great Britain: an invitation to take part in a new World's Fair which the Belgians were calling the 'Exposition Universelle et Internationale de Bruxelles 1958'.

Five months later, on 24 November 1954, Her Majesty's Government's formal acceptance of the invitation was presented to the Ambassador, on the occasion of a visit to London by Baron Moens de Fernig, the Commissioner-General appointed by the Belgian government to undertake the work of organizing the exposition.

It would be the first such event since the end of the Second World War. It would be held at a time when the European nations involved in that war were moving ever closer towards peaceful cooperation and even union; and at a time, conversely, when political tensions between the NATO and Soviet bloc countries were at their height. It would be held at a time of unprecedented optimism about recent advances in the field of nuclear science; and at a time when that optimism was tempered by unprecedented anxiety about what might happen if these same advances were put to destructive, rather than benign, use. Symbolizing this great paradox, and standing at the very heart of the exhibition site, was to be an enormous metal structure known as the Atomium; conceived and designed by a British-born Belgian engineer called André Waterkeyn, it would stand more than one hundred metres tall and resemble, in its shape, the unit cell of an iron crystal magnified 165 billion times.

In the original letter of invitation, the purpose of the exhibition was described thus:

to facilitate a comparison of the multifarious activities of different peoples in the fields of thought, art, science, economic affairs and technology. Its method is to present an all-embracing view of the present achievements, spiritual or material, and the further aspirations of a rapidly changing world. Its final aim is to contribute to the development of a genuine unity of mankind, based upon respect for human personality.

History does not record how the British Secretary of State for Foreign Affairs reacted when he first read these impressive words. But Thomas's guess was that, seeing four years of stress, argument and expense ahead of him, he let the invitation slip from his fingers, put his hands to his forehead and muttered: 'Oh no . . . Those bloody Belgians . . .'

Thomas was a quiet man. That was his distinguishing feature. He worked at the Central Office of Information on Baker Street, and behind his back, his colleagues sometimes referred to him as 'Gandhi' because there were days when it was believed that he had taken a vow of silence. At the same time, and also behind his back, some of the secretaries had been heard to call him 'Gary' because he reminded them of Gary Cooper, while a rival faction knew him as 'Dirk', on account of a closer resemblance, in their eyes, to Dirk Bogarde. It could be agreed, at any rate, that Thomas was handsome, but he would have been astonished if anyone had ever told him this and, once in possession of the knowledge, he would have had no idea what to do with it. Gentleness and humility were the qualities which first struck people upon meeting him and it was only later (if at all) that they would begin to suspect a certain self-assurance, bordering on arrogance, lying beneath them. In the meantime, he was most often described as a 'decent sort' and 'the unassuming, dependable type'.

He had worked at the COI for fourteen years, starting in 1944, when it was still called the Ministry of Information and he was only eighteen years old. He had started out as a post boy, and worked his way up surely – but very, very slowly – to his present rank as junior copywriter. Now he was thirty-two, and spent most of his working days drafting pamphlets on public health and safety, advising pedestrians of the best way to cross the road and cold-sufferers of the best way to avoid spreading germs in public places. Some days he looked back on his childhood and thought about his start in life (Thomas was the son of a pub landlord) and considered that he was doing very well; other days he found his work tedious and contemptible, and it felt as though he had been doing the same things for years, and he couldn't wait to find some way of moving on.

Brussels had livened things up a bit, that was certain. The COI had been given overall responsibility for the content of the British pavilion at Expo 58 and this had immediately led to a frenzy of head-scratching and soul-searching around that maddening, elusive topic of 'Britishness'. What did it mean to be British, in 1958? Nobody seemed to know. Britain was steeped in tradition, everybody agreed upon that: its traditions, its pageantry, its ceremony were admired and envied all over the world. At the same time, it was mired in the past: scared of innovation, riddled with archaic class distinctions, in thrall to a secretive and untouchable Establishment. Which way were you supposed to look, when defining Britishness? Forwards, or backwards?

It was a difficult conundrum; and the Foreign Secretary was not the only person to be found sitting at his desk, in the years leading up to Expo 58, muttering, 'Those bloody Belgians . . .' on long afternoons when the answers did not seem to come easily.

Some positive steps were taken. James Gardner, many of whose ideas had proved so inspiring at the Festival of Britain seven years earlier, was engaged as designer of the pavilion; and before long he came up with a geometric exterior which, by general consent, caught just the right combination of modernity and continuity. It had been allocated a very favourable position in the

Exposition park on the Heysel plateau just north of Brussels. But what should go inside it? Millions of visitors were expected to flock to the Expo, from all over the world, including the African and Soviet bloc countries. The Americans and the Soviets were bound to produce national displays on a massive scale. What sort of self-image did the British want to project, given the opportunity of such a vast global stage, and such a curious and diverse audience?

Nobody appeared to know the answer. But by common consent, Gardner's pavilion was going to be a thing of beauty: that was beyond dispute. And, if it was any consolation, there was one other thing that everybody was agreed about: the pub. Visitors to the Expo would need to be fed and watered, and if the national character was going to be expressed at all, this meant that somehow or other, next to the pavilion, they were going to have to build a British pub. And just in case anybody missed the point, the name of the pub would leave no room for ambiguity: it was going to be called the Britannia.

This afternoon, in the middle of February 1958, Thomas was checking the proofs of a pamphlet he had helped to put together for sale outside the pavilion: 'Images of the United Kingdom'. There was a small body of text, interspersed with attractive wood-cut illustrations by Barbara Jones. Thomas was checking the French version.

'*Le Grand-Bretagne vit de son commerce,*' he read. '*Outre les marchandises, la Grande-Bretagne fait un commerce important de "services": transports maritimes et aériens, tourisme, service bancaire, services d'assurance. La "City" de Londres, avec ses célèbres institutions comme la Banque d'Angleterre, la Bourse et la grand compagnie d'assurance "Lloyd's", est depuis longtemps la plus grand centre financier du monde.*'

Thomas was just wondering whether the *la* in that last sentence was a mistake, and should be changed to the masculine, when his telephone rang, and Susan from the switchboard gave him the surprising news that Mr Cooke, Director of Exhibitions, wanted to see him in his office. At four o'clock that very afternoon.

The door was ajar, and Thomas could hear voices on the other side. Smooth, softly spoken, well-educated voices. The voices of Establishment men. He raised his hand to knock on the door, but fear made him hesitate. For the last ten years or more, he had been surrounded by voices like this at work: so why was he hesitating now, his hand almost shaking as it hovered over the wood panelling? Why was this situation any different?

It was strange how the fear never really seemed to go away.

'Come in!' one of the voices called, in response to his over-deferential tap.

Thomas took a deep breath, pushed the door open and stepped inside. It was the first time he had ever been admitted to Mr Cooke's office. It was predictably grand: a hushed, calming environment of oak furniture and red leather, with two enormous sash windows reaching almost to the floor, offering a distant view of the windswept treetops of Regent's Park. Mr Cooke was seated behind his desk, and his deputy, Mr Swaine, was seated to the right of him, next to the window. Standing before the fireplace, his grey-pink bald patch unforgivingly reflected in the gilt-framed mirror, was a man Thomas didn't recognize. His dark worsted suit and stiff white collar gave little away: they were of a piece, however, with the navy-blue tie, discreetly embellished with what could confidently be identified as the crest of an Oxford or Cambridge college.

'Ah, Foley.' Mr Cooke rose to his feet and held out a welcoming hand. Thomas shook it weakly, more disconcerted than ever by this display of warmth. 'Thank you for dropping by. Extremely decent of you. Lots on your plate today, I'm sure. You know Mr Swaine, of course? And this is Mr Ellis, of the Foreign Office.'

The unfamiliar man stepped forward and offered his hand. The grip was wary, lacking conviction.

'Good to meet you, Foley. Cooke has been telling me a lot about you.'

Thomas didn't see how this could possibly be true. He returned the handshake and nodded helplessly, lost for words. Finally he sat down, in response to a gesture of invitation from Mr Cooke.

'Now then,' said Mr Cooke, facing him from across the desk. 'Mr Swaine tells me that you've been doing good work on the Brussels project. Excellent work.'

'Thank you,' Thomas mumbled, inclining his head towards Mr Swaine in a movement that was somewhere between a nod and a bow. Raising his voice slightly, in the knowledge that something more was expected of him, he added: 'It's been a challenge. An exciting challenge.'

'Well, we're all excited about Brussels,' said Mr Swaine. 'Tremendously excited. You can be sure of that.'

'Brussels, in fact,' said Mr Cooke, 'is what we've brought you here to talk about. Swaine, you'd better fill him in.'

Mr Swaine now rose to his feet and, placing his hands behind his back, began to pace the room in the manner of a Latin teacher about to run through a list of verbal conjugations.

'As you all know,' he began, 'the British exhibit at Brussels is divided into two sections. There is the official government pavilion, which is our baby here at the COI. We've all been busting a gut on this one for the last few months – not least young Foley here, who has been composing no end of captions and tour pamphlets and whatnot, and making a jolly fine job of it too, if I may say so. The government pavilion, of course, is essentially a cultural and historical display. We're pretty close to the wire, now, and we still haven't – ahem – still haven't *quite* fine-tuned all the fiddly bits, but the . . . the essential shape of the thing is more or less settled. The idea is to sell – or should I say, to *project* – an image of the British character. Looking at things . . . looking at things, as I said, both historically and culturally – and also scientifically. We're trying to look back, of course, on our rich and varied history. But we're also trying to look forward. Looking forward to the . . . to the . . .'

He tailed off. The word seemed to be on the tip of his tongue.

'To the future?' Mr Ellis suggested.

Mr Swaine beamed at him. 'Precisely. Back into the past, but also forward to the future. Both at the same time, if you catch my meaning.' Mr Ellis and Mr Cooke nodded at him in unison. They both appeared to catch his meaning without difficulty. Whether Thomas caught it or not seemed to be of little consequence, at that moment. 'And then,' Mr Swaine continued, 'there is the British Industries pavilion, which is a different kettle of fish altogether. That's being knocked up by British Overseas Fairs, with the help of some of the high-up industrial bods, and the aim there is quite . . . quite particular, by comparison. We see the Industries Fair as being very much in the nature of a shop window. A large number of firms have been eager to take part, and they are all paying for the opportunity to be part of the display, so the idea is . . . well, the idea is to rustle up a good deal of business, we hope. It seems that this will be the only substantial privately sponsored pavilion in the whole fair, and naturally we're very pleased that Britain is leading the way on this one.'

'Of course. "A nation of shopkeepers," ' said Mr Ellis. The quotation was delivered drily, but there was a certain thin satisfaction in his smile, all the same.

Mr Swaine seemed rather nonplussed by this intervention. For several seconds he stared absently into the fireplace which – even on this dismal February afternoon – remained cold and empty. In the end, Mr Cooke was obliged to prompt him:

'All right, Swaine, so we have the official pavilion and we have the industrial pavilion. Isn't there something else?'

'Ah! Yes, of course.' He snapped out of it and resumed his pacing. 'There is something else, most definitely. Something which comes slap in the middle of the two, in fact. Naturally, I'm referring . . .' He turned to Thomas. 'Well, Foley, you don't need me to tell you. You know exactly what comes between the two pavilions.'

Thomas did indeed. 'The pub,' he said. 'The pub is what comes between.'

'Exactly!' said Mr Swaine. 'The pub. The Britannia. A quaint old hostelry, as British as . . . bowler hats and fish and chips, representing the finest hospitality our nation can offer.'

Mr Ellis shuddered. 'Those poor Belgians. That's what we're giving them, is it? Bangers and mash and last week's pork pie, all washed down with a pint of lukewarm bitter. It's enough to make you want to emigrate.'

'In 1949,' Mr Cooke reminded him, 'a Yorkshire inn was constructed in Toronto, for the International Trade Fair. It was considered a great success. We hope to repeat that success; and indeed build on it.'

'Well, to each his own,' Mr Ellis conceded, with a shrug. 'When I visit the fair, I shall be hunting down a bowl of *moules* and a decent bottle of Bordeaux. Meanwhile, my concern – *our* concern, I should say – is that this dubious venture should be properly organized, and overseen.'

Thomas wondered about the force of that plural pronoun. On whose behalf was Mr Ellis speaking? The Foreign Office, presumably . . .

'Exactly, Ellis, exactly. We are of one mind.' Mr Cooke conducted a vague search of his desk, found a cherrywood pipe and slipped it into his mouth, apparently with no thought of lighting it. 'The trouble with this pub, you see, is its . . . *provenance*. Whitbread are going to set it up and run it. So in that sense it's nothing to do with us. But the fact remains that it's on our site. It will be seen, inevitably, as part of the official British presence. To my mind . . .' (he puffed on the pipe as though it were burning merrily) '. . . this presents a definite problem.'

'But not an insoluble problem, Cooke,' said Mr Swaine, stepping forward from the fireplace. 'By no means insoluble. All it means is that we have to *be* there, in some shape or form, to put our stamp on it – as it were – and make sure that . . . well, that things are as they should be.'

'Quite,' said Mr Ellis. 'So, in effect, what is required is that someone from your office should be on hand – and indeed, on site – to run things. Or keep an eye on them, at the very least.'

It was very obtuse of him, but even at this stage Thomas could not see where he was supposed to fit into all this. He watched with increasing stupefaction as Mr Cooke opened the manila file beside him and began to flip languidly through its contents.

'Now, Foley,' he said, 'I've been looking through your file here, and one or two things . . . One or two things seem to rather leap out at me. For instance, it says here –' (he raised his eyes and glanced at Thomas questioningly, as though the information he had just lighted upon could hardly be credited) '– it says here that your mother was Belgian. Is that true?'

Thomas nodded. 'She still is, if it comes to that. She was born in Leuven, but she had to leave at the beginning of the war – the Great War, that is – when she was ten years old.'

'So you're half-Belgian, in other words?'

'Yes. But I've never been there.'

'Leuven . . . Is that Flemish-speaking, or French?'

'Flemish.'

'I see. Speak any of the lingo?'

'Not really. A few words.'

Mr Cooke returned to his file. 'I've also been reading a little bit about your father's . . . your father's background.' This time he actually shook his head while skimming over the pages, as if lost in rueful amazement. 'It says here – it says here that your father actually runs a pub. Can that be true, as well?'

'I'm afraid not, sir.'

'Ah.' Mr Cooke seemed torn between relief and disappointment.

'He did run a pub, yes, for almost twenty years. He was the landlord of the Rose and Crown, in Leatherhead. But I'm afraid that my father died, three years ago. He was rather young. In his mid-fifties.'

Mr Cooke lowered his gaze. 'I'm sorry to hear that, Foley.'

'It was lung cancer. He was a heavy smoker.'

The three men stared at him, puzzled by this information.

'A recent study has shown,' Thomas explained carefully, 'that there may be a link between smoking and lung cancer.'

'Funny,' Mr Swaine mused, aloud. 'I always feel much healthier after a gasper or two.'

There was an embarrassed pause.

'Well, Foley,' said Mr Cooke, 'this is pretty dreadful for you. You certainly have our commiserations.'

'Thank you, sir. He's been much missed, by my mother and me.'

'Erm – yes, there is your father's loss, of course,' said Mr Cooke hastily, although it appeared that this was not what he'd actually been referring to. 'But we were commiserating with you, rather, on your . . . start in life. What with one thing and another – the pub, and the Belgian thing – you must have felt pretty severely handicapped.'

Temporarily lost for words, Thomas could only let him speak on.

'You made it into the local grammar, I see, so that must have been something. Still, you've done frightfully well, I think, to get where you have since then. Wouldn't you agree, gentlemen? That young Foley here has shown a good deal of pluck, and determination?'

'Rather,' said Mr Swaine.

'Absolutely,' said Mr Ellis.

In the silence that followed, Thomas felt himself sinking into a state of absolute indifference to the conversation. He gazed through the sash window and out into the distance, towards the park, and while waiting for Mr Cooke to speak he had a savage craving to be there, walking alongside Sylvia, pushing the pram, both of them looking down at the baby as she lay deep in a dreamless, animal sleep.

'Well, Foley,' said the Central Office of Information's Director of Exhibitions, slapping the file shut with sudden decisiveness, 'it's pretty obvious that you're our man.'

'Your man?' said Thomas, his eyes slowly coming back into focus.

'Our man, yes. Our man in Brussels.'

'Brussels?'

'Foley, have you not been listening? As Mr Ellis here was explaining, we need someone from the COI to oversee the whole running of the Britannia. We need someone on site, on the premises, for the whole six months of the fair. And that someone is going to be you.'

'Me, sir? But . . .'

'But what? Your father ran a pub for twenty years, didn't he? So you must have learned something about it in that time.'

'Yes, but . . .'

'And your mother comes from Belgium, for Heaven's sake. You've got Belgian blood coursing through your veins. It'll be like a second home to you.'

'But . . . But what about my family, sir? I can't just abandon them for all that time. I've got a wife. We've got a little baby girl.'

Mr Cooke waved his hand airily. 'Well, take them with you, if you like. Although a lot of men, quite frankly, would jump at the opportunity to get away from nappies and rattles for six months. I know I would have done, at your age.' He beamed a happy smile around the room. 'So, is it all settled, then?'

Thomas asked if he could have the weekend to think about it. Mr Cooke looked bemused and offended, but he agreed.

Thomas found it hard to concentrate on his work for the rest of that afternoon, and when five-thirty came around he still felt agitated. Instead of getting the tube right away he went to the Volunteer and ordered half a pint with a whisky chaser. The pub was smoky and crowded and before long he found himself having to share his table with a young brunette and a much older man with a military moustache: they seemed to be conducting an affair and not making much of a secret of it. When he got tired of listening to their plans for the weekend, and of having his shoulder jostled by a crowd of music students from the Royal Academy, he drank up and left.

It was well after dark, and already a filthy night. The wind was almost enough to blow his umbrella inside-out. At Baker Street station Thomas realized that he was going to be very late getting home, and there would be trouble if he didn't telephone. Sylvia answered almost at once.

'Tooting, two-five-double-one.'

'Hello, darling, it's only me.'

'Oh. Hello, darling.'

'How are things?'

'Things are fine.'

'What about Baby? Is she sleeping?'

'Not at the moment. Where are you? There's a lot of noise in the background.'

'I'm at Baker Street.'

'Baker Street? What are you still doing there?'

'I popped in for a quick one. Felt the need, to be honest. It's been quite a day. This afternoon they called me upstairs and dropped a bombshell. Got a bit of news to tell you when I get home.'

'Good news, or bad?'

'Good – I think.'

'Did you remember to pop out to the chemist at lunchtime?'

'Damn. No, I didn't.'

'Oh, Thomas.'

'I know. I'm sorry, it slipped my mind.'

'There's not a drop of gripe water left. And she's been bawling all afternoon.'

'Can't you go to Jackson's?'

'Jackson's closes at five.'

'But their boy delivers, doesn't he?'

'Only if you telephone them to ask. I can't call them now, they'll have shut up shop ages ago. We'll just have to manage until tomorrow.'

'I'm sorry, darling. I'm an ass.'

'Yes, you are. And you're going to be dreadfully late for dinner.'

'What have you made?'

'Shepherd's pie. It's been ready for more than an hour, but it'll keep.'

Thomas hung up and left the phone booth; but then, instead of heading straight for the escalators, he lit a cigarette and leaned against a wall and watched the other people hurrying by. He thought about the conversation he'd just had with his wife. It had been affectionate, as always, but something about it had disturbed him. Increasingly, these last few months, he had felt that the axis of his relationship with Sylvia had shifted. It was the arrival of Baby Gill that had done it, undoubtedly: of course this event had brought them closer together, in some ways, but still . . . Sylvia was so preoccupied, now, with the day-to-day responsibility of looking after the baby, ministering to her endless, unpredictable needs, Thomas could not help feeling that he was somehow being marginalized, squeezed out. But what was he to do? The transient image that had visited him in Mr Cooke's office – that image of the two of them, pushing the pram together in Regent's Park – had been vivid enough: but what sort of man was in thrall to such visions? What sort of man preferred a stroll in the park with his wife and baby daughter to the pressing business of getting on in the world? Carlton-Browne and Windrush had overheard him, one morning, talking with Sylvia on the telephone about Baby's hiccups, and they had given him a terrible ribbing about it for days afterwards. With good reason, too. There was no dignity in any of that, no seriousness. In this day and age, a chap had responsibilities, after all. A role to play.

It would be madness not to take the Brussels job. By the time he reached the front door of his house, fifty minutes later, he had already decided that. But there was something else, too: he was resolved not to tell Sylvia about Mr Cooke's proposal. Not just yet. Not until he had made up his mind whether she and the baby should come with him. In the meantime, he would keep it to himself. Over dinner, he told her that the 'bombshell' he had mentioned on the telephone was a small improvement in the terms of his pension contributions.

What's gone is gone

When she had fled with her mother from Belgium to London in 1914, she had been Marte Hendrickx. But the English found these names too difficult: her mother had anglicized them both, in turn, and by the time of her eighteenth birthday she was Martha Hendricks. Since her wedding day, in 1924, she had been Martha Foley. For more than thirty years, therefore, her own name had felt like a peculiarity. And now that the man whose surname she had taken was dead, this feeling of self-estrangement was more acute, more insistent than ever.

Today Martha Foley, if that's who she was, sat inside the bus shelter and waited patiently for the bus to arrive. It was 11.32. The bus was not due until 11.43. She did not mind having to wait. She did not like leaving things to chance.

She was fifty-three years of age. Fifty-four in September. She could have made herself beautiful, had she wanted to. But she chose, instead, to dress in sensible, middle-aged clothes, to wear flat shoes, to cut her greying hair in a matronly, austere fashion (rather like the Queen Mother's) and to eschew all make-up apart from thoughtlessly applied bright-red lipstick and the occasional dab of face powder. She was a grandmother, now, after all. She had to conserve some dignity.

Martha Foley looked placidly at the ribbon of road stretched before her, at the leafy outskirts of her home town, at the modest contours of the Surrey hills swelling up in the near distance. This morning was as deathly quiet as only an English Sunday morning could be.

Another six minutes before the bus arrived. Martha stretched out her legs and gave a little silent sigh of satisfaction. She loved this English quiet. She could never get enough of it.

*

At five past one, Thomas poured himself some whisky, and topped it up with a quick dash of soda from the siphon in the drinks cabinet. For Sylvia and his mother he poured glasses of nut-brown sweet sherry.

'There you are, Mother, get that down you,' he said.

Sylvia came in, patting her hair. She had checked the roast and it was almost done, now. All that was left was the gravy.

'And how are you, Mrs Foley?' she said, reaching down to kiss her mother-in-law on her powdered cheek. 'Buses on time this morning, were they? You know, as soon as we get a car, Thomas will be able to run out to Leatherhead and fetch you. Then you won't have to make that awful long journey any more.'

'I don't mind,' she said. 'I don't mind a bit.'

'It's good that she keeps her independence,' said Thomas.

His mother looked across at him sharply. 'You make me sound ancient. That's the sort of thing you should be saying in twenty years' time, when I'm really old.'

'Anyway,' said Thomas, trying to conciliate, 'we're a long way from getting a car yet. A long way. We'll be paying this place off for years.'

'Well, it will be money well spent,' said Mrs Foley, looking around her. 'It's a beautiful home.'

After this comment had hung in the air and died down there was a long hiatus, during which the clock on the mantelpiece seemed to be ticking extremely loudly. Feeling himself running out of conversation already, Thomas glanced longingly towards the copy of today's *Observer* which he had been obliged to lay aside, only half-read, on the occasional table. It had been an especially thought-provoking edition. A strongly worded article by Bertrand Russell, in support of the Campaign for Nuclear Disarmament, had been balanced by a more even-handed editorial on the opposite page, which maintained that in the rush to condemn the proliferation of weapons, people should not forget the amazing benefits that nuclear technology was going to bring them. A potentially infinite source of clean, cheap energy, for one thing. Thomas still didn't know where he stood in this particular debate and, with the arguments currently fresh in his mind, would have liked to have been able to chew them over with someone. If he had been at work, he could perhaps have taken it up with Windrush or Tracepurcel in the office canteen: but Sylvia, on the whole, was too unsure of herself to offer an opinion about such things. In fact their minds, he sometimes thought, were starting to run on completely different tracks. It was not right. He hardly expected her to be an expert on world politics or nuclear science – he could scarcely claim that distinction himself – but he felt it was important (a responsibility, even) to sustain an interest in these matters. Reading about them, keeping himself informed, was an essential part of Thomas's daily life. He had to believe that somewhere out there, beyond the silent confines of suburban Tooting, was a world of ideas, movements, discoveries and momentous changes, a world that was in a constant state of discussion with itself; a discussion to which one day he might (who could say?) make his own tiny contribution.

'I'd better start thinking about the carrots,' said Sylvia, putting her glass down.

She was about to rise to her feet, but Thomas beat her to it.

'They're out in the yard, aren't they?' he asked, and was on his way before his wife could do anything to stop him.

Left to each other's company, Sylvia and her mother-in-law sized each other up warily.

'What a lovely picture,' said Mrs Foley in a bright voice, after they had both taken a few sips of sherry.

It was a new photograph of Baby Gill, taken two weeks ago at the little studio on the High Street, and only delivered in its smart beechwood frame yesterday morning. She was sitting up on a sheepskin rug, bright-eyed, wearing a lacy cap which concealed the fact that her hair was currently still on the thin side. It was a monochrome print, but the photographer had artfully tinted the baby's cheeks with touches of rose-pink.

'She's going to be a beauty,' Mrs Foley predicted.

'Gosh. I don't know about that,' said Sylvia, lowering her eyes as if it were her own looks that were being complimented.

'She has your colouring, you see. Her skin's going to be peachy, just like yours. Now if she'd taken after Thomas, we'd be in trouble. He had terrible skin when he was younger. Dreadful. Well, you can still see he gets pimples even now. It comes down on his father's side.' This was all stated in a perfectly matter-of-fact way. Experience – of which she had a great deal – had taught Mrs Foley many things, but never the need to be tactful. 'Sleeping now, is she?'

'Yes. I should go and check on her, really.'

It would have been a lame excuse for leaving the room. Fortunately, a better one presented itself when the telephone rang in the hallway.

'Excuse me.'

It was her mother, Gwendoline, calling from Birmingham. Thomas, in the midst of peeling the carrots, popped his head out from the kitchen and hissed, *Tell her to call back,*' but she took no notice. It seemed that some serious family news was being imparted, but Thomas did not find out what it was until later, when they were all sitting at the dining-room table and the joint had been carved.

'I'm sorry about the interruption,' said Sylvia, spooning the vegetables onto Mrs Foley's plate, 'but Mother had something rather distressing to tell me.'

'Not too many of those for me, dear,' said Mrs Foley, keeping a watchful eye on the potatoes. 'This girdle's tight enough as it is. I don't want to be getting stout.'

'Why, what's happened, darling?' Thomas asked.

'It's Cousin Beatrix.'

'Oh yes?'

Thomas's ears always pricked up when he heard Beatrix's name. She was by some way the most interesting (and least respectable) member of Sylvia's family, a compulsive romantic adventuress rarely held back by the fact that she had an infant daughter to look after. The pleasure of tutting over the latest Beatrix scandal was one of the few that Thomas and Sylvia could share together: from both of them, her exploits provoked routine outbursts of disapproval and secret pangs of envy in equal measure.

'Don't tell me,' he said. 'She's walked out on that poor old Canadian already and found yet another victim. I knew it wouldn't last more than a year or two.'

But it transpired that the news was much more dramatic than that. 'She's had a dreadful accident,' Sylvia told them. 'She was stopped at a roundabout in her car when some enormous truck ran into the back of her.'

'My God,' said Thomas, 'was she badly hurt?'

Sylvia nodded. 'She's broken her neck, poor soul. She's going to be in hospital for months.'

There was a solemn, respectful silence.

'It sounds like she's lucky to have escaped with her life,' said Mrs Foley.

'I know. We should be thankful for that, at least.'

In the further silence that followed, Thomas said: 'Talking of being thankful . . .'

'Oh. Yes, of course.' Sylvia put her hands together and closed her eyes. The others did the same. 'For what we are about to receive, may the Lord make us truly thankful.'

'Amen,' intoned Thomas and his mother.

They began to eat; and before long, another of those aching conversational voids had made itself felt.

'These place mats are charming,' said Mrs Foley, in something like desperation. 'Alpine scenes, aren't they?'

'Quite,' said Thomas, without looking up from his food.

'I bought them in Basle,' said Sylvia. 'Of course, they weren't the only souvenir I brought back from that holiday.' She smiled a flirty, conspiratorial smile at her husband, but he was bent over his Yorkshire pudding, and did not register that he had heard her comment.

Rebuffed, Sylvia continued to watch him for a moment, her gaze held by the intensity of his efforts to soak up as much gravy as possible before putting the fork in his mouth. His self-absorption pierced her: filled her with an acute, dizzying combination of love and disquiet. This was the man she had entrusted her life to. Sometimes she wondered if she had made a mistake.

Sylvia had little experience of relationships with men, and what little she had had been unfortunate. She had married late, at the age of thirty-two. Throughout most of her twenties she had lived at home in Birmingham, with her mother and father, during which time she had squandered (it now seemed to her) many of the best years of her life on an engagement to a much older man, a commercial traveller from the north. They had met one Friday afternoon in the café of a department store, where he had insisted on paying for her coffee and eclair. After that first encounter she had not seen him for some months, but a passionate series of letters had been exchanged, culminating in another coffee-bar meeting and an offer of marriage. Sylvia shuddered now to think of her own naivety. They continued to see each other two, perhaps three times a year. The letters had kept coming, at irregular and increasingly distant intervals. Finally an envelope had arrived in the post one morning, enclosing an anonymous note which informed her that her betrothed already had a wife, three children, and a string of similar fiancées up and down the country.

Sylvia had plunged, after this, into a long period of depression, which her doctor had advised would probably best be cured by fresh air and strenuous exercise. With the help of her parents she had arranged, in the summer of 1955, to travel to Switzerland for an extended walking holiday in the Alps. She had travelled with two other women, both of them spinster daughters of her father's work colleagues. She had not known either of them beforehand; nor, having made their acquaintance on the trip, had she come to like them very much. But all had not been lost. At the end of the holiday, while resting in Basle for a few days, the three women had plucked

up the courage to visit a beer cellar, and there they had encountered
Thomas. An Englishman – a bachelor, no less – who was on holiday
alone, and seemed only too glad to fall in with some welcoming
female company. What's more, he had the most charming manners,
and the most impressive jawline. One of Sylvia's companions
thought there was more than a hint of Gary Cooper in his pale-blue
eyes; the other saw a striking resemblance to Dirk Bogarde. Sylvia
noticed neither of these: but she did see – potentially – a future husband, and from the ferocious competition which ensued over the
next few days she was the one who emerged triumphant. All the
same, she did not rush into an engagement this time; she kept
Thomas on tenterhooks for weeks, after returning home; but there
had been no doubt in her mind that she would acccpt him, after a
decent interval. He seemed to be a splendid catch. His job at the
COI was steady, prestigious and not badly paid. And the prospect of
moving to London had, at first, felt glamorous and exciting . . .

Sylvia became aware that her mother-in-law was saying something to her.

'I'm sorry, Mrs Foley? I didn't quite catch that.'

'I was asking,' Mrs Foley repeated, dabbing at her lips with a
gingham napkin, 'if you had thought any more about the mangle. I
hardly use it any more, as I said. I know that some people consider
them old-fashioned, but the old ways are usually the best ways, you
know. And I'm sure you must have much more laundry to do since
Baby came along.'

'Well,' said Sylvia, 'that's very kind . . . What do you think, darling?'

After lunch, Baby woke up, and Sylvia went upstairs to feed her.
Thomas made his mother a cup of tea and thcy wcnt out to inspect
the garden. A hint of late-afternoon sunshine was breaking through
the blanket of clouds, and it was warm enough to sit, for a minute
or two, at the little wrought-iron table he had optimistically bought
last summer, in anticipation of quiet afternoons spent reading the

newspaper while Baby played happily in the (as yet unconstructed) sandpit. The garden looked a mess.

'You really need to do some work on this,' said his mother.

'I know.'

'What on earth's that big hole over there?'

'I started a goldfish pond,' said Thomas.

'I thought you were planning to grow vegetables.'

'I am. I'm going to plant some potatoes and beans. It's too early yet.'

Then he told his mother about the meeting with Mr Cooke and Mr Swaine and Mr Ellis of the Foreign Office. He told her that they were asking him to go to Belgium for six months.

'What does Sylvia say?' she asked him.

'I haven't mentioned it to her. I'm waiting for the right moment.'

'Could you take them with you?'

'It's been suggested. I don't think it sounds ideal. We're not sure what the accommodation's going to be like yet. It could be pretty basic.'

His mother looked very doubtful. 'You shouldn't have told me first. You should have discussed it with your wife.'

'I'm going to.'

She held up a warning finger. 'Don't neglect her, Thomas. Be a good husband to her. This –' (she gestured into the near distance, beyond the unfinished goldfish pond, beyond the air-raid shelter in which Thomas kept his few garden tools, beyond the railway embankment, and towards the dreary flatlands of Tooting itself) '– is not her home, you know. Not really. It's not what she's used to. And it's no fun being a long way from home with a man who doesn't care for you.'

Thomas knew that she was talking about her own experience, about her marriage to his father. He didn't want to hear it.

'Your father had affairs, you know.'

'Yes. I know.'

'I put up with it. But that doesn't mean that I didn't mind.' Mrs

Foley shivered, and wrapped her shawl more closely around her shoulders. 'Come on. I think we'd better get inside. It's getting chilly.'

She was about to get up, but Thomas laid a restraining hand on her arm, and said earnestly: 'I'll be in Brussels, Mother. Close to Leuven, close to where the farmhouse was. Only about half an hour away. I can go there and – I know the house isn't there any more – but I can see where it used to be, and . . . talk to people, and . . . take pictures . . .'

Mrs Foley rose stiffly to her feet. 'Please don't do that. Not on my account. I don't think about any of those things any more. What's gone is gone.'

These are modern times

Four-thirty on Tuesday afternoon found Thomas walking through St James's Park, on his way to a meeting in Whitehall. Despite the steady downpour of rain, there was an unaccustomed jauntiness to his step, and under his breath he was singing to himself a cheerful tune he had caught on the Light Programme the night before: 'The Boulevardier' by Frederic Curzon.

Things had progressed pretty smoothly since the weekend. Over last night's dinner, he had finally told Sylvia about the Brussels assignment. She had been shocked, at first: the thought of coming with him did not seem to cross her mind (nor did he suggest it), and the prospect of being left alone for six months certainly alarmed her. But Thomas's reassurances were convincing: there would be letters, there would be telephone calls, there would be weekends when he flew home to see her. And the more he told her about the fair itself, the more she came to see that this was an opportunity he could not afford to turn down. 'So, really,' she had said – at last beginning to see the thing clearly, as pudding was dished up and she poured condensed milk over her slender portion of apple pie – 'it's a great honour that Mr Cooke has singled you out in this way. He didn't ask any of the others. And you'll be rubbing shoulders with people from all sorts of places: Belgians, French – even Americans . . .' And Thomas had realized, when she said this, that from one point of view Sylvia was actually willing him to go, already: that in her eyes, painful though the separation would be for both of them, he would grow in stature from this experience. No longer a mere government pen-pusher, he would become, for six short months, something much more interesting, and indeed glamorous: a player (however small) on the international stage. The idea appealed to her – even titillated her. And perhaps it was this knowledge, more than anything else, that lightened his step that Tuesday afternoon, and added a few imaginary inches to his height as he strode across the footbridge towards Birdcage Walk. He felt a sudden, unexpected kinship with London's seagulls as they swooped low over the water beneath him, revelling in the freedom of flight.

Half an hour later, Thomas was seated in Conference Room 191 of the Foreign Office, as close as he had ever come in his life to a centre of power.

The conference table was huge, and every seat was taken. The air was thick with cigarette smoke. Some of those present Thomas had already met in the waiting room downstairs. Others were public figures whom he recognized: Sir Philip Hendy, director of the National Gallery; Sir Bronson Albery, the famous theatrical manager; Sir Lawrence Bragg, the physicist and director of the Royal Institution. Several times in the last few months, back at the COI's Baker Street offices, Thomas had caught glimpses of James Gardner, designer of the British pavilion; but he had not, until today, met the man with whom Gardner spent most of the meeting locked in combat – Sir John Balfour, GCMG, Commissioner-General for the United Kingdom's participation at Expo 58.

The trouble began early on. Thomas could tell that there was a general sense of panic in the air. The fair was due to open in three months' time, and there was obviously a good deal of work still to be done. Sir John had a thick pile of paperwork on the table in front of him, the very sight of which seemed to fill him with a palpable disgust.

'Now I have to say,' he began, crisply but with an edge of weariness to his voice, 'that our Belgian friends have been most prolific with their communications over the last few weeks. This mountain of paper represents but a small proportion of their output. And we have been more selective still in making copies for everyone. So perhaps it would be in order for me to summarize. Let's start with the musical side of things, shall we? Is Sir Malcolm here?'

Sir Malcolm Sargent, chief conductor of the BBC Symphony Orchestra and musical advisor on the British contribution, had not been able to come to the meeting, it transpired.

'He's in rehearsals, I'm told,' said a young man in a pin-striped suit, whom Thomas took to be a junior clerk. 'Sends his apologies and all that. But the concert programmes are well in hand, he says.'

'Did he give you any details?'

'A few names were mentioned. Elgar, obviously. A bit of Purcell. The usual suspects, by the sound of it.'

Sir John nodded. 'Ideal. I must say there are some pretty . . . peculiar ideas coming out of the Belgian side.' He glanced at the uppermost of his sheets of paper. 'A week-long festival – *week*-long, it says here – of electronic music and *musique concrète*, featuring world premieres by Stockhausen and – how the devil do you pronounce this – Xenakis?' He looked around the room, frowning incredulously. 'Has anyone heard of these chaps? And what is "concrete music" when it's at home, I'd like to know? Can anyone enlighten me?'

There was a general shaking of heads around the table; in the midst of which Thomas became distracted, on suddenly becoming aware of two curious figures seated at the far end. What was it about them, in particular, that caught his attention? They were following the discussion as closely as anybody – perhaps more closely – and yet they seemed somehow detached from it. Although they never spoke to each other, or appeared to acknowledge each other's presence, they were sitting rather closer to each other than was strictly necessary, and gave the impression of being in some sort of conspiracy. They were both (he would have guessed) in early middle age. One of them had slicked-back dark hair, and a moon-shaped face whose expression managed to be both vacant and intelligent at the same time. The other looked more benign, and less watchful; he had a noticeable scar down his left cheek, but the look of it was not at all sinister, and it did not detract in the least from his general air of dreamy good nature. They were the only two people who, throughout the entirety of the proceedings, were never named or introduced, and once he had noticed them, Thomas found their presence strangely distracting.

'Well, I don't know about you, but I think that's an excellent proposal,' Sir John was saying.

Thomas realized that he had not been following the discussion. It appeared that Britain was being asked to make its own contribution to the contemporary music week, and the general feeling around the table was that a military tattoo would fit the bill perfectly.

'The Grenadier Guards, perhaps?' someone suggested.

'Perfect,' said Sir John, nodding to the secretary at his side, who duly made a note of the decision.

At which point, from one corner of the table, came what could only be described as a derisive snort. 'Ha!'

Sir John looked up, in wounded surprise.

'Mr Gardner – would you like to register an objection?'

The lean, ascetic figure in question, who peered through conservatively horn-rimmed glasses but wore his hair rakishly long, waved his hand dismissively and said: 'Really, Sir John, it has nothing to do with me. No, I don't want to register an objection. But your secretary can register my amusement if she likes.'

'And what, might we ask, is so amusing about a military tattoo?'

'In this context? Well, if you can't see that, Sir John, all I can say is . . . you are probably the ideal person to be chairing this committee.'

Thomas was expecting a ripple of laughter, but there was only shocked silence.

'Mr Gardner,' said Sir John, leaning his elbows on the table and putting his fingertips together to form a pyramid, 'I was going to defer discussion of your latest suggestions for the British pavilion, but perhaps after all this would be a good moment to consider them.'

'They're just ideas,' said Gardner, offhand.

'The Brussels World's Fair,' Sir John reminded him, 'opens in three months' time. Work on the construction of the pavilion is running weeks behind schedule. Isn't it a bit late to be pitching in with new ideas? Particularly ideas like . . .' (he glanced down at his paperwork) '"A history of the British water closet."'

'Oh,' said Gardner, 'didn't you like that?'

'It seems a trifle . . . well, "whimsical" would be a polite way of putting it.'

'Don't feel that you have to be polite if you don't want to, Sir John. After all, we're all friends here.'

'Very well. I shall rephrase that, and say that this suggestion appears to me . . . downright stupid and offensive.'

Several of the men (there were no women, apart from Sir John's secretary) seated around the table looked up at this point, their interest keenly aroused.

'I respectfully disagree, Sir John,' said Gardner. 'Britain's contribution to the disposal of human waste has never been properly recognized. That's not just my opinion, it is a historical fact.'

'Gardner, you're talking rot.'

'Well –' (there was an embarrassed cough from a pallid, under-nourished young man sitting to the left of Mr Gardner, who seemed to be part of his team) '– not exactly, Sir John.'

The Commissioner raised an eyebrow.

'Not exactly?'

The man who had spoken up seemed more embarrassed than ever. 'What I mean is, Jim – I mean Mr Gardner – does have a point. Toilets are crucial to everyday life. I mean, we all use them, don't we? We all . . .' (he swallowed hard) '. . . do them, after all.'

'*Do them*, Mr Sykes? Do *what*?'

'There's no point in pretending otherwise, really, is there?'

'What on earth are you talking about?'

'Well, you know. We all do . . . number twos.'

'*Number twos?*'

'Precisely!' Gardner jumped to his feet and began pacing the perimeter of the table. 'Sykes has put his finger on it. We all do them, Sir John. Even you! We all do number twos. We may not like to talk about them, we may not even like to think about them, but years ago, somebody *did* think about them, he thought about them long and hard – if you'll pardon the expression – and the result was that we can now all do our number twos cleanly, and without embarrassment, and the whole nation – the whole world! – is a better place as a consequence. So why shouldn't we celebrate that fact? Why shouldn't we celebrate the fact that, besides conquering half of the globe, Britons have also fought a historic battle against their number twos, and emerged victorious?'

He sat down again. Sir John stared across the table at him coolly.

'Have you quite finished, Gardner?' Taking his silence as consent, he added: 'Might I remind you that at the entrance to this pavilion, which you propose to deface with this obscene display, visitors will find a portrait of Her Majesty the Queen?'

Gardner leaned forward. 'And might I remind you, Sir John, that even her Majesty – *even her Majesty . . .*'

Sir John stood up, his brow furrowed with rage. 'If you finish that sentence, Gardner,' he said, 'I shall have to ask you to leave this room.' There was a tense, extended silence, as both men locked eyes across the table. When it became apparent that Mr Gardner was not going to add anything, Sir John slowly sat down again. 'Now,' he continued, 'I expect you to forget all about this ludicrous idea, and concentrate on devising a display which does something to reflect not just the glory but the dignity of the people of these islands. Is that understood?' Distinctly flustered, not pausing for an answer, he turned over his next sheet of paper and read the first few lines out quickly and automatically, without thinking about them: 'Next – the ZETA project. "Proposal for transporting and exhibiting a replica of Britain's . . ."'

'*AHEM!*'

Sir John glanced across the table again. The warning cough had come from one of the two mysterious men who had earlier caught

Thomas's attention: the one with the moon-shaped face and the slicked-back hair. He held a minatory finger up to his lips, and shook his head, almost unnoticeably. Whatever had prompted the gesture, Sir John took immediate notice of it, and turned the sheet of paper over in a casual movement, laying it face down on the table.

'Quite right, of course. Not a priority at all. We can leave that until later. We have a far more important matter to consider, which is . . . Ah, yes! The pub. The famous pub.' His features relaxed, and he looked enquiringly among the assembled faces. 'Now, we should have a new recruit to our team, is that correct? Mr Foley, are you amongst us?'

Thomas half-rose to his feet, then realized that this probably looked ridiculous, and sat down again. His voice, when he managed to find it, seemed impossibly thin and tentative.

'Yes, that would be me, Sir . . . Sir John.'

'Good. Splendid.' A long, expectant silence ensued. When it became clear that Thomas had no intention of breaking it, Sir John said: 'We're ready to hear your thoughts, I believe.'

'Ah. Yes.' Thomas looked around the circle of distinguished faces currently trained on him, and swallowed hard. 'Well, the Britannia, as you probably know, will be – in some ways – the focal point of the British exhibit. The original idea, as you probably know –' (why was he repeating himself?) '– was to build a replica of – and here I quote – "an olde English inne" – to show visitors the finest in traditional British hospitality. One or two factors, however, brought about a change from the initial plan. One is that the Belgians themselves are, apparently, in the process of constructing a village on the festival site, which they are calling "La Belgique Joyeuse" – which translates, roughly speaking, as "Gay Belgium" – and this will include replica buildings from the eighteenth century and earlier, including an authentic inn. Another, erm, factor, is that the COI – and, I think, Mr Gardner himself, though I wouldn't like to put words into his mouth – have always been concerned that the British contribution, while doing justice, obviously, to our great traditions, should not be too – well, too backward-looking. And so it was decided that the designers of the Britannia should be briefed to take a slightly more modern approach. Britain, after all, is a modern country. We are at the very forefront of innovation in the sciences and technology.' (He was getting into his stride now, and, to his own amazement, rather beginning to enjoy himself.) 'But our great strength is our ability to move forward, without ever breaking our links with the past. This is the paradox that the designers have worked so hard to express with the interior of the Britannia.'

A mild interruption was presented at this point.

'Looking at these photographs,' said one of the more elderly committee members, seated to Thomas's right, 'this is not what I picture when I think of an English inn. Not at all.' He sifted through some black-and-white prints, shaking his head. 'Surely . . . some horse brasses, some wooden beams, the froth of a fine English ale overflowing the sides of a pewter tankard . . .?'

'But that's exactly what we wanted to avoid,' said Thomas. 'The Britannia is being built on a most attractive site, overlooking an artificial lake. We wanted to give it the feeling of a . . . of a yachting club, if you like. There will be big windows, and white walls. The interior is light and spacious and airy because this is the modern way, don't you see? These are modern times! It's 1958! Britain will be presenting its new face to the world under the shadow of the Atomium, and we must rise to the challenge. We have to move forward. We have to move on.'

Sir John was regarding Thomas, suddenly, with marked interest and approval.

'Excellently phrased, Mr Foley, if I may say so. You are quite right. Britain has to find its place in the modern world and we must show the other countries how this can be done without resorting to fashionable nonsense such as . . . concrete music, or whatever it is called. I think Mr Lonsdale's designs are capital. Quite capital. And you, I believe, are going to be on site for the entirety of the fair, looking after the Britannia in a managerial capacity. Is that correct?'

'That is correct, sir, yes.' From the corner of his eye Thomas noticed, as he said this, that the two mysterious gentlemen were exchanging a fleeting glance. 'The brewery has engaged its own landlord, and its own serving staff, but I will be there, as a representative of the COI, to oversee things and make sure everything is above board and . . . ship-shape, as it were.'

'Splendid. And have you visited the site yet?'

'I'm flying out to Brussels for a preliminary view on Thursday, sir.'

'Excellent. We wish you all the very best of British luck with that assignment, Mr Foley. And I'm sure that I myself will be seeing more of you in Brussels.'

Thomas smiled his thanks, and inclined his head. It was a careful, restrained gesture, and one which gave no indication of the sensations of wild pride and excitement that were coursing through him at that moment.

Trying to build up a picture

'Top-notch speech in there, Mr Foley.'

'Quite right. Absolutely first-class.'

Thomas whirled around to see where the voices were coming from. Standing on the rain-soaked pavement outside the Foreign Office, wondering which direction to take, he had had no idea that anyone was waiting in the shadows behind him. Now two figures emerged from the darkness, dressed identically in long beige raincoats and trilby hats. Thomas was somehow not surprised to identify them as the two anonymous men from the committee meeting.

'Filthy night, isn't it?' the first one remarked conversationally.

'Shocking,' Thomas agreed.

'Mind if we walk with you?' asked the second.

'Not at all. Which direction are you heading?'

'Oh, we thought we'd leave that up to you.'

'It makes no difference to us.'

'I see,' said Thomas, even though he didn't. 'Well, I hadn't quite decided.'

'Tell you what.' The first of the men raised his arm and immediately, as if from nowhere, a black Austin Cambridge pulled up against the kerb beside them. 'Why don't we give you a lift home?'

'That's decent of you,' said Thomas. 'Are you sure?'

'Absolutely, old man.'

'No trouble at all.'

The three of them squeezed onto the back seat. It was very tight. Thomas, seated in the middle, could scarcely move his arms.

'Where to this time, gents?' the driver asked.

'Tooting, please,' said the first man, unprompted. And when

Thomas looked at him in surprise, he said: 'Sorry. You don't have to go home if you don't want to. We can take you anywhere you like.'

'No, no,' he demurred, 'Tooting's fine.'

'Don't want to keep the little woman waiting, after all, do you?'

'Got something nice bubbling away for you on the stove, I dare say.'

'Lucky man.'

'Cigarette, Mr Foley?'

While they were all in the process of lighting up, the moon-faced man said:

'Well, we might as well introduce ourselves. My name's Wayne.'

'As in the film star,' said his companion. 'Comical, really, isn't it? You can't picture him in a stetson.'

'And this is Mr Radford,' said Mr Wayne.

With some difficulty, given the confines of the back seat, Mr Radford shook Thomas warmly by the hand and said: 'Delighted to make your acquaintance.'

'Are you both members of the Brussels Committee?' asked Thomas, at which they chuckled.

'Oh, goodness me, no.'

'Heaven forbid.'

'Far from it, old boy. But we take a keen interest, you know. From a distance.'

'We've sat in on quite a few of the meetings.'

'Starting to get to know most of the characters involved.'

'That Mr Gardner's a bit of a card, isn't he?'

'Likes to put the cat among the pigeons.'

'Dependable chap, though.'

'Absolutely. Salt of the earth.'

'Solid as a rock. Underneath, you understand.'

They fell silent. Mr Radford wound down his window, in an attempt to dispel some of the smoke. But it was so wet and blustery outside, he soon wound it up again. The traffic was light and the driver was making rapid progress. In only a few minutes they were driving along Clapham High Street. While the Cambridge was stopped at a red light, Mr Wayne glanced out of the window and said: 'I say, Radford, isn't that the coffee place we were in a couple of days ago?'

'I believe so, yes,' said Mr Radford, peering through the rain.

'Do you know, I just feel like a cup of coffee.'

'I was just thinking the same thing.'

'What about you, Foley?'

'Do you fancy a cup of coffee?'

'Well, I . . . I was rather hoping to get home in time for . . .'

'That's settled then. Driver! Can you drop us off here, please?'

'Wait for us round the corner, if you would.'

'We'll only be a jiffy.'

The three of them spilled out of the car and hurried across the pavement, which glistened in the rain. The establishment they had chosen advertised itself as Mario's Coffee Bar. Inside there were half a dozen tables, all empty, and a bored dark-haired girl behind the counter, trying to fill in the time by painting her fingernails green.

'Coffee for me, please,' said Mr Wayne, politely but firmly. 'White, two sugars.'

'And the same for me,' said Mr Radford. 'Foley, what will you have?'

'I don't really drink much coffee,' said Thomas.

'Three white coffees, two sugars each,' said Mr Wayne.

'And put some of that frothy milk on top, if you would,' said Mr Radford. 'You know, the way the Italians drink it.'

'We're all continentals now, I suppose,' said Mr Wayne, as he sat down.

'Quite,' said Mr Radford, joining him, and shaking some of the rain off his overcoat. 'All the European nations starting to come together.'

'Treaty of Rome and all that.'

'Very much what this Brussels business is about, when you think about it.'

'Quite. Bit of history in the making.'

'Lucky to be a part of it.'

'What's your view, Foley?'

'My view?'

'On this Belgian shindig. Expo 58. Do you regard it as a historic opportunity for all the nations of the world to come together, for the first time since the War, in a spirit of peaceful cooperation?'

'Or do you consider it little more than a sordid marketplace powered not by idealism at all, but by the forces of capitalism?'

Thomas had barely had time to sit down himself when these questions were fired at him. His clothes were soaking even after such a short walk, and he could feel the steam rising off his body.

'I shall . . . Well, I shall have to think about that,' he said.

'Very good answer,' observed Mr Wayne approvingly.

'Spoken like a true diplomat.'

The waitress arrived with the sugar bowl.

'Coffees'll be with you in a minute,' she said. 'The machine's on the blink. We can't seem to get any heat out of it.'

On her way back to the counter she stopped by a jukebox and inserted a few coppers. A burst of music followed after a few seconds: it was fast and driving, with loud drums pounding out a rhythm beneath three or four simple chords, and a male vocalist half-shouting, half-singing something about a Streamline Train over the whole din. Mr Wayne put his hands over his ears.

'Good God.'

'What a cacophony.'

'What on earth is it?'

'I believe they call it "rock'n'roll",' said Mr Radford.

'Sounds more like skiffle to me,' said Thomas.

'Well well,' said Mr Wayne. 'I had no idea you were an authority on musical trends.'

'Who, me? Not at all. My wife listens to this sort of music occasionally. I'm more of a classical man, myself.'

'Ah, yes. The classics. Nothing like a bit of classical music, is there? I expect you like Tchaikovsky?'

'Of course. Who doesn't?'

'What about the more modern bods? Stravinsky, say?'

'Oh, yes. First rate.'

'Shostakovich?'

'Haven't heard much.'

'Prokofiev?'

Thomas nodded, without really knowing why. He couldn't see where any of this was leading. The waitress brought their coffees and they all stirred in their sugar and took their first sips.

'Of course,' said Mr Radford, 'a lot of chaps would rather read than listen to music.'

'Curl up with a good book,' agreed Mr Wayne.

'Do much reading?'

'A bit, yes. Not as much as I should, probably.'

'Read any Dostoevsky? Some people swear by him.'

'What about Tolstoy?'

'I'm afraid I'm rather parochial in my tastes. I like Dickens. I read Wodehouse, for a bit of light relief. Do you mind telling me what this is all about? You seem to be asking me an awful lot of questions about Russian writers and composers.'

'We're just trying to build up a picture.'

'Finding out about your likes and dislikes, that sort of thing.'

'It's just that I need to get home to my wife before too long.'

'Of course, old man. We understand that.'

'You'll probably be wanting to see as much of her as you can, in the next few weeks.'

Thomas frowned. 'Why's that?'

'Well, after all, she won't be coming to Brussels with you, will she?'

'No, that's true.'

'Six months is a long time, to be doing without . . . home comforts.'

'The pleasures of married life.'

'That's if you like married life, of course.'

'Some men don't, you know. I mean, they marry, but it's not really their cup of tea.'

'Their real interests lie elsewhere.'

'It's a sordid subject.'

'Terribly sordid.'

'For instance, chap I knew, married for ten years, three children, hardly spent any time at home. More likely to be found in the gentlemen's toilet at Hyde Park Corner.'

'What a ghastly prospect.'

'Ghastly. Do you know it?'

'Know it?' Thomas repeated.

'The gentlemen's toilet at Hyde Park Corner.'

He shook his head. 'No.'

'Very wise. Best to steer well clear of it, I should think.'

'Give it a wide berth.'

'Are you by any chance asking me if I'm a homosexual?' asked Thomas, his face pinkening with indignation.

Mr Wayne thought this a splendid joke. 'My dear chap, what on earth makes you say that?'

'What a fantastic notion!'

'The idea never entered our heads.'

'Nothing could have been further from our thoughts.'

'Why, you're obviously no more a homosexual than you are a member of the Communist Party.'

Thomas was mollified. 'That's all right, then. Because there are some things you shouldn't joke about.'

'Couldn't agree more, old man.'

'By the way,' said Mr Radford, 'you're not a member of the Communist Party, are you?'

'No, I'm not. And once again, will you *please* tell me what this is all about?'

Mr Wayne took one more sip of his coffee and consulted his pocket watch.

'Look, Foley, we've kept you chatting for far too long. You've got absolutely nothing to worry about. You, me and Mr Radford – we're all on the same side.'

'Batting for the same team.'

'It's just that you must understand – this knees-up in Brussels, well, it's a wonderful idea in principle of course, but there are dangers involved.'

'Dangers?'

'All these different countries coming together in the same place for six months – it's a marvellous idea in theory, but someone has to consider the risks.'

'What risks?'

'You said it yourself in the meeting.'

'I did?'

'We're living in modern times. Science is achieving miraculous things.'

'But don't forget – science is a two-way street.'

'A double-edged sword.'

'Precisely. We all have to be vigilant. It's the price we pay.' Mr Wayne stood up, now, and held out his hand. 'Anyway, goodbye, Foley. Or perhaps *au revoir* would be more appropriate.'

Thomas and Mr Radford both rose to their feet. There was a flurry of confused handshaking.

'You can get the bus from here, I take it?' said Mr Radford. 'Only Tooting's a little bit out of our way.'

'Yes, of course,' Thomas mumbled, more out of his depth than ever.

'We won't keep you any longer. You head off back to your supper.'

'Back to the bosom of your family.'

'And don't worry about the coffees. Everything's on us.'

'Our treat.'

'Small price to pay for the pleasure of your company.'

Thomas thanked them uncertainly, and headed for the door.

The rain outside looked even heavier than before. He turned up the collar of his coat in anticipation. Just as he was opening the door to let in the first gusts and raindrops, Mr Radford called after him:

'Oh, and Foley?'

Thomas turned. 'Yes?'

'Just remember one thing: this conversation never took place.'

Welkom terug

Entering the modest arrivals hall at Melsbroek airport late on Thursday morning, Thomas looked out for a besuited figure who might correspond to his image of David Carter, the British Council representative who had arranged to meet him there. However, no such figure presented himself. Instead, Thomas found himself being approached by a young, attractive woman in uniform.

'Mr Foley?' she said, extending her hand. 'My name is Anneke and I am here to escort you to the British pavilion at the Exposition site. Would you follow me please?'

Without waiting for his reply she turned and began walking towards the exit, two or three paces ahead of Thomas. He hurried to catch up.

'I was expecting Mr Carter,' he said, 'but this is a very pleasant surprise.'

Anneke allowed him a smile which was neither warm nor cold, just highly professional.

'Mr Carter has been detained,' she said. 'He will meet you at the site.'

Anneke's uniform was smart, discreet and studiedly sexless. The heels were high, but not too high. The navy-blue skirt was cut well below the knee. Beneath the trimly tailored maroon jacket she wore a white shirt with collar and tie. The whole ensemble was crowned by a cheerful – but sober – pill-box hat. It was an unexceptional uniform, but Thomas found himself feeling slightly revolted by it. He felt that Anneke would have been much easier to talk to had she been wearing something else.

'So you are one of the famous Expo hostesses,' he said.

'Are we famous already, even in England?' she asked. 'I will tell my colleagues. They will be excited.'

Thomas was entertained by a passing image of a group of these young women, all in their early twenties, all wearing the same uniform, sitting around a table in some Brussels café or works canteen, giggling together over their English celebrity. It made him feel very elderly.

Outside the arrivals hall, the sunshine of early spring was breaking through tentatively. Anneke came to a halt and looked to the left and right, newly indecisive.

'There should be a car waiting for us,' she explained. 'I will go and find it.'

Left to his own devices for a few minutes, Thomas attempted to savour what should have been a significant occasion for him: the first time he had ever stood on the soil of Belgium, his mother's country. He had been looking forward to this moment all week, and was grateful for the opportunity to enjoy it alone. But soon he began to feel foolish. There was nothing significant about it really. This was just a country like any other: it had been naive to suppose that he would feel anything like an immediate sense of belonging. In any case, perhaps the paradox of Belgium was going to be that it made him feel more British than ever.

The car arrived: it was a pale-green Citroën, the driver's door emblazoned with the distinctive, irregular star-shaped logo of Expo 58. Anneke jumped out and opened the rear passenger door for him. They set off quickly in the direction of Heysel.

'Just a short journey,' Anneke promised him. 'Twenty minutes or less.'

'Fine. Will we be passing near Leuven, by any chance?'

'Leuven?' Anneke seemed surprised. 'Leuven is not far away, but it lies in the other direction. You wanted to visit there?'

'Perhaps not today,' said Thomas. 'Another time, I hope. My mother was born there. My grandparents had a farm nearby.'

'Ah, so your mother was Belgian! Do you speak the language?'

'No, not at all. Just a few words.'

'Well then, I suppose I should say, *Welkom terug*, Mr Foley.'

'*Dankuwel, dat is vriendelijk,*' said Thomas, carefully.

Anneke gave a delighted laugh: '*Goed zo!* But I won't test you any more. It wouldn't be fair of me.'

After that, their conversation flowed more easily. Anneke told him that she came from Londerzeel, a village to the north-west of Brussels, where she still lived with her parents. She was one of 280 young women who were lucky enough to have been chosen as hostesses. All of them spoke four languages – French, Dutch, German and English – and most were being sent to seaports, railway stations and airports, where it would be their job to greet the expected thousands of visitors from overseas and ensure that they had an easy onward journey to Expo 58. The hostesses were considered to be among the Expo's most important ambassadors, and their rules of conduct were strict: during their working hours, they were not allowed to chew gum, to knit or sew, to smoke, drink alcohol, or to read novels, newspapers or magazines.

'In fact,' said Anneke, 'I'm not even supposed to appear in public in the company of a man, without written permission from the authorities. Which in your case, fortunately, I have.'

She smiled at Thomas again; and the smile, this time, had less of a professional sheen to it, and more of human warmth. Thomas was starting to realize that she was very pretty indeed.

'Look!' she said suddenly, leaning towards him and pointing out of the window. 'Can you see it?'

All Thomas could see, at first, was a line of treetops standing tall and steady in the middle distance; but then, rising above the topmost of them, something distinctly man-made could be glimpsed: the upper half of what appeared to be a gigantic silver globe. And as their car sped forward and the perspective changed, three more such globes emerged, set at different heights, and connected to each other by glistening steel tubes. The whole of the structure could not be glimpsed, yet, but already Thomas had the sense of something immense and majestic, something sublime and unearthly that had been imagined on an epic scale by the creators of some science-fiction comic or film, and then transported, by a miracle of human ingenuity and engineering, into the natural world.

'The Atomium,' said Anneke proudly. 'We will have a better view of it when we enter the Expo park.'

She sat forward and spoke to the driver in French.

'I was asking him not to take you directly to the British pavilion,' she explained (although Thomas had been able to understand quite well). 'I think you should enjoy a little tour first.'

Shortly afterwards the car pulled up outside a wide entrance gate, surrounded by dozens of flagpoles to which no flags had yet been attached. A half-finished sign announced that this was the Porte des Nations. The car was waved through by an enthusiastic security guard who seemed to know the driver well; and before long they were inside the Park itself, driving at a cautious ten kilometres an hour down a wide, tree-lined boulevard called the Avenue des Nations.

The caution was necessary, for the road was clogged, and there was industry and activity everywhere. At first Thomas could not comprehend anything of what he was seeing: it was all a mêlée of trucks, scaffolding, cranes, girders, piles of bricks, slabs of concrete, planks of wood being carried hither and thither by workmen wearing cloth caps or knotted handkerchiefs on their heads. He had never seen such a density of building work being carried out in such a small space. Instructions, reprimands, cries of warning and encouragement were being shouted out in every language imaginable. Only after he had taken a few seconds to adjust to the pace and the bustle could Thomas start distinguishing some details. The first building to attract his full attention was on their left: indeed, it thrust itself at them, being a spectacular diorama in steel, glass and concrete, more than one hundred metres in diameter, approached by a broad, welcoming walkway studded with flagpoles. In scale, ambition and design it called to Thomas's mind a profoundly modern version of the Roman Colosseum.

'The American pavilion,' Anneke explained. 'And here is the Soviet one, right next door. Which,' she added, with a gleam in her eye, 'is a typical example of the Belgian sense of humour.'

The Soviet pavilion presented a powerful contrast. It conceded nothing in terms of scale, but the heroic simplicity of its design offered a kind of reprimand to American pretension and vulgarity. It was a giant cuboid, constructed from steel and glass, swelling towards the sky almost as far as Thomas's eye could see as the car eased its way past and he craned his neck out of the window, looking upwards in open-mouthed astonishment. The walls of the pavilion were of corrugated glass, giving it a lightness and openness which belied its dimensions: as if in implied rebuke to Westerners who might have assumed that the very concept of transparency was unknown in the USSR.

After this, they took a left turn down a smaller road, and past a building which – though not as imposing as the two they had just seen – struck Thomas as more beautiful than either: less arrogant, for one thing, and smoother in its curves, clearer and more confident in its outline. Anneke agreed.

'This is my favourite of the pavilions so far,' she said. 'It belongs to Czechoslovakia. I am looking forward very much to visiting this one.'

They took another left, and drove straight up the Avenue de l'Atomium. And this time, when he saw the celebrated structure in all its shimmering, eerie magnificence, getting larger and larger as they approached, Thomas felt his heart swell with awe and excitement, and the full import of the adventure he was embarked upon started to strike home. The previous Sunday he had been pouring sherry for his wife and mother in Tooting, the overture to an endless family lunch in which nothing of note had been said, nothing of interest had happened. Even then, he had begun to feel himself driven almost to distraction by the smug quietude of that deathly suburb, the overwhelming sense of indifference towards the great events that were taking place out in the wider world. But now, only four days later, he had already been drawn by some miracle into the very epicentre of these events. Here, for the next six months, would be thrown together all the nations whose complex relationships, whose conflicts and alliances, whose fraught, tangled histories had shaped and would continue to shape the destiny of mankind. And this brilliant folly was at the heart of it: a gigantic latticework of spheres, interconnected, imperishable, each one emblematic of that tiny mysterious unit which man had so recently learned how to divide, with consequences both alarming and wonderful: the atom. The very sight of it set his heart pounding.

'Do you like it?' Anneke was saying, as the car drove around it in a full circle. 'Do you like it, Mr Foley?'

'I love it,' said Thomas, leaning out of the window again. 'I absolutely, utterly adore it.'

The words sounded strange to him as soon as they were uttered. When had he last spoken so extravagantly? Perhaps it was not this place that was stirring him to such heights of enthusiasm – nor the Atomium, for that matter – but Anneke herself.

Rapidly he suppressed this alarming thought. The car drove past the modernist pavilions of France, Brazil, Finland and Yugoslavia, and then the Italian pavilion, which bucked the trend and sought instead to re-create the atmosphere of a mountain village. They drove through the Scandinavian section, past the Turkish and Israeli pavilions; in another few minutes they had traversed the whole of South America and even the Far East. Thomas was beginning to feel dizzy, travel-sick. The clashing architectures were beginning to blur.

'And what's this one?' he asked, as they drove past yet another modernistic construction, this one a semi-circular affair clad in gleaming metallic bricks, approached by an escalator running upwards through a glass tunnel.

'Ah! For we Belgians,' Anneke told him, 'this is a very important part of the Exposition. It will be the section devoted to the Belgian Congo and Ruanda-Urundi. On the other side there is a tropical garden with a native village inside. All very authentic, with little huts and grass roofs! They're even bringing some of the natives over to live here, for the time of the Expo. I can't wait to see them. I have never seen a real black before. They look so strange and funny in photographs.'

Thomas said nothing in reply to this, but it gave him an uneasy feeling. There were plenty of black faces on the streets of London these days, and while he knew people who felt unhappy about it (a heated conversation with Mr Tracepurcel in the office canteen sprang to mind), he prided himself on being free of skin prejudice. If what Anneke said was true, he considered that this part of the Exposition struck the wrong note.

Before he had time to think of a reply, in any case, the car turned a corner, and Thomas saw something that he recognized at once: James Gardner's British pavilion – looking, he had to admit, even more quirky, original and impressive in real life than it had in the photographs. Its three triangular sections seemed every bit as modern and dynamic as the buildings that surrounded it, yet somehow they also called to mind a cathedral, or a succession of church steeples. Dazzled though he had been by all the other buildings, Thomas felt a special glow rise up inside him when the car came to a halt here: it was the glow of homecoming.

Anneke opened the car door for him, but then, instead of leading him towards the main entrance of the pavilion (where workmen were ranged upon tall ladders, lifting panes of glass into place) they ducked around a corner, and made their way through a clump of beech trees towards the interior of the British site. Here more buildings were grouped around a small artificial lake, and, standing in the corner, looking about as incongruous as anything could look in the hectic, heterogeneous miniature universe through which Thomas had just travelled, was a sight at once familiar and alien: the weatherboard exterior of a public house, its name spelled out in bold capitals at the upper level: THE BRITANNIA.

'Mr Foley?' said a well-bred English voice, and Thomas found that he was being approached by a young man in a white linen suit, who came trotting down the stairs of the pub and extended a firm, energetic handshake. 'My name's Carter. So sorry I couldn't meet you at the airport.'

'Think nothing of it,' said Thomas. 'I've been well looked after.'

Anneke smiled her thanks at him, and said to Mr Carter, 'Delighted to meet you.' Then, turning back to Thomas: 'I have to go now. A car will collect you from the British Council at four o'clock, and take you back to the airport. With a hostess, of course, to assist you with all the arrangements.'

'Will it be you?' asked Thomas, suddenly not caring how direct the question sounded.

Anneke looked away, trying not to smile, and said simply: 'I will see if I can arrange it.'

Both Thomas and Mr Carter watched her retreating figure wistfully as she disappeared through the trees, back towards the car. Carter let out a low whistle of appreciation.

'What a pip,' he said. 'And unless I'm much mistaken, old boy, you've made a bit of an impression there.'

'Really?' said Thomas. 'I mean . . . I didn't intend to.'

'Of course you didn't. But this is a dangerous place, you know. Can't you feel it? Strange things could happen here, if we don't all keep our heads.' Before Thomas could ask him what he meant, exactly, by this remark, Mr Carter laughed and clapped him on the back. 'Now come inside, and see what the Britannia is going to be offering its customers. You look as though you could do with a pint of British best.'

Rum sort of cove

Empty of customers, the Britannia seemed much larger than Thomas had been expecting. It did, however – much to his relief – appear to be more or less finished. There were some wall decorations missing, and a trio of workmen were putting finishing touches to some of the fittings behind the bar, but there was no doubt that it was in a state of near-readiness. After viewing so many plans, drawings and photographs of the interior over the last few months, it was the latest in today's succession of pleasures to see the thing, finally, in real life.

The first impression was good. Very good. There was an immediate sensation of light and space. In the ground-floor saloon, three of the walls were covered with pine planking and white plaster; the fourth was in natural brick. The flooring was of a black-and-green chequer pattern. The long, red-topped bar of light and dark wood stretched down much of one side, fronted by its row of bar stools. Along the other walls was the familiar bench seating, with round, glass-topped tables and a few individual chairs in yellow and black. A number of naval prints already hung on the walls; there were also model ships in glass cases, and a larger model of a Britannia airliner suspended as if in flight.

Mr Carter beamed happily. 'Splendid, isn't it? You'll have trouble keeping me away from this place for the next six months. A little bit of Blighty transported over to boring old Bruxelles.'

He led Thomas upstairs. The Britannia was two-storeyed, and the upper floor contained a large reception room for private parties, together with a smaller bar or Exhibitors' Club. These rooms were carpeted in black and orange, with fixed seating as well as armchairs in black leather. There not being much to see here, Mr

Carter took Thomas out onto the projecting upper deck, with its planking in naval fashion, its hand rails, lifebuoys and shaded verandah. From here you could view the whole of the terrace below, soon to be thronged with visitors, strolling between James Gardner's British Government pavilion and the Industries pavilion, or sitting at tables beneath the brightly coloured sun umbrellas. Beyond, amid the trees, was the ornamental lake, and at its far end a great steel mast pointing proudly but irrelevantly towards the sky.

Mr Carter walked towards the railing at the edge of the verandah and leaned against it, looking out over the lake. Thomas spent a moment or two inspecting the carpentry on the supporting pillars, then joined him.

'This is going to be some shindig, isn't it?' said Carter, gazing across the lake and through the trees on the other side, where more trucks and lorries could be seen trundling backwards and forwards along the Avenue des Trembles. 'I don't think I've ever seen anything quite like it.' He turned to Thomas. 'Cigarette?'

'Very decent of you, old man.' They lit up, sharing a match. 'People are starting to say they're bad for you, you know.'

'Oh, they'll say that about anything. Rotten spoilsports, the lot of them. So . . .' (he inhaled deeply, and gave Thomas a more appraising glance than he had given before) 'the COI are sending you over to keep an eye on this place, are they?'

'Something along those lines,' said Thomas. 'I dare say there's no need. Probably a colossal waste of time and money.'

'I wouldn't be so sure about that,' said Mr Carter. 'Have you met mine host?'

'Mr Rossiter, the landlord? Not yet. I was rather hoping to meet him today.'

'You can. He's down in the cellar. We'll go down in a tick.'

'Anything I should know about him?'

'I wouldn't want to spoil your first impression. So, how did they manage to single you out for this mission – if you don't mind my asking? Six months in Belgium. Did you draw lots in the office, and end up with the short straw?'

'It's not that bad, is it?'

Mr Carter reflected for a moment. 'Oh, of course, it could be worse. I've been with the Council nearly ten years and had some pretty hairy postings. Amman. Bergen. All sorts of places. The worst you can say about the Belgians is that they tend to be on the eccentric side.'

'Eccentric?'

'Surrealism is the norm here, old man,. They pretty much invented it. And the next six months are going to be wackier than most.'

'Ah yes. Anneke – the hostess – was saying something about that. Putting the Americans and the Russians right next to each other. She said it was a Belgian joke.'

'Hmm,' said Mr Carter, stubbing his cigarette out on the balcony rail. 'I wonder what the punchline will be. One thing's certain – both those pavilions are going to be crawling with spies. Come on, then, let's go and meet the Wing Commander.'

With this enigmatic comment, he led Thomas back down to the ground floor and then towards a wide trapdoor which was standing open in one of the recesses behind the bar. From here a set of wooden steps led down to a capacious, brightly lit cellar. The two men clattered down the steps and found themselves confronted by many long rows of metal stillions, all awaiting the arrival of beer barrels. In front of one of them, a confused argument was taking place. A tall, swarthy man, very sweaty in his short-sleeved white flannel shirt, was protesting in French; opposite him, with his back towards Thomas, stood a stouter, shorter man with his hands on his hips. The back of his neck showed red and angry above the line of his stiff white collar.

Thomas knew enough about pub management to be able to follow the argument. The tall French-speaking man was from the company which had been responsible for providing the stillions and the other man was complaining about the automatic tilting system that had been installed with them. He said that the action was jerky and was liable to set the beer swaying in the barrels. If this happened, the beer would be cloudy when it was pulled up through the pipes into the bar. Why not tilt the barrels with simple wooden scotches instead, he wanted to know. The French-speaking man said that this was a very old-fashioned method. The other man didn't seem to understand his answer. Eventually the French-speaking man gave up the attempt to explain his position and walked away up the wooden steps, muttering to himself and making an angry, dismissive gesture before disappearing altogether.

It was only then that the landlord of the Britannia noticed his two visitors.

'Good afternoon, gents,' he said, warily. 'Er . . . *bonsoir, mes amis. Comment* . . . I mean, what can I do for you?'

'Carter,' said Mr Carter with a bland smile, holding out his hand. 'From the British Council. We met yesterday.'

'Ah, yes! I do recall,' said the landlord – who clearly didn't.

'This is Mr Foley,' said Mr Carter. 'I was telling you about him. He's going to be working here as well.'

'Ah, capital!' said the landlord, shaking Thomas by the hand. 'Rossiter's the name. Terence Rossiter. Aha!' He took Thomas's tie between thumb and forefinger of one hand, and drew it towards him for a closer inspection. 'Now this I recognize. Radley College, isn't it? Or is it Marlborough? Tell me it's a school tie, anyway, and I'm not making a complete chump of myself.'

'It is a school tie, yes. Leatherhead Grammar.'

'Ah. My mistake. Grammar-school boy, eh? Well, stands to reason, what would an old Radleian be doing working in a pub? Come upstairs, gents, I'll see what we've got on hand to slake your thirst.'

They sat at one of the glass-topped tables in the first-floor saloon, and Mr Rossiter fetched three pint bottles of pale ale, apologizing for the lack of beer on draught. Whitbread had created a special new brew for the Expo – a strong, dark bitter known inevitably as Britannia – but they were still awaiting delivery of the first barrels.

'It won't be here until a week before we open,' Mr Rossiter explained. 'I'd hoped to get the tilting issue resolved before that, but I have no idea what that Froggy fellow was on about, to be honest. It doesn't half complicate things when you find yourself dealing with a whole lot of foreigners.'

'I think he was saying,' Thomas ventured, 'that he considered your suggestion of wooden stocks to be rather old-fashioned.'

'Old-fashioned, is it? Well, it was good enough for the Duke's Head in Abingdon, which was my domain for eleven years after the War, with no complaints from the customers, thank you very much.'

He drank deeply from his pint glass, an action which caused a good deal of foam to cling to each end of his gingery moustache. This moustache, Thomas could not help thinking, was a most impressive creation: it sprung out at a perfect horizontal, and each half must have been getting on for two inches long. Its extremities were quite free-standing, having no contact with Mr Rossiter's face at all. The face itself was ruddy, marked with innumerable networks of tiny red veins. The nose was purple. It was tempting to draw the conclusion that Mr Rossiter's vocation as a landlord was well chosen, if constant proximity to liquor was his object.

'The fact is,' Mr Rossiter continued, 'that these Belgian types don't know their arses from their elbows, if you ask me – not about beer, and not about anything else. I know what I'm talking about. I almost lost a leg at El Alamein and spent two years of the War in a hospital sort of place near Tonbridge. There were a couple of Belgians in there with me for a few months and I can tell you now, they were the queerest, craziest types I ever encountered. Mad as coots, the pair of them.'

'Part of the purpose of this fair, as I understand it,' said Mr Carter, 'is that the peoples of the different nations will be living alongside each other for a period of time, and thereby coming to understand their differences, and similarities, and perhaps reaching a greater understanding –'

'Well, that's poppycock,' said Mr Rossiter. 'No offence intended, but there you have it. I'm a plain-speaking man, as I'm sure you've noticed. I dare say that what you propose is fine in theory – but it won't work out like that, I can tell you. Six months from now we're all going to be packing up with no better understanding of each other than when we started. On the other hand, if the people in charge want to chuck away a few million setting up this crazy fair, good luck to them. I'm quite happy to lend a hand in exchange for a decent cut.'

Mr Carter shot a rather embarrassed glance in Thomas's direction.

'Of course, you know the capacity in which Mr Foley will be working here . . .'

'He can start behind the bar. At the moment the only other person engaged to work here is my niece, Ruthie. I've told the brewery many times that we're going to be short-staffed and I'm pleased to hear that they've finally taken some notice.'

'I don't think you quite understand,' said Mr Carter. 'Mr Foley is not a barman. He works for the COI.'

'The what?'

'The Central Office of Information.'

Mr Rossiter looked from one man to the other.

'I don't get it.'

'The fact is,' Thomas began, speaking in as reasonable tone as he could, 'that this very fine pub, besides having an existence . . . in its own right, as it were, is also part of the British exhibit at the fair. And so, my superiors thought it was appropriate – I think this was all explained to you in a letter – that someone from the COI should be in residence here, for the duration, to . . . to –'

'To keep an eye on me, I suppose,' said Mr Rossiter, finishing the sentence phlegmatically.

'That wouldn't be my way of putting it,' said Thomas. It sounded lame even to him.

'So you're not here to help at all? You're just going to be snooping around and looking over my shoulder?'

'My father was a publican,' said Thomas. 'I know a good deal about it. I shall be happy to help you out in a practical capacity, whenever you need it.'

Mr Rossiter was not convinced, and was not happy. Grudgingly, after his two guests had taken a few more sips of their beer, he showed them over the rest of the premises: the kitchens, in particular, where the Britannia's restaurant manager, Mr Daintry, would be preparing his menu of 'traditional English fare' (Thomas caught Mr Carter's eye as this phrase was mentioned, and saw him make the sign of the cross). After that, the landlord protested that he had work to be getting on with, and disappeared once again into the cellar: to brood, no doubt, on the intractability of the Belgians when it came to stillions, wooden stocks and tilting arrangements.

'Rum sort of cove,' said Thomas, as they left the pub and began to stroll towards the boundary of the British site.

'I did warn you. But I think he'll be all right. You'd better keep on eye on his tippling, that's all. He's the sort who might be too pie-eyed to stand up by nine o'clock, if you're not careful. And remember – no British licensing laws here. So he'll be able to go at it for twelve hours at a time.'

The rest of the day passed quickly. Mr Carter took Thomas to the British Council offices in central Brussels, where they had lunch in the staff restaurant. They discussed plans for a small party to celebrate the opening of the Britannia, on the second evening of the Expo itself.

The car which came to return him to the airport contained no hostess, and Thomas was obliged to conclude that he would not see Anneke again that day; until, when they pulled up forty-five minutes ahead of his flight, he found her waiting for him outside the departures hall. By now, any hint of that brittle professionalism with which she had first greeted him had vanished. As they said their broken goodbyes, she swayed slightly from side to side in an almost girlish manner, her hands behind her back, sometimes lowering her gaze as if she did not trust herself to look him too often directly in the eye. Her eyes were green, he noticed, pale green with a hint of amber, and her smile was wide, bright and flawless. The only thing about her that was less than perfect, in fact, was the way she was obliged to dress. Stumblingly, just before they parted, he tried to say something to this effect.

'I hope we will be meeting a few more times during the Expo,' Anneke said.

'Yes,' Thomas answered. 'Yes, I'd like to see you again.' It didn't seem enough, so he added: 'Perhaps without your uniform on.'

Anneke's cheeks flushed crimson.

'I meant –' Thomas stammered, '– I meant that I'd like to see you in ordinary clothes.'

'Yes.' Anneke tried to laugh, but she was still blushing. 'I know what you meant.'

There was a long final pause, before she said, 'You're going to miss your flight,' and then a long, fervent, final handshake before Thomas broke away and hurried inside. He glanced back at her one more time. She waved.

Calloway's Corn Cushions

Over the next few weeks, Thomas's error, perhaps, was to make his excitement at the prospect of leaving for Brussels just a little too obvious. It should have been no surprise that Sylvia began to resent him for it; and her previous cheerful, resigned tolerance of their imminent separation began to harden into something more tight-lipped and melancholy.

On the Saturday morning of the weekend before his departure, Thomas was propelled by one of Baby Gill's more vigorous bouts of screaming out of the house and along the street in the direction of Jackson's the chemist, in search of yet more of the gripe water for which she seemed to have developed an insatiable need. There was a sizeable queue at the counter and, resigning himself to a wait of at least ten minutes, he was not best pleased to find that the customer in front was Norman Sparks, one of his next-door neighbours. Mr Sparks, a bachelor, shared his home with his sister and was, in Thomas's eyes, a crashing bore of the first water. Shortly after their arrival in the neighbourhood, Thomas and Sylvia had been invited round to the Sparks' for dinner: an experiment which had not been repeated, for it had been a long and arduous evening. Mr Sparks's sister, Judith, was a sickly woman of about thirty who barely said a word to anybody (including her brother) and retired to bed shortly after nine o'clock, even before pudding had been served. As soon as she had gone, her brother proceeded to describe to his guests, in the most intrusively intimate detail, the nature of his invalid sister's many ailments, which between them, he lamented, kept her more or less bedbound for most of the day. The tactless, bantering way in which he handled the subject had confirmed Thomas's already growing dislike of his new acquaintance;

a dislike further strengthened by the feeling that Sparks had spent much of the meal regarding his wife with what could only be described as a leer. Since then, all the same, he had kept up a reasonably polite front towards his neighbour. By nature, Thomas was not inclined towards antagonism. He would mutter a civil, 'Morning, Sparks,' if ever they passed in the street, and indulged him with the occasional idle chat across the back garden fence in sunny weather. None the less, he had not forgotten those hungry glances thrown in Sylvia's direction over the dinner table.

'Morning, Sparks,' he said to him now. 'How's that poor sister of yours keeping?'

'Oh, no better, no worse,' Mr Sparks replied, with his accustomed breeziness. 'Bed sores – that's the latest thing. Big red ones. All over her *b-t-m*. I've been rubbing cream on them every day for the last two weeks.'

Thomas stared at him. 'Really,' he said, as flatly as he could. He was acutely conscious that every customer in the crowded shop was being made privy to this dialogue, and felt that a swift change of subject was called for. 'Still, you're looking well, at least. No troubles of your own, on the health front, I assume?'

'Spoken too soon,' said Mr Sparks, shaking his head with a rueful smile. 'Corns. I'm a martyr to them. It's my feet, you see. The awkward size of my feet.'

Thomas glanced down. There was nothing unusual about his neighbour's feet, so far as he could see.

'You astonish me,' he remarked.

'I'm a three-quarter size,' Mr Sparks elaborated. 'Eight and a halves are too small. Size nines are too big. There's nothing I can do about it. I'm a unique specimen.' There was a note of quiet pride in this conclusion.

'So they either rub, or pinch, I suppose,' said Thomas, sympathetically.

'They rub, or they pinch. Precisely. I'm caught between the devil and the deep blue sea.'

'Can't you get a pair made specially?' Thomas asked – in response to which, Mr Sparks burst out laughing.

'D'you think I'm made of money, old man? I couldn't afford anything like that. Not possibly. Why, I can barely keep me and Judy going as it is. No, those little beauties' – he pointed at a shelf behind the counter, where there was a pile of little boxes bearing the label *Calloway's Corn Cushions* – 'those are my only salvation.' Suddenly it was Sparks's turn to be served, and with a lamentable attempt at a flirtatious smile for the girl on Saturday-morning duty, he said: 'A packet of Mr Calloway's finest, please, my lovely. And another tube of that wretched ointment – for the relief of the tender nether quarters of the unfortunate Miss Sparks, if you would.'

After this, to Thomas's annoyance, Sparks waited for him outside the chemist's shop, with the clear design of their walking back together. A further conversation was inevitable: Thomas managed to steer it gently away from Miss Sparks's physical complaints and towards the less distasteful subject of football. Then, when they reached the gate of his own little front garden, a further misfortune presented itself: Sylvia was outside, trowelling the soil in their tiny flower bed, getting ready to plant a few rows of bulbs. She straightened up when she saw them, a hand on her aching back, and said: 'Good morning, Mr Sparks. I put the kettle on only two minutes ago. Would you care to join us for a cup of tea?'

Frowning, Thomas followed his wife and his neighbour indoors He knew exactly what was going on here: his imminent departure was weighing on Sylvia's mind and, subconsciously, bestowing unnecessary attentions upon Mr Sparks was her way of punishing him for it. 'I'm sure you like it strong and sweet, don't you, Mr Sparks?' she said, bringing the teapot in from the kitchen, and bending over him much too closely while she filled his cup. Sylvia had quickly regained her figure after giving birth, and even improved upon it: the breasts from which she fed the baby were fuller and more rounded than before, a fact which could scarcely escape Mr Sparks's notice as he inclined himself slightly but eagerly towards her, his nose almost brushing the neckline of her dress, obviously breathing in her scent. 'Milk and two lumps, please, Mrs Foley,' he said hoarsely, looking up and holding the gaze of her hazel eyes for several moments too long. Thomas looked on with indignant surprise.

'I must say, Foley', Mr Sparks said, after Sylvia had returned to the kitchen to cut some slices of walnut cake, 'that you're a damned fool, if you want my honest opinion.'

'Why so?' Thomas asked, pretty sure that he wanted nothing of the sort.

'Leaving the little woman all by herself while you swan off to Belgium, of all places. If I were you I wouldn't leave her alone for more than ten minutes.'

Thomas stirred his tea, masking his irritation.

'I don't quite see what you're driving at, old man,' he said.

'Well, after all, six months is a deuce of a long time,' said Mr Sparks. 'Aren't you worried that she's going to miss you?'

'How considerate of you to think it,' said Sylvia, coming back with the cake. 'But I believe that aspect of it hardly troubles Thomas at all.'

'Well, I don't think it at all gallant of him.'

'I shall be coming back at weekends, you know,' said Thomas. 'Some weekends, at any rate.'

'And I suppose there are such things as letters, and telephones.'

'Of course there are. We shall maintain a passionate correspondence.'

'All the same,' said Mr Sparks, 'there are some . . . routine little tasks that only a man can carry out. And I would just like you to know, Mrs Foley, that if you ever have any requirements in that direction, I am always at your disposal. Just one ring on the doorbell, and I shall come running.'

'Why, Mr Sparks, whatever can you be suggesting?' asked Sylvia, with a delighted smirk.

Mr Sparks blushed to his roots. 'Oh – I only meant,' he mumbled, 'that if you were to need a light bulb changing, or a shelf putting up, or anything in that line . . .'

'I see,' Sylvia replied, allowing herself the remains of a smile as she sipped her tea. 'Well, that is very kind of you. What do you think, darling? Isn't that a handsome offer of Mr Sparks's?'

Thomas gave her a glassy stare, and merely observed, after a few moments' pause: 'Sparks was telling me that he's a martyr to corns, these days. Almost prostrated with them, he is. He was limping like nobody's business on our way home.'

If this remark was intended to dampen the sympathy that seemed to be developing by the minute between Sylvia and Mr Sparks, it actually had the opposite effect. Sylvia flashed him a look of sincere concern, and said: 'That's dreadful. Corns can be a terrible worry. My mother's suffered for years. And her mother before her. It runs in the family.'

'Does your mother use these?' asked Mr Sparks, and produced his packet of corn cushions. 'They stick over the affected area, you see, but with a hole in the middle, so that –'

Thomas had heard enough. Letting out a contemptuous sigh, he took a large bite from his cake, and then went to answer the telephone as soon as it started ringing in the hallway. On his return he found that the medical demonstration had run its course, and Mr Sparks had, instead, resumed his campaign of promising devoted assistance to the abandoned bride.

'You might feel yourself rather confined here,' he was saying. 'Of course, if you need me to drive you anywhere – the station, for instance . . .'

'You mean to tell me that old banger of yours is still running, Sparks?' said Thomas (who was not yet able to afford a car). 'I thought it fell to pieces ages ago.'

'Who was that on the telephone?' Sylvia asked.

'Nobody. Just a bit of crackle at the other end of the line.'

'Oh. That happened to me earlier today, while you were out.'

'Really?'

'Yes. And twice yesterday.'

It was time for Mr Sparks to leave, and to apply his ministering hands to his sister's afflicted regions. Thomas made a point of escorting him to the garden gate, to make sure that he really was leaving the premises. When he returned to the hallway, Sylvia was standing by the telephone, the receiver to her ear.

'Insufferable ass,' Thomas muttered, not entirely to himself. And then, to Sylvia: 'Everything all right?'

'Yes. I was just a little worried about the telephone.'

'Is the dial tone there?'

'Seems to be.'

'Then it should be fine.'

'I've been noticing these funny noises, that's all. Ever since the engineer came.'

On his way towards the kitchen, Thomas stopped and turned.

'Engineer? What engineer?'

'A man came from the GPO, on Thursday morning. He was here for about half an hour, fiddling with the wires.'

'Really? Why didn't you tell me?'

Sylvia didn't say why she hadn't told him, although they both knew the reason: because they had barely been speaking to each other all week.

'Did he just turn up on the doorstep,' Thomas asked, 'without any warning?'

'No. The two gentlemen told me that he would be calling.'

'Which two gentlemen?'

'The two gentlemen who came the day before.'

Thomas began, slowly and glimmeringly, to understand what must be happening.

'I see,' he said, grimly. 'And I suppose they told you they were from the GPO as well?'

'Yes. Why? Nobody would tell a lie about something like that, would they?'

Sylvia followed Thomas into the kitchen and they sat down together at the table. She began to tell him, in full, the story of her strange encounter with the two nice men from the General Post Office on Wednesday afternoon. They had arrived at about three o'clock, she said, and told her that they were investigating a series of complaints in the area, relating to crossed lines, interrupted calls and general interference and unsatisfactory conditions on the local telephone service.

'And that's all you talked about?' Thomas wanted to know. 'Nothing but telephones?'

'Why yes, of course,' said Sylvia. 'I told them that we hadn't had any problems in particular – none that I could think of – but they said that an engineer would call the next day anyway, just to make sure, and to carry out some . . . routine maintenance work. And then they asked me to fill in a form –'

'A form?'

'Yes.'

'What, name, address, that sort of thing?'

'Yes. And there were some other questions, like . . . I don't know, funny things like if I belonged to any political parties, and where I'd been on my holidays, and things like that.'

Thomas sighed, and said drily: 'They wanted all that information, just to mend the telephone?'

'Yes, I did think that was a little odd.' She looked up at him, deferential, trusting: 'You don't think there was anything   queer about it, do you?'

Thomas rose to his feet. 'I shouldn't think so,' he said. 'Probably just making sure everything's ready for the new long-distance calls, or something.'

He was touched by the look of relief that lit up Sylvia's face. Her naivety could sometimes be frustrating; but it was also capable of moving him, or at least making him feel powerful and necessary – which, if truth be told, he found a pleasant sensation. As for his growing suspicion that someone would most likely be keeping a careful eye on the daily comings and goings during his absence, that too, in its way, was strangely comforting.

The remainder of the weekend passed quietly enough. That night they went to the pictures – at the suggestion of Mrs Foley, of all people. 'It's your last Saturday evening together for a while,' she said to her son. 'For Heaven's sake do something special. Give your wife a treat.' Sylvia had been shocked, initially, by the thought of abandoning Gill for a whole evening, but Thomas's mother had reassured her, and offered to sit with the baby herself. 'I shall enjoy it,' she had insisted. 'It will make a change from sitting at home by myself. And what is the point of you having a guest room, if nobody ever sleeps in it?' Thomas and Sylvia had taken the tube to Leicester Square and limbered up for his immersion in European cuisine by going to an Italian restaurant for lasagne and Chianti. After that, they had argued over the choice of film. Thomas wanted to continue the Italian theme by seeing *Cabiria – Her Nights, Her Men*, which was playing at the Continental: a suggestion which Sylvia vetoed firmly as soon as she learned that it was an X-certificate film, and that the main character was a prostitute. Her preference was for *Peyton Place*, which Mrs Hamilton at the Post Office had already seen four times, and which she could not recommend too highly: 'The way they live . . .' she had sighed to Sylvia the last time she had come in to cash a postal order. 'The way they live in America. The great big motor cars, and the big wide roads. The beautiful houses, and everything in colour, and the men so handsome. There's one actor plays the schoolteacher, and he's such a good man, and has such strong principles, and at the same time you can just imagine him, with those wide shoulders, in those wonderful well-cut suits, taking you in his arms and . . .' She had tailed off, dreamily, before thumping Sylvia's postal order with her rubber stamp and handing over her two shillings and sixpence. Thomas, hearing this conversation repeated over tiramisu, remained unconvinced.

Many years ago, without realizing it, he had acquired from somewhere the deep-rooted conviction that America was a shallow, vulgar, uncivilized place. He understood the allure of the image it was at pains to present to the world – a bold, insistent image, projected in Technicolor and VistaVision – but he was immune to it. Something within him rebelled against the idea of seeing a film which celebrated this way of life, even in the guise (hypocritical, he was sure) of a lurid melodrama which purported to expose its cracks and fault lines. So they ended up, by way of compromise, going to see *Chase a Crooked Shadow*, a British picture starring Richard Todd and Anne Baxter. It was filmed in black-and-white and, although most of the action took place in a Spanish villa, Thomas found some of the exterior shots to be curiously evocative of Hertfordshire. There was a twist at the end which wrapped the plot up neatly, and gave them something to talk about as they lit up their cigarettes on the tube home. It was a tidy, comfortable little film which left them both feeling dissatisfied, and it ended this valedictory evening on a note of anticlimax.

Mrs Foley returned to Leatherhead the next morning, and for the rest of the day, husband and wife did their best to keep up a façade of domestic normality. Sylvia spent most of the afternoon ironing her husband's shirts, vests and underpants, while Thomas, bringing his armchair into companionable proximity with the ironing board, read the Sunday newspaper, which was full of stories about Mr Khrushchev and his demand that America call off its nuclear missile tests in the Pacific. His attempts to interest Sylvia in this subject were unsuccessful. She seemed depressed and distracted, and forgot to butter his toast before putting sardines on it. All she would talk about, over the tea table, was the sumac tree in the back garden, the branches of which were still bare, even in mid-April. 'Supposing it never grew leaves again?' she said at one point, unexpectedly. 'Supposing that happened to all the trees, in the garden and on the common and everywhere? Suppose that they never came back? What if there were no more leaves?' Thomas could not be sure if she was merely following some random, unhealthy train of thought of her own, or if these observations were somehow connected to the subject of nuclear missile tests, as broached by himself. It was really impossible to know. In fact the only things he *could* tell, for certain, were that Sylvia was deeply upset, and that neither of them had the gumption to do anything about it.

Motel Expo

On its approach to Melsbroek the next afternoon, Thomas's plane flew low over the north-western suburbs of Brussels. He craned his neck towards the window and looked out, through the swirls of cigarette smoke, in the hope of glimpsing the Expo site, but the angle of approach was all wrong. Instead he saw miles and miles of farmland, divided up into irregular geometric patterns by long, straight hedgerows and canals; he saw the occasional tidy, unassuming village; and he also saw, more surprisingly and less explicably, a collection of temporary buildings which lay sprawling at the edge of one of these villages: long, low buildings, grouped into rows of four and criss-crossed by neat, angular carriageways. There must have been about forty rows altogether, standing on a broad, flat, barren stretch of land which looked as though it had been cleared expressly for this purpose. Thomas might have said this was a prisoner-of-war camp, from the look of it: but the construction was much too recent, and in any case he was not sure that there had ever been such things in Belgium. In a few seconds the plane had passed over these buildings and they were gone from view.

After retrieving his two over-filled suitcases, he was met in the arrivals hall by another of the Belgian hostesses: but it was not Anneke, this time, and her duties seemed to extend no further than accompanying him to the taxi rank, and relaying his instructions to the driver. The journey was slower than expected: the French-speaking driver complained that traffic on these roads had been building up for many weeks, and now, with only three days to go until the opening day of the fair, it was becoming intolerable. Thomas muttered his agreement at a few appropriate moments but made no attempt to revive the conversation when it fizzled out. In a manila envelope on his lap were the typewritten directions to his accommodation. They told him that he would be staying in Cabin 419 of something called the 'Motel Expo', and that he would be sharing it with another Englishman by the name of A. J. Buttress. But this gave Thomas no idea what to expect, except that the word 'cabin' had a rather austere ring to it, and the number 419 implied that, whatever this cabin turned out to look like, it would only be one among many.

After about twenty minutes' driving, to his left, Thomas could once again see the glistening spheres of the Atomium rising above the trees, full moons of silver against the grey of the shifting afternoon sky. His spirits stirred. Tomorrow he would stand beneath them again, and the knowledge gave him a swift, electric thrill. In some complex, shrouded way, this monument represented everything that the fair itself – and the next six months of his own life – stood for: progress, history, modernity, and what it would feel like to be inside the engine that drove all of these things. And yet how could that feeling be reconciled with the life he had temporarily abandoned, the life that Sylvia remained marooned in? The two things seemed profoundly contradictory.

Ten minutes later his taxi turned off the main road and nosed its way into a small village by the name of Wemmel, which consisted of only a few dozen respectable, red-bricked houses, most of them generously provided with plots of land on which goats, chickens and sheep were grazing and otherwise passing the time contentedly, oblivious to the great events about to unfold in their vicinity. The taxi passed through the village and turned left; and then, after less than one minute's drive along a sinuous lane lined with poplar trees, it drew up outside a large complex of makeshift buildings which Thomas recognized at once, even though he had only seen it from the air. He regretted the fleeting comparison with a prisoner-of-war camp, now. Apparently this was to be his home until October.

Just beyond the barrier which opened up to allow them entry was one lonely wooden hut containing a small reception desk. Behind it sat a grave-looking man who bore a slight resemblance to a young Joseph Stalin.

'Welcome, Mr Foley. Welcome to the Motel Expo Wemmel. As you can see we are still in the final stages of completion but I think everything will be to your satisfaction. Breakfast will be served in the canteen daily from seven o'clock until nine o'clock in the morning. A laundry service is provided and we also provide a chapel where Sunday services will be performed in English as well as other languages. The gate will be locked at midnight and after that you must ring for assistance. Overnight guests are not permitted. This is your key.'

Thomas's cabin was at the far end of the site. As he trudged towards it with his suitcases, he was obliged to dodge and duck his way through the teams of workmen who were still putting the finishing touches to the motel: some were applying a final coat of light-blue paint to the woodwork, others were perched at the tops of ladders, nailing brightly coloured canopies to the eaves in order to give the rough, breeze-block structures a more festive atmosphere. A man with a wheelbarrow filled to overflowing with moist, reddish earth almost ran over his toe while crossing his path. Another workman was still painting numbers onto a few remaining doors: he had got as far as 412, so Thomas was able to find his own cabin easily enough by counting onwards.

Inside, he was immediately struck by the overwhelming sense of quiet. He sat down on the twin bed nearer the window – the other already had a suitcase placed on it – and looked around him. A wardrobe, a table, a tiny bathroom containing toilet, basin and shower. A skylight in the roof threw a faint rectangle of pallid sunlight onto the linoleum floor. No blankets or sheets on the bed – just one of those funny Continental quilt things. Duvets, were they called? The sounds of the workmen were distant, now, and served only to emphasize the more immediate silence. There did not seem to be anyone in the neighbouring rooms. All was still, very still.

Thomas lay down flat on the bed, ran his hands through his hair, and exhaled deeply. The journey was over, the moment of arrival had passed. Now what?

In a moment he would unpack. Then he would take a taxi to the Expo site and perhaps visit the Britannia: certainly look for somewhere to dine, and someone to dine with. It was four-thirty. Three-thirty back in London. He wondered what plans Sylvia would be making for dinner, which he supposed she would eat by herself in the kitchen.

He had done the right thing by coming here. He was sure of that. Though he knew it would be hard on her, terribly hard. At least she had Baby Gill for company, that was one consolation. He would write to her in a day or two, in any case; perhaps sooner . . .

'Sorry, old man. I didn't mean to interrupt your beauty sleep.'

Thomas stirred slowly and stiffly on his bed. A clatter from the bathroom had awoken him. Outside it was almost dark. He raised himself onto one elbow and peered towards the bathroom door. He saw a friendly-looking man of about his own age, with wavy blond hair, a V-necked sweater and a pipe clamped between his teeth. The man beamed back at him.

'Long journey, eh?' he said.

Thomas sat up, suddenly and thoroughly awake.

'I'm terribly sorry,' he said. 'I was just having a little lie down and . . .'

'Buttress,' said the man, extending his hand.

'Foley,' said Thomas.

They shook hands.

'Might as well call me Tony,' said the man. 'After all, it looks like we're going to be pretty intimate.'

'Rather. I'm Thomas, in that case.'

'Right you are. Mind if I light up in here?'

'Good Lord, not at all, old man. I'm ready for a gasper myself.'

'Good man.'

Tony lit his pipe, and Thomas lit his cigarette, and within a few seconds the interior of the cabin was agreeably thick with smoke.

'Well,' said Thomas, dragging on the cigarette thoughtfully. 'What do you make of this place, then? Not exactly Pontin's, is it?'

'Not exactly. Puts me more in mind of Colditz, to be honest.'

'Just what I thought when I saw it from the plane, when we were coming in to land.'

'Good flight?'

'Not bad. What about you?'

'Could have been worse.' Tony opened his suitcase and began to take out a few clothes. 'So, what's your role in this Expo hoo-hah going to be, if you don't mind my asking?'

'Back in London,' said Thomas, 'I work for the COI. They want me to be here to keep an eye on this pub. You know, the Britannia.'

'Ha! So they've got you pulling pints for six months, have they? You've landed on your feet, old boy.'

'I dare say I have. What about you?'

'Nothing so cushy, I'm afraid,' said Tony, who had wandered over to the wardrobe now. 'I say, how would it be if I had the shelves on the left, and you had the ones on the right? We don't want your socks getting mixed up with my smalls, after all.'

'Sounds good to me.'

'Then we can both hang our shirts up in the middle. Spirit of compromise, and all that.'

'Makes perfectly good sense.'

'Jolly d. I can see you and I are going to rub along quite painlessly.' By now Tony had his head in the wardrobe, placing socks, underwear, ties, cufflinks and other accessories onto the different shelves. His voice was muffled and indistinct. 'Anyway, I'm here on secondment from the Royal Institution,' he said. 'Sounds rather grand, I know, but I'm Scientific Consultant to the British pavilion, if you can believe that.'

'I can believe it,' said Thomas, 'but I'm not sure what it means.'

'There's a lot of pretty advanced equipment in there,' Tony explained, emerging from the wardrobe and looking around to see if there was anything else to pack away. 'The jewel in the crown being the ZETA machine.'

Thomas's interest was suddenly piqued, as he remembered the cloud of secrecy which had descended in the committee room as soon as Sir John had mentioned this project. Not wanting to sound too inquisitive, however, he adopted a casual tone and said: 'Oh, yes. Think I read something about that in the papers a few months ago.'

'There was quite a fanfare about it back in January.'

'What does it do, exactly?'

'What does it do? Well, to put it in the simplest possible terms, it's a bloody great oven. They're trying to achieve temperatures of about one hundred million degrees centigrade.'

Thomas let out a low whistle. 'Pretty darn hot.'

'Yes. Though all they've managed so far is about three million.'

'Still – plenty high enough to burn your Yorkshire pudding to a cinder, I would have thought.'

'I'll say. Though the ultimate plan is a bit more serious than that. You see, at those sorts of temperatures, you start to get neutron bursts. Nuclear fusion, in other words – which is the Holy Grail, as far as the researchers are concerned. All mankind's energy problems solved at a stroke.'

'And will it happen? Can it be done?'

'Some people think it already has. The venerable old Sir John Cockroft, who heads up the team, told the press he was 90 per cent certain that they'd cracked it. Hence all the ballyhoo in January. Of course, the Yanks and the Soviets are both trying to do the same thing, and seem to be lagging well behind, so the actual workings of the contraption have to be kept terribly hush-hush. What we're showing in the pavilion is only a replica. But still, you know, someone has to make sure it's working properly. All the lights have to flash on and off at the right time, and so forth, to make sure that Joe

Public is suitably impressed. Funny, really. You're here to look after a replica pub and I'm here to look after a replica machine. Both in the conjuring business, really, aren't we?' He chuckled quietly and then, while Thomas was still reflecting on this observation, started to rummage in his jacket pocket, finally producing a small, white, slightly crumpled envelope. 'By the way,' he said, 'you'd better have this, before it goes out of my head. Old Joe Stalin out there handed it to me at the reception desk. Looks like an invitation, unless I'm much mistaken.'

The British are part of Europe

The invitation had been typed on the notepaper of the British Embassy in Brussels, and read:

> *Dear Folly*
> *The Commissioner-General has the greatest of pleasure in inviting you to attend a small reception in the restaurant of the Atomium on the evening of Tuesday 15 April, to celebrate the imminent opening of the British Government Pavilion to the General Public. Drinks 6.45, Dinner 7.30. Dress: Lounge Suit.*
> *Yours*
> *Mr S. Hebblethwaite*
> *Secretary-General*
> *RSVP by return.*

Thomas would remember it, for years afterwards, as being one of the great moments of his life. It was not long after dusk, and he had entered the Expo Park by the Portes des Attractions, showing his newly issued delegate's pass to the security guard (who would never ask to see it again). Passing by the as yet silent and unopened amusement park on his left, he entered the Place de Belgique, then took a right turn. This avenue, too, was quiet: the cable cars stood empty and motionless high above him, their bodies thrown into brilliant relief by the fluorescent light which gleamed out from innumerable futuristic lampposts placed along the walkways. As for the Atomium, it was now directly ahead of him, and Thomas caught his breath when he saw it: each one of the aluminium spheres was festooned with a criss-crossing network of silver lights, and the effect was at once festive, majestic and other-worldly, as if this were a

Christmas celebration on the planet of some far-flung galaxy. Raising his eyes hundreds of feet to the topmost sphere, Thomas could see the warmer, yellower lights of the restaurant: the very place towards which his eager footsteps were now leading him.

A liveried footman welcomed him into the ground-floor reception area, and showed him to the lift, which was furnished with a glass roof so that the passenger might have a sense of the speed of his passage up through the central column. And indeed, it seemed incredibly fast: Thomas's ears were already popping when the lift hissed and braked its way to a gentle halt. The doors whooshed open and he stepped out into the restaurant.

A British Embassy functionary was waiting outside the lift with a typewritten list of invited guests.

'Ah. Good evening, Mr, er . . .' (he consulted the sheet of paper) 'Mr Folly, isn't it?'

'Foley.'

'Really? Are you sure?'

'Quite sure.'

'OK then. Tickety-boo.' (He crossed Thomas's name off the list.) 'I'm Simon Hebblethwaite, Sir John's secretary-general. Have you been introduced to Sir John?'

'Not as such, no. We . . . we attended a meeting together in London.'

'Ah. Well, anyway, it's jolly good of you to come, at such short notice. Someone from the Industries pavilion had to drop out at the last minute, and it would have looked bad to have a spare place at the table.'

'I see. Yes, that would have been awkward.'

'Well, do help yourself to a drink. There's a few bottles of fizz. I should get a couple of glasses down before it runs out and we have to fall back on the standard French plonk.'

Thomas took a glass of champagne from one of the waitresses and, realizing at once that it would be hard to get into conversation with any of the already tightly knit groups that had formed throughout the room, he wandered over to one of the vast plate-glass windows. It didn't bother him, for now, that his invitation to this dinner had obviously been an afterthought, or that nobody here had any interest in him. He could have stood for ever by that window, sipping champagne and looking down on the multicoloured lights of this incredible new metropolis: so busy, so modern, shimmering with life and promise. He felt that he was looking into the future, from the clearest and loftiest vantage point that the technological ingenuity of man could devise. He felt like a king of the universe.

For dinner, he took his allotted place at a table for four. The entire restaurant seemed to have been booked out for this occasion, and although Thomas's table – like all the others – was next to a window and offered the usual panorama of the Expo site, it was also about as far removed from Sir John Balfour and the other VIPs as it was possible to be. He found it surprising, then, that he was seated next to James Gardner, the designer of the British pavilion: for Thomas, this felt like a special and very intimidating honour. Also at the table were one Roger Braintree, introduced as Secretary to the Commercial Counsellor of the British Embassy in Brussels, and a tall, softly spoken Belgian lady called Ilke: Ilke Scheers, who held some position (never quite explained) on one of the committees responsible for advising on the musical component of the different nations' contributions.

'Well, ladies and gentlemen,' said Mr Gardner to the other three, raising his glass. 'Let us drink a toast to Expo 58. By golly, we made it! Here we are, bang on time, and only a few more nails and screws to bash in before Thursday. Nothing short of a miracle, if you ask me. Let's allow ourselves a small pat on the back.'

'To Expo 58,' Thomas echoed.

'And to Great Britain,' said Miss Scheers gallantly, 'whose contribution will, I'm sure, be one of the finest.'

They began to eat. The first course involved prawns, and onions, and something liquid and grey: closer identification than that was difficult. Thomas found it rather pleasant. Roger Braintree ate his portion quickly and determinedly, with a scowl of concentration on his face. He seemed to regard it as an unwelcome interruption, rather than a conversational overture, when Miss Scheers turned to him and said: 'And will you be attending the opening ceremony on Thursday, Mr Braintree?'

'Not if I can help it,' he replied, through his latest mouthful.

Miss Scheers flinched slightly, as if from an insect bite.

'You don't want to be present, on this historic occasion? Something to tell your grandchildren?'

'Do you?'

'Of course. An opportunity to see our King. To hear his speech.' Roger Braintree grunted and speared another prawn. 'Being British, I would have thought you enjoyed a certain amount of pomp and pageantry.'

'Well, we get plenty of that at home.'

'But *this*, Mr Braintree . . . Surely this is unique, and unrepeatable? So many nations coming together, when a few years ago we were all fighting each other. America and the Soviet Union, standing side by side. The exchange of ideas, the declaration of commitment to a shared vision of the future . . .'

Roger Braintree said nothing at first. Then, after dabbing at his lips with a napkin for a few moments, his only comment was: 'You have a very European way of looking at things.'

'The British are part of Europe, I think?'

'Yes, but we prefer things to be rather more . . . solid, than our continental allies. Might I trouble you to pass the bread, please?'

Meanwhile, Thomas was easing his way into conversation with Mr Gardner. The designer had a fearsome reputation at the COI, but was proving far more approachable than Thomas had expected. Instinctively, at first, he had been addressing the great man as 'sir', but Gardner took exception to this and insisted that there should be no formality.

'We're not in Whitehall now,' he said, refilling his wine glass for the third or fourth time. He raised the glass to Thomas again, without making a toast this time, and asked: 'So, how's this pub of yours coming on?'

'Well, it's not really *mine*, I wouldn't say . . .'

'Oh, come on. Enough of the English modesty.'

'It's shaping up very well, anyway. Almost there now. We're still waiting for delivery of a couple of things. One of the anchors from HMS *Victory* is supposed to have shown up, but there seems to have been a hitch.'

'A replica, I presume?'

'Yes, of course. We've had it made up in Wolverhampton. Bit of a headache, to be honest, but the brief, as you know, was that there should be plenty of historical stuff on display.'

'Ah, yes. We do love our imperial past, we Brits. Still – full marks to you for still making everything as fresh as you could. Not going with the thatched cottage, olde English sort of thing. I'm sure you had a few battles to fight. God knows, I did. But you can see what we're competing with.' He gestured at the window, with its vista down the brightly lit avenue towards the Porte Benelux. 'The Belgians have really pulled the stops out. This is all as bang up-to-date as anything I've seen. No wonder old Braintree here doesn't like it.' (Mr Braintree had, in fact, departed by now, pleading a prior engagement; and Miss Scheers had soon afterwards made her excuses and joined another table.) 'Good God, you heard what an uphill struggle that poor Belgian bird was having trying to get him to express a bit of basic well-mannered enthusiasm. All too typical, sadly. The number of times I've come up against people like him. This bloody British antipathy to anything new, anything modern, anything which smacks of *ideas* rather than boring old facts. I mean – no offence – but why do you think they've stuck me here with you, at the opposite end of the room from Brave Sir John and his not especially Merry Men? I'm only the designer of the pavilion, after all. And to them, that makes me some sort of crank. A weirdo. I'm telling you,' he continued – warming to his theme – 'our lot are about thirty years behind the Belgians. I mean, take this place we're sitting in. Bit gimmicky, but still a thing of beauty and wonder, don't you think? The designer was born in Britain, if you can believe that. Wimbledon, of all places. But he would never have come up with anything like this if he'd stayed there. The Brits just don't believe in progress, you see. That's why the Roger Braintrees of this world can't be doing with me. They pay lip service to it, all right, but when it comes down to it they don't trust the word – or the idea. Because it threatens a system which has been serving them very well for the last few centuries. And so, unlike him, yes I *will* be attending the opening ceremony on Thursday morning. With a bit of a "typically English", cynical smile on my face, of course, because we all know exactly what the King is going to say. He's going to say that humanity is standing at a crossroads, and we face two paths, one which leads to peace and one which leads to destruction. What else is he supposed to say? But that doesn't matter. What matters is that we're here – and in years to come, we can say that we were here. Taking part.' Mr Gardner was interrupted, at this point, by a waitress arriving with a plate of cheese. He picked up a couple of slices with his knife and slid them carefully onto Thomas's plate, then sighed. 'What wouldn't I give for a bit of nice, tangy Cheddar, and some Wensleydale,' he said. 'Have you tried this Dutch stuff? It tastes like candle wax.'

We deal in information

On the morning of Thursday, 17 April 1958, the Brussels World's Fair was declared open by King Baudouin Albert Charles Léopold Axel Marie Gustave de Belgique. The King entered the Exposition site by the Porte Royale, and was then driven along the Avenue de la Dynastie, accompanied by the Prime Minister and members of the royal family. The avenue was lined with cheering crowds – amongst them Thomas Foley and Tony Buttress – and the royal procession was marked with a fly-past of aeroplanes which formed a letter 'B' in the colours of the Belgian flag – although, as regards this last detail, Sylvia, watching at home on her black-and-white television, had to take the commentator's word for it. She was transfixed, in any case, by the novelty of watching the event live on television so early in the morning (ITV had commenced transmission several hours earlier than usual, for this very purpose) and spent the whole of the broadcast watching out eagerly – but with a mounting sense of desperation – for a glimpse of her husband in the crowd; dandling Baby Gill on her knee as she did so, and rousing her interest (or driving her to distraction) with endless repetitions of the question, 'Where's Daddy? Where's Daddy?' as the uncomprehending infant gazed intently at the flickering screen, mesmerized by its play of abstract, monochrome shapes. They were joined, for the second half of the broadcast, by Norman Sparks, who had taken the morning off work to mark the occasion. He apologized for disturbing them, but his own television was suffering problems with the vertical hold, and would Mrs Foley mind too much if he took the liberty of watching the rest of the ceremony on their set? Mrs Foley was only too happy to oblige. She placed Gill on her neighbour's lap while she went to pop the kettle on, and he cooed and gurgled at her with a natural ease, as if he did this sort of thing every day. The baby responded with besotted giggles.

Having driven the length of the avenue, King Baudouin proceeded into the Grand Auditorium, where, shortly after ten o'clock, he delivered his inaugural speech. A speech in which he expressed his view that humanity was standing at a crossroads, and that it faced two paths, one which led towards peace and one which led to destruction. He recommended, on the whole, taking the first of these paths. It was a fine, wise and memorable speech, most people agreed afterwards. A copy of it would later be made available to every hostess who worked at the fair, on a 45-rpm record.

When the speech was over, but before the crowd had really begun to disperse, Thomas slipped away and pushed and thrust himself through the thronging morass as best he could, making for the Britannia. It took a good half hour to complete the 500-yard journey.

Terence Rossiter was already there, standing behind the bar and polishing glasses in preparation for the midday opening. In this task he was being assisted by a tall, wiry woman of about twenty-five, with platinum-blonde hair and a hard, world-weary expression. Thomas assumed that this must be Mr Rossiter's niece, as mentioned on his first visit to the Britannia some weeks ago.

'Not at all,' the landlord told him. 'Ruthie was all set to come over, but then she got a better offer. Only last week, in fact. Quite out of the blue. Secretarial work, very well paid, just the sort of thing she's been looking for. So she could hardly turn it down. Damn nuisance from my point of view, but we didn't have to worry for long. Miss Knott heard of the vacancy on the grapevine, before it was even advertised, and put herself forward. We could hardly say no. Not many people would be willing or able to come to Belgium for six months, at just a few days' notice. And she seems very capable.' He turned to call her over from the other end of the bar. 'Shirley! Come and meet our lord and master.'

The blonde woman shimmied over on what appeared to be unfeasibly high heels, and shook Thomas by the hand.

'This is Mr Foley. He works for the Central Office of Information, and is here to see that we don't do anything treasonable or unpatriotic while going about our business.'

'Delighted, I'm sure,' said Shirley, giving Thomas a long but not particularly friendly glance.

'The pleasure's all mine,' Thomas answered.

Shirley said nothing to this, but turned and (after one more backwards glance) went back to her work.

'Has His Majesty finished pontificating, then?' Mr Rossiter asked.

'He has. You didn't go to watch him arrive?'

'My loyalties are with the Queen of England,' Mr Rossiter answered, 'not the King of Belgium.'

Having made his position quite clear, he too resumed his polishing. Thomas was just about to ask if there was anything he could do to help, when his attention was caught by a small pile of invitation cards sitting on a shelf behind the bar. They were for the Britannia's opening party tomorrow night, and he had written and designed them himself, back in London, before sending them off to the printers. After that, they were to have been shipped over to the British Council office in Brussels, so he was surprised to find that any of them had ended up here.

'How did you come by these, Mr Rossiter, if you don't mind my asking?'

The landlord glanced at the cards and said: 'Mr Carter brought a few dozen of them over last week. He said we should feel free to pass them on to any interested parties. I distributed a few among the staff, but didn't use any myself.'

'Good,' said Thomas. 'That's fine. I'll just –' (he thumbed through the cards, and removed a couple) '– I'll just take one or two, while I'm here, for . . . for contingency purposes.'

He kept one of the cards aside for Tony Buttress. Later that day, he slipped the other one into an envelope, addressed it to Anneke, and dropped it at the Hall d'Accueil, where messages could be left for the hostesses and other members of the Expo staff. On the card he wrote: 'I do hope you can come. Kind regards, Mr Foley.' But after delivering it, he worried that the wording might sound presumptuous. They had only met once, after all.

The party was going well. So well, in fact, that by ten o'clock on Friday night, Shirley and the other bar staff were starting to look exhausted. Thomas stood at the bar with Mr Carter and waited patiently to be served. All around them, guests were chattering in loud voices and in a distracting medley of different languages. When Shirley did finally get round to drawing up two more pints of Britannia bitter for them, she found that the barrel was almost empty, and had to summon Mr Rossiter for help in switching to a new one. This process itself took a good while – not least because the landlord had been partaking freely of his own refreshments for several hours, and they could all see that by now he had a glazed, unsteady look in his eye.

'Jeez,' said a voice to Thomas's left. 'Is this how slowly they do everything in Britain?'

'I think things are rather busier, at present, than anyone was expecting,' Thomas replied, stiffly.

'Is that so? Well I am "rather" thirsty, and getting "rather" tired of standing here and being ignored by this ill-mannered blonde.'

Thomas turned to get the measure of this speaker for the first time. With one remark, it seemed, all his prejudices about Americans had been confirmed. The man was young, in his late twenties or early thirties, and his hair was crew cut. He wore horn-rimmed spectacles and was brandishing a wad of Belgian francs in Shirley's direction in a way that struck Thomas as being particularly arrogant. The jacket of his suit was wide-shouldered, his collar was starched and his tie was narrow.

'May I see your invitation?' Thomas asked.

The American turned. 'Excuse me?'

'The reason this party is so crowded, and this bar is so busy, is that there seems to be a large number of people here who were not on the original guest list.'

'Is that so?' The American turned away again, and whistled loudly to attract Shirley's attention.

'I suppose,' said Thomas, 'that you're attached to the American pavilion.'

'You suppose correctly.'

'May I ask in what capacity?'

'Well. Why not take a look at my card?' The American reached into his pocket. 'Or even this – because, what do you know? It seems to be an invitation to this party. And look what it says here – my name. Edward Longman, Research Engineer, US pavilion.'

He held the card up for Thomas's inspection, briefly, defiantly. Thomas was suitably abashed.

'Look, old man, I'm terribly sorry, I –'

'Old? I'm only twenty-seven, pal. Though I shall be well into my thirties by the time I manage to get a drink in this dive.'

Shirley at last placed two pints of bitter in front of Thomas and Mr Carter.

'Serve this gentleman next,' said Thomas, handing her a twenty-franc note. 'And when you've done that, take a fifteen-minute break.'

'I can't,' she said. 'We're too busy.'

'Never mind that. You look worn out.'

'But Mr Rossiter will –'

'Mr Rossiter will just have to like it. Come and join us. We're sitting at that table in the corner.'

'All right. Thanks ever so, Mr Foley,' Shirley said, and took the money off him with a grateful smile.

Thomas stayed at the bar a few minutes more, chatting with Mr Carter and trying to engage Edward Longman in conversation; but he abandoned the attempt when it became clear that all his overtures were going to meet with monosyllabic rebuffs. He said goodbye to his British Council colleague and went back to rejoin Tony Buttress at their corner table. By the time he reached it, Shirley was already there. She was drinking bitter lemon and Tony, well into his third pint, was laughing somewhat stupidly and gazing into her eyes with woozy enthusiasm.

'Hallo, Thomas old boy,' he said. 'Got any ciggies on you?'

Thomas took out his packet of Player's Navy Cut, and offered it around.

'What's so funny?' he asked Tony.

'She's just been telling me her name,' he explained. Shirley stared back at him with tired resignation, as if she had heard this joke many times before. 'Took me a while to get it.'

'Get it?'

'Well, haven't you cottoned on yet? Shirley. Shirley Knott. *Surely not*. Don't you see?'

'Ah.' Thomas smiled. 'Do you know, it's taken me till now to real-ize . . .'

'Do people ever tease you about it?' Tony asked her.

'Oh, no. Never. I don't know why – it never seems to come up.'

Finally noticing the sarcasm, Tony said: 'Look, I didn't mean any offence. I just found it, you know, rather amusing . . .'

Shirley leaned towards him and Thomas was surprised to see her manner change, with impressive rapidity, from the abrasive to the flirtatious.

'Never mind, luvvie. You've got nice eyes. I could forgive most things to a man with eyes like that.' Tony blushed and drew back slightly. 'What brings you here, anyway? To the Expo, I mean.'

'Oh, I'm in the British pavilion. Got a technical job there.'

'Technical? What do you mean?' Shirley asked, and Thomas thought that if she was faking her interest, she was making a very convincing job of it. Before Tony had a chance to enlighten her fur-ther, however, a commanding, but musical voice interrupted the conversation.

'Mr Foley, I believe? Mr Thomas Foley?'

Thomas and his companions looked up. Standing over them was

a very tall, dark-haired man with a slim, athletic build. He wore a light-grey suit and carried, in one hand, a pint glass of beer, and in the other, a packet of Smith's *Salt'n'Shake* potato crisps. When he smiled down at them, he showed a set of brilliant white teeth. Even Thomas could see that this man was handsome; almost dangerously so.

He stood up to shake hands with him uncertainly.

'That's right,' he said. 'I'm Thomas Foley. To whom do I . . . have the honour of speaking?'

'My name is Chersky. Andrey Chersky. But I don't suppose for a moment that you have heard of me. Here – my business card.'

Thomas looked at the card. It was in Russian, so – apart from confirming Mr Chersky's identity – it did not enlighten him very much.

'May I join you for a few moments?' Mr Chersky asked.

'Of course.'

He sat down, and at the same instant, Mr Rossiter hurried over to the table.

'What do you think you're doing?' he said to Shirley.

'Mr Foley said –'

'I don't give a damn what he said. Can't you see how busy we are? Get back behind that bar.'

With an angry sigh, Shirley rose to her feet. She held out her hand to Tony Buttress.

'It's been lovely meeting you,' she said. 'Do come by again, won't you?'

'Of course.'

She said a short farewell to Thomas, and also to Mr Chersky, holding his eyes in a brief, appraising glance. But it was Tony whose gaze followed her the most wistfully as she squeezed through the crowds of customers on her way back to the bar.

'A most . . . attractive girl,' said Mr Chersky, to no one in particular, as he took his first sip of beer. Then he addressed Thomas: 'Forgive me for imposing my company on you like this, but I've been most anxious to meet you this evening.'

'Really?' said Thomas, nonplussed.

'Allow me to explain. I am a journalist, and an editor. I will be in Brussels for the next six months, attached to the Soviet pavilion, where I have the task of producing, every week, a magazine for the entertainment and instruction of our visitors. The name of the magazine . . . Well, you can probably guess it. *Sputnik*.' He smiled. 'I know. It is not the most original name. But sometimes the obvious thing is also the right thing to do.'

He stopped, at this point, to look at his packet of crisps. The name on the packet seemed to intrigue him, and he read it out slowly and wonderingly. '*Salt'n'Shake* . . .' he intoned. 'This "'n'" . . . what does it mean? I thought my English was rather good, but . . .'

'It's short for "and",' Thomas explained.

'Then why don't they print "and"?' Mr Chersky asked. 'Is it to save ink?'

'No, it's just to . . . well, I don't know – give things a more informal, chatty sort of feel.'

'I see. A kind of affectation.' Mr Chersky tore the packet open and extracted a crisp, which he now regarded with equal bemusement. 'And one is supposed to eat this, yes?'

'That's the general idea,' said Tony.

Thomas realized that the two men had not been properly introduced, and remedied the situation at once. After which, Mr Chersky began to nibble tentatively at his crisp, and offered the packet around.

'What a curious taste,' he said. 'Is this really what the British like to eat? It's extremely bland, and I would imagine has very little nutritional content.'

'They're only meant to be a snack,' said Thomas.

'Besides,' said Tony, 'you haven't put any salt on.'

'Salt?'

'Well, with this brand, you see, there's supposed to be a little blue envelope thingy in there, with salt inside.'

Mr Chersky rooted around in the packet, and found the salt

sachet at the bottom. Looking to the others for guidance, he cautiously tore it open, found the salt inside, and shook it over the remaining contents.

'Fascinating,' he said. 'I should have expected nothing less from the British. Such a resourceful nation. This is the genius that enabled you to conquer the globe.' He took the torn sachet and placed it carefully inside his wallet. 'I shall keep this to show to my colleagues,' he explained. 'Or perhaps even send it to my nephew back home.'

'Tell me more about your magazine,' Thomas prompted.

'Of course. You may take a look at our first issue.'

From an inside jacket pocket, he produced a single large sheet of paper, unfolded it carefully, and laid it out on the table before them. *Sputnik* consisted of only four pages, but within those pages there were many different articles printed in small, dense type. Much of it, inevitably, was given over to pieces eulogizing recent achievements in satellite technology, but there were also some paragraphs about other scientific inventions and about advances in the mining industry, together with a short essay on modern Soviet cinema.

'You're publishing in English, then?' Thomas asked.

'Yes, of course. Also French, Dutch, German and Russian. We have an experienced team of translators working for us at the embassy in Brussels. Please –' (he slid the magazine over to Thomas) '– I would like you to keep it.'

'Really? That's terribly decent of you.'

'In return,' said Mr Chersky, with his most charming smile, 'I would very much appreciate your advice. You see, your employer, I believe, is the Central Office of Information in London, and this is an organization which we admire very much in Russia. The kind of propaganda you deal in is really something that in my country, at the moment, we can only aspire to. So . . . elegant, and so subtle. We have very much to learn from your activities.'

'Now hold on a minute,' said Thomas. 'What we do at the COI can hardly be described as *propaganda*.'

'Really? But what else would you call it?'

'Well, as our name suggests, we deal in information.'

'Yes, but it's not as simple as that. In your publications and your exhibitions, you select certain pieces of information, and reject others. You present them in a certain way. These are political choices. We're all doing it. That's why we are all sitting here in Brussels. We've come to sell ourselves to the rest of the world.'

'No, I deny that. I deny it emphatically.'

'Very well. I have six months to bring you around to my point of view. In the meantime, will you help me?'

'How can I help?'

'I'm sure,' said Mr Chersky, 'that your time at Expo 58 is going to be extremely busy. And I cannot offer to remunerate you, in any concrete way, for the assistance you might be good enough to offer. But it is my sincere hope, nevertheless, that you might sometimes be prepared to cast your eye over our simple publication, and share with me any thoughts you have about how we could improve it. If, for this purpose, we might enjoy the occasional friendly meeting, I would be more than grateful.'

'Well,' said Thomas – highly flattered, although he was trying not to show it – 'I'm all for friendly meetings.'

'Really?' Mr Chersky smiled another of his brilliant smiles. 'And perhaps . . . Perhaps this fine establishment itself could be our rendezvous.'

'Why not? Capital idea. Absolutely capital.'

'Mr Foley, you do me the greatest of honours.'

'The pleasure's all mine. What are we here for, after all, if not to promote precisely this sort of exchange?'

'You are right,' said Mr Chersky, 'And although I did put forward a more cynical interpretation in my earlier comments, allow me to offer at least a partial retraction. Tonight is not the time to be cynical! The next six months are not the time to be cynical! I will go further, and say that 1958 is not the time to be cynical!'

'Hear, hear!' said Thomas.

'To 1958!' said Tony, raising his glass.

'Nineteen fifty-eight!' the others echoed, and they all drank deeply.

Thomas felt a hand on his shoulder, at this moment, and looked up. It was Anneke. He rose to his feet quickly and turned to face her. Unable to think of a more appropriate form of greeting, he shook her briskly by the hand.

'How very, very nice to see you again,' he said, conscious that the eyes of both Tony and Mr Chersky were turned enquiringly towards them. She was wearing her hostess's uniform, which seemed to be very damp, and her mousy blonde hair was scattered with raindrops. 'But – dear me – you're rather wet, I'm afraid.'

'I know,' she said, 'it's started to rain outside. Hadn't you realized?'

'I hadn't. But please, pull up a chair, make yourself comfortable.'

'That's very kind of you,' she said. 'And it was very kind of you, as well, to send me this invitation. But I cannot stay.'

'You can't?'

'I only finished work half an hour ago. And in ten minutes from now, my father will be waiting to collect me from the Porte de L'Esplanade, to take me home. But I had to come by, to say thank you.'

Feeling very bold, Thomas took her gently by the arm. 'Shall I walk with you, at least some of the way?'

'That would be nice. Thank you.'

Together, they stepped outside. It was a relief to leave behind the multilingual babble of the Britannia.

'It is a success, your party?' Anneke asked.

'Yes, I think so. No shortage of guests, at any rate.'

'I hear a lot of people talking about the British pavilion, and the British pub.'

'Really? That's very gratifying.'

The rain was getting heavier all the time. They took temporary shelter beneath one of the trees by the side of the ornamental lake.

'I had a suggestion to make,' said Anneke, 'since I was not able to stay very long tonight. On Monday evening I'm not working and I was going to come to the Expo with my friend Clara. We thought we would visit the Parc des Attractions. Would you like to join us?'

'Yes, of course,' said Thomas. 'Thank you. That would be splendid.'

'Perhaps you also have a friend, someone you could bring with you?'

'Naturally. I'll ask Tony, my room-mate.'

'Good.'

She smiled at Thomas, and a confusion of different feelings shivered through him. He had not seen Anneke for many weeks, and tonight she looked even more beautiful than he remembered, notwithstanding that dreadful uniform. But it also occurred to him, for the first time, that he should really not delay much longer in telling her that he had a wife and baby back in London.

'I was so pleased that you invited me to the party,' Anneke said. 'I was worried that you might have forgotten about me. After all, you must already have met a lot of hostesses.'

The conversation, Thomas realized, could take a dangerously intimate turn if it continued in this vein.

'Blast this rain,' he said, by way of distraction. 'I don't think you should keep your father waiting. If only we had an umbrella . . .'

Suddenly a hand was thrust out from the darkness, holding that very object.

'Here you are, old man.'

Two familiar figures stepped out from the shadows.

'You can use ours if you like.'

'Only too happy to be of service.'

It was Mr Radford and Mr Wayne. Thomas stared at them stupidly. How long had they been lurking in the undergrowth? Had they been following him ever since he left the pub? Or even before that?

'Evening, Foley,' said Mr Wayne, extending his hand. 'We thought it wouldn't be long before we ran into you.'

'Not interrupting anything, I hope?'

'Hate to break in on a tender moment.'

'My name's Radford,' said Mr Radford, shaking Anneke's hand. 'Wayne.'

'Anneke,' she answered, looking from one to the other in confusion. 'Anneke Hoskens.'

'Would you like us to escort you to your meeting point?' said Mr Wayne. 'It's a filthy night.'

'A girl could catch her death on a night like this,' said Mr Radford. 'Here, you take my arm, and get under this umbrella.'

'And I'll tag along behind, with Mr Foley. 'We don't mind a bit of rain, do we?'

'Erm . . . no. I suppose we don't.'

'Of course not. We British are made of stern stuff.'

Mr Wayne headed off at an uncompromising pace, tugging Anneke alongside him on his arm, and entertaining her, presumably, with whatever smalltalk he had at his disposal. Mr Radford, meanwhile, was in his usual interrogative mode.

'Good party, Foley?'

'Not bad. Pretty decent.'

'Any surprises? Uninvited guests, that sort of thing?'

'A couple, yes.'

'Like that Russian chap, for instance.'

Thomas looked askance at him. 'How did you know about that?'

'Wants to have a few meetings with you, I gather.'

'So he says. Is there a problem?'

'Good heavens, no. A free and frank cultural exchange between the different nations . . . that's what this event is all about. It's why you're here, isn't it?'

'I believe so, yes.' Mollified, Thomas added: 'Good of you to see it like that, I must say. After all, you heard what the King said yesterday. We're never going to make any sort of progress until we all start to trust each other.'

'Trust?' said Mr Radford. 'Who said anything about trust? Of course you mustn't trust him.'

'Why not?'

'Because we don't know anything about him yet. Apart from the fact that he has the freedom to wander into your pub all by himself, when most of the Soviets are being kept locked up in their hotel at this time of night – which makes him suspicious, to start with. Good Lord, man, I wasn't saying that you should trust him. Whatever gave you that idea?'

'I just thought –'

'See him as often as you like. The more often, the better. Just keep your eyes and ears open, and if he ever lets slip something that might be considered . . . you know, interesting – let us know.'

'How will I contact you?'

'Oh, don't worry about that. We'll always be around. Now look, you'd better go and say a fond farewell to your little Belgian piece. Charming girl, by the way. Excellent choice. And don't worry about the abandoned bride back home, either. Very little chance of her finding out, I'd say. Highly unlikely. You're on a safe wicket there.'

With which reassuring words he gave a hideous wink, tipped the rim of his trilby hat at Thomas and slipped away.

I can love whoever I want

On Monday evening, Thomas and Tony decided to walk from their motel to the Expo site. It would only take half an hour or so, and there was a beautiful sunset to enjoy along the way.

The Atomium was ahead of them as they walked, its lights glimmering and twinkling in the encroaching dusk. Thomas felt a tremor of excitement pass through him: partly from sheer joy at the sight of this bizarre, impudent monument, of which he knew he could never tire; partly from nervous anticipation at the thought of everything the next few hours might hold.

'By the way, as far as Miss Hoskens is concerned,' Tony said, not for the first time that day, 'I think you're playing a pretty dangerous game.'

'I told you, I'm not playing any sort of game.'

'Well, what are your intentions, exactly?'

'She's a charming girl, that's all, and while I'm here in Brussels I see no harm in having an honest, serious friendship with her.'

'Ha! Friendship, you say? I'm sorry, old boy, but I saw the way she was looking at you on Friday night, and there was more than friendship in those luminescent Belgian eyes.'

Thomas was forever discovering hidden depths in his new friend. Where had he picked up the word 'luminescent', he wondered?

'Even that Russian bod noticed it,' Tony continued, 'and he didn't strike me as being over-preoccupied with matters of the human heart. I tell you, you're going to hurt that girl, if you're not careful. Not to mention your wife. Marriages have broken up over less.'

'With all respect, what do you know about married life? Either its responsibilities or its pleasures?'

'Nothing, I'm pleased to say. Footloose and fancy free, that's me, and I intend to stay that way. Which is why *I*, at least, can look forward to this evening with a clear conscience. And if this friend of hers is half as good-looking as Anneke herself, there'll be no stopping me. I don't know if you'd noticed, but I reckon I've spruced myself up pretty nicely this evening. Best shirt. Smartest tie. A few splashes of the old cologne behind the ears and a thorough going-over with that new stripey toothpaste with the miracle ingredient. I don't know how she's going to resist me.'

Thomas smiled, although he had only been half-listening. Tony's comment about Mr Chersky had reminded him of some of the things that had been said on Friday night: in particular, the way Mr Radford had asked him to keep an eye on their new Russian acquaintance and report anything suspicious. Was this what had alarmed those two strange, eternally vigilant, omnipresent Englishmen? Perhaps Chersky had really been using his (rather implausible, it now seemed) eagerness to seek out editorial advice as the most brazen of pretexts for introducing himself, not to Thomas, but to Tony: the man whose job in Brussels was to oversee the display of valuable British scientific equipment, the very workings of which were shrouded in well-kept secrecy. Contemplating this, Thomas had a sudden, vertiginous sense of radical instability: as if he was standing again by the window in the Atomium's topmost globe but gazing down, this time, not on the various pavilions and attractions of Expo 58, but on a hallucinogenic, perpetually shifting world of doubtful loyalties and concealed motives. Even the seemingly innocent conversation he'd had with Tony over the weekend about CND . . . Thomas had been – not shocked, exactly, but certainly surprised to learn that he had taken part in one of the Aldermaston marches. Of course, that didn't make him a Communist, or anything like that. But still, he imagined it was the kind of thing that made the likes of Mr Wayne and Mr Radford a bit jumpy. It only added to his sense that he was being drawn deeper and deeper into a world he didn't really understand. The business with Anneke was much the same. It was true, looked at from an objective point of view, that he shouldn't be spending time with her like this. He was a married man, and he took his vows very seriously. But he could see little harm in it, for precisely that reason. He would know when to stop. He would know when to draw the line. Surely they would both have the strength to pull back, when things threatened to get out of control?

When Thomas and Tony reached their meeting point at the gate to the Parc des Attractions, there was no more time to reflect. Nor did the next couple of hours do much to alleviate his vertigo. Together with Anneke and her friend Clara, they rode the *montagne russe* and the big dipper. They span around on a giant wheel and they whizzed around in circles on model spaceships. They hurtled around the track in dodgem cars and deliberately crashed into each other, giggling wildly like fourteen-year-olds. Thomas had never known such dizziness. The years fell away from him and soon he had forgotten everything: the British pavilion, the Britannia, his office in Baker Street, his house in Tooting, Sylvia, his mother, Baby Gill . . . Dazzled by the company of the two girls, his head spinning with the adrenalin rush of the different rides, he felt that he had miraculously entered some sort of eternal present, in which nothing that he did need have any consequences, or come to an end.

They were hungry and thirsty. 'Let's go to the Oberbayern!' said Clara. The two Englishmen didn't know what she meant, but they followed the Belgian girls trustingly.

The place Clara had proposed was a gigantic replica of a Bavarian beerhouse and dance-hall. Waved inside by a doorman in traditional costume, they found themselves entering a space that had the dimensions of a medium-sized factory. It was packed to the rafters, and the noise was overwhelming. Through a dense cloud of pipe and cigarette smoke, Thomas could just about see that trestle tables filled every available inch of space, apart from a raised platform, about the size of a boxing ring, alongside one of the walls, on which a lederhosen-clad orchestra was pounding out a repetitive folk tune.

Clara and Anneke made their excuses and went to the ladies' room, while the two men pushed through the crowd and struggled to find four places together at one of the tables.

'Good God,' said Tony, once they were safely seated. 'This is mayhem.'

A waiter appeared and they ordered four beers, which were promptly delivered in tankards holding at least a quart apiece.

'Well, cheers, old boy,' said Thomas. 'This is certainly turning out to be a night to remember.'

'I'll say.'

'How are you getting on with Clara?'

'Well, to be perfectly frank . . . She's just not really my type.'

Thomas nodded sympathetically. 'Yes, I could see that. She seems awfully nice.'

'Oh, don't get me wrong. She is awfully nice.'

'Very friendly.'

'Terribly friendly. It's just that . . . you know.'

'Yes. I know what you mean.' He tried to think of a tactful way of phrasing it. 'She's a well-built girl, isn't she?'

'Very much so. Sturdy. Useful sort of girl to have around on a farm, or something like that.'

'What's she doing here, exactly?'

'Well, she comes from the same town as Anneke and applied to be a hostess as well. But they didn't take her. So she's working in this sort of cod historical village they've put together. "La Belgique Joyeuse".'

'Ah, yes – Gay Belgium. I've heard a lot about it. They say that if you haven't experienced Gay Belgium, you haven't lived.'

'Well, Clara's working in one of the shops there. Poor girl, she has to get dressed up as an eighteenth-century baker every day. Got ticked off this afternoon for wearing a wristwatch, apparently.'

'So what are you going to do? She seems awfully stuck on you.'

'I don't know. I'll play it by ear. Anyway, Mum's the word – here they come.'

The contrast between the two girls, as they approached the table, could hardly have been clearer. Anneke was wearing a pale-blue summer dress, short-sleeved, which showed off the slenderness of her arms and ankles. Freed from her ridiculous pill-box hat, her hair was able to fall to her shoulders in a tousled cascade. Her eyes gleamed and her skin, though freckled, had a bronzed and healthy glow. Clara's ruddy face, meanwhile, radiated simple good nature. Her legs were stocky and the cut of her knee-length skirt was ill-chosen, but there was a permanent, overbearing cheerfulness about her which somehow contrived to take your mind off these failings. Thomas liked her. But then she had not been clinging on to his arm for the last two hours.

Clara proved a useful guide to the entertainment on stage. She said that she had grown up in a German-speaking part of Belgium, and was familiar with many of the songs the orchestra was playing. Like Anneke, she tucked in enthusiastically to her plate of *bratwurst* and sauerkraut. Thomas thought it strange that Belgians should be so ready to embrace the culture of a country which had occupied their own less than fifteen years ago, and committed many atrocities, but he did not say anything. It was not the right time to get involved in such discussions.

The orchestra had begun to play a particularly insistent and catchy song. Everyone who wasn't eating began to clap their hands to the beat of the music. Clara leaned across the table and said – or rather shouted – that this tune was called 'Ein Prosit' and was a traditional Bavarian drinking song. She and Anneke were starting to clap along, too. The music got louder and louder, and the tempo faster and faster, as the chorus repeated itself incessantly. Many of the diners were singing along, and suddenly, a few yards away from Thomas, two young women jumped to their feet, clambered onto the table and began to dance, scattering fragments of food and attracting more than the occasional glance as they did so. The diners laughed and cheered and stamped their feet. Many of them also got up to dance, and the singing got louder still:

> *Ein Prosit, ein Prosit*
> *Der Gemütlichkeit*
> *Ein Prosit, ein Prosit*
> *Der Gemütlichkeit.*
> *OANS ZWOA DREI! G'SUFFA!*
>
> (A toast, a toast
> To cheer and good times
> A toast, a toast
> To cheer and good times.
> ONE TWO THREE! DRINK UP!)

Anneke and Clara jumped up and held out their hands for the men to join them. But Tony shook his head, grinning broadly, while Thomas took a long draught of beer and hid his face behind the enormous tankard. The women shrugged and began to dance with each other anyway.

'This is mass hysteria!' shouted Tony, looking around in amazement. 'Isn't this the kind of thing that brought Hitler to power?'

'Ssh! No politics tonight, please.'

Finally, when it seemed impossible that the music could get any louder or any faster, a crashing major chord brought the whole thing to a welcome conclusion. Amid the cheers, clapping and laughter, Anneke and Clara flopped back down into their chairs, flushed and sweating, and made an immediate lunge for their beer glasses.

'*Die Gemütlichkeit!*' said Clara, swinging her glass at everyone's in turn.

'Good times, and good cheer!' said Anneke.

They all drank deeply, then sat back and smiled long, satisfied, slightly tipsy smiles.

The orchestra started up another tune, and on a balcony high above the diners, a choir of about twenty men and women – all in traditional costume – materialized as if from nowhere and took up the melody in three-part harmony. Clara sighed delightedly.

'Ah – "Horch was kommt von draußen rein"! I adore this tune.'

It did indeed come as something of a relief, after the crazed monotony of the last performance. It was hardly what Thomas would have described as sophisticated music, but still, there was something lilting and supple about the melody that appealed to him. The audience began to clap along again, but less robotically than before.

'Bavaria must be a very cheerful place,' he remarked. 'I've never heard a piece of music from there that didn't sound jolly.'

'Ah, but the words are rather tragic,' Clara explained. 'There is a lover – in some versions a man, though I like to think of her as a woman – and today her sweetheart is getting married to someone else, and she says that for her this is a day of mourning. But she is quite defiant about it. She won't relinquish her feelings for this man.'

And, as a new verse started, Clara began to sing along:

> *Laß sie reden, schweig fein still*
> *Hollahi hollaho*
> *Kann ja lieben wen ich will*
> *Hollahi aho.*

'"I can love whoever I want," she says.' Clara had been addressing her words to all of them, up until this point, but now she stared pointedly at Tony, and repeated: 'I can love whoever I want.' She stood up, took him by the hand, and pulled him to his feet. 'Come on, let's dance. You must feel like dancing.'

Tony followed, looking rather like a sheep being led off to the abattoir, and throwing a helpless, beseeching glance back in Thomas's direction.

Now Anneke stood up and held out her arms.

'So, Thomas, do you ever dance?'

'Very rarely,' Thomas said. He was about to add, 'I think the last time was at my wedding,' but the words died on his lips. Instead he allowed Anneke to lead him gently towards a clear space between the tables. He took hold of one her hands, and put his other arm around her waist. Through the thin cotton of her dress he could feel the beginnings of the curve of her bottom. This did not seem right, so he moved his hand upwards, until he could feel the base of her spine, which seemed just as inappropriate, if not more so. So he raised his hand away from her back a fraction, and barely touched her at all. Clara, he noticed, was leaning in tightly to Tony as they danced, her head resting upon his shoulder, a quietly blissful smile on her face.

'This has been a wonderful evening,' said Anneke.

'Yes, it has,' said Thomas, but before the conversation could proceed any further, he was interrupted by a familiar voice with a shrill Cockney accent, saying: 'Hello, Mr Foley! Fancy seeing you here.'

It was Shirley Knott, the barmaid at the Britannia. And her dancing partner was, of all people, Ed Longman, the rude American guest from Friday night.

'Hello!' said Thomas, to both of them. He could not resist adding, to Mr Longman: 'So – you managed to get served, I see.'

Mr Longman grinned. 'English hospitality. Took me a while to get the hang of it, but now that I have, I'm a *real* fan.' He gave Shirley's waist a tight squeeze, and looked warmly into her eyes.

It occurred to Thomas that almost everybody in this vast dance-hall was drunk, to some degree or another, and that the whole room was alive with the promise of transient international or even intercontinental romances on the point of budding into life. He was quite relieved when the music came to a halt again, and everyone could return to their seats once more. He waved goodbye to Shirley and Mr Longman, and sat down opposite Anneke, who smiled at him and then began powdering her face and examining the results in her compact mirror.

Tony appeared at his side and leaned in towards him.

'Look, old boy, I'm going to shoot off.'

'What?'

'Clara's gone to the ladies' and this is my only chance to escape.'

'You can't do that! She'll be devastated.'

'I know it's not exactly the decent thing to do, but you will help me out here, won't you? The woman's a positive man-eater.'

'What shall I tell her?'

'I don't know . . . Tell her I got an urgent message that the ZETA machine was about to explode, or something. Just . . . try and square things with her, OK?'

Thomas suspected that his friend was asking the impossible, and so it proved. His use of the word 'devastated' had been no exaggeration, and as he walked with the two women, a few minutes later, through the thinning crowds towards the meeting point where Anneke's father would be waiting to drive them both home, he caught a glimpse of tears glistening against Clara's now pallid cheeks. He glanced at Anneke, who had noticed them too. It was a subdued trio, then, who said goodbye at the Porte des Attractions. Although, if there was one thing that could not be described as subdued, it was Anneke's goodnight kiss. It may have been delivered chastely to his cheek, but there was still an unmistakeable tenderness to it that made his heart flutter. And as she walked away with her friend, she turned and blew him another one.

When they had gone, Thomas stood there for a few moments, his hands in his pockets, hot dog wrappers and empty cigarette packets scuffling past him in the breeze. He sighed and puffed out his cheeks.

He had been at the Expo for more than a week, and had not written Sylvia a single letter yet. Time to remedy that situation, he decided.

The girl from Wisconsin

22nd April 1958

Dearest Syllabub,

I'm dreadfully sorry not to have written to you before now. As we both found out last week, telephone communications between Brussels and London are likely to prove challenging – and jolly expensive. Lovely as it was to hear your voice, I think we had better confine ourselves to letters for the time being.

Anyhow, you will be pleased to know that I have settled in, and the powers that be are giving me a busy time of it so far. Accommodation is a bit on the Spartan side. Motel Expo is a gruesome collection of breeze-block cabins in the middle of a muddy field about two miles from the Heysel site. It is run along militaristic lines – the lights go out and the barriers come down at midnight, with no exceptions. Tony B and I have talked about setting up an escape committee.

Tony B is Tony Buttress, my room-mate, as mentioned on the phone. I have fallen on my feet here – he really is a very decent sort. He is here as a sort of scientific advisor to the British pavilion, and is terribly knowledgeable about everything. Atomic science seems to be his main area, however. We find ourselves thrown together a good deal. Last night we took on the Parc des Attractions – dodgem cars, Ferris wheel, fake Bavarian beerhouse, the whole shebang. All ripping good fun, but it's taken it out of me today, I must say. Head like a ball of wet cotton wool. I'm obviously not as young as I was.

My duties at the Britannia remain somewhat ambiguous. I am not supposed to be involved in the day-to-day running of the pub but sadly the character of our landlord, Mr Rossiter, makes it necessary. During the early hours of opening he is more or less reliable, but as the day draws on I'm afraid that he begins to tipple. In fact, why be euphemistic about it – the word 'tipple' does nothing like justice to his capacity. By five or six o'clock in the evening you can guarantee that he will be royally sloshed. Luckily his chief barmaid seems a very sensible and competent girl. She rejoices in the name of Shirley Knott. (Think on it for a while, and you will see the pun.)

The fair itself is rapidly getting into full swing. The queerest sorts of groups and organizations are passing through. This week they are playing host to an International Congress of Opticians. A number of them came to the Britannia yesterday at lunchtime. One of them was so short-sighted that he banged his head on our model aeroplane and had to be treated for concussion.

Write soon, my love.

Thomas xxx.

2nd May 1958

Thomas my dear,

How wonderful to hear from you at long last! I was beginning to wonder if you had forgotten our address, or if the postal service in Belgium had perhaps gone on strike. But I realize now, of course, that you have just been awfully busy. I understand completely how full your days must be at the beginning of the fair.

I was delighted to hear that you have already started to make new friends. I know that you are very interested in the subject of Atomic Energy yourself, so you must be able to have all sorts of interesting conversations with Mr Buttress, of the kind which I sadly am not able to provide you with. Now that I reflect on how quiet and dull everything must seem to you here, I understand why you were so keen to take the job in Brussels. Although it still would have been nice if you could have taken me with you.

You did not mention Baby Gill in your letter but I imagine you would like to hear some news of her. The news, in fact, is very exciting – she has started to crawl! As you may remember (or perhaps not), just before you left she was beginning to sit up very well. And so, on Saturday morning, I had her with me in the kitchen, while I was making a pot of tea to take out to Mr Sparks in the garden, and I left her on the floor not thinking very much of it. I took Mr Sparks his tea, stopped to exchange a few words with him, looked round behind me and there she was! She had followed me all the way into the garden, and halfway down the garden path! What a prodigy!

I suppose you might be wondering what Mr Sparks was doing in our garden all this time. Well, really, he has been most obliging since you went away. It all began when your opening ceremony was broadcast last Thursday morning. Naturally I sat down to watch the whole proceedings, and after a while Mr Sparks came to join me because he has been experiencing some difficulty with the reception on his television set. We both looked out for you, but could not see you anywhere in the crowds. I presume you were there? Afterwards, Mr Sparks asked if he could visit our garden, and as soon as he saw it I could tell there were some things that had caught his attention. Little jobs, I mean, that you had left unfinished before your departure – such as the digging of the goldfish pond. And then he asked, in the nicest possible way, if I thought it would disoblige you if he undertook to complete one or two of these tasks. Of course, I had no way of consulting you, but I was sure what your answer would be. And so, on Saturday morning, he came around here with his spade and his other tools, and dug the rest of the pond out in no time at all, to a tremendous depth. For such a slight man, he is surprisingly strong! On Sunday he filled the pond with water and next weekend he has promised to drive me to the aquarium in East Sheen to buy some fish and also some water lilies and other foliage. I am sure you will be pleased to see it looking so attractive when you return.

Anyway, now Baby has woken up and I can hear her crying. Write back soon, my sweet, but don't worry about me, I am coping quite well and I have been far from feeling lonely.

Your loving,

Sylvia x.

19th May 1958

Dear Syllabub,

Thank you for your last letter, which I found most reassuring. How lucky we are to have a neighbour as thoughtful as Mr Sparks. I do hope you are not taking advantage of him, my angel, and encouraging him to come round *too* often to help with these little jobs? It would be wrong to deprive his sister of his caring attentions, after all. Anyway, I'm sure you are the best judge of the situation.

Once again I fear I have left it much too long before replying. I am so sorry, but we have been run off our feet for the last two weeks. As I'm sure you will understand, we are especially busy at the Britannia whenever there are crowds of our own countrymen visiting the fair, and just lately things have been especially busy on that front. Last week the British pavilion was subject to a visit of delegates from the Bristol Chamber of Commerce. And if that was not enough, a few days later, the London Symphony Orchestra were giving a concert of British music in the Grand Auditorium here, and blow me if the whole blessed orchestra did not decide to drop by for a pint at the Britannia after the performance! Everyone had to work flat out to make sure that the whole crew were adequately fed and watered – right down to the chaps who play the bass fiddle and the triangle. Mr Rossiter was having a snooze in the cellar at the time so it was all hands on deck, I can tell you. Even Anneke pitched in and helped.

Oh, but I haven't mentioned Anneke before, have I? Anneke is my guardian angel – at least, that is how I like to think of her. She was the hostess who came to meet me at the airport the very first time I arrived here, and we seem to keep running into each other ever since. She was at the pub on this occasion to have a drink with her friend Clara, and it was jolly decent of them both to lend a hand, I think.

In fact, there is a bit more to it than that. For Clara, you see, has the most frightful crush on Tony B, which means that she is always hanging around the British pavilion trying to catch sight of him, while he spends most of his time doing his best to keep out of her way. I feel a bit sorry for the poor girl, not least because, quite apart from all that, her job at the fair – dressing up as a shopkeeper from Ye Olden Dayes as part of a sort of living museum they have put together here, called Gay Belgium – is not really as nice or as prestigious as Anneke's.

Anyway, I mustn't drivel on too much about these two, not least because I have scarcely yet mentioned my new Russian friend, Mr Chersky. A newspaper editor from Moscow who reckons that yours truly, believe it or not, is just about the bee's knees, journalism-wise. Can you believe that? Well, it's a longish story, so I shall save it for another letter in any case.

I hope I have told you enough, at any rate, to convey the impression that life here is pretty exciting, as well as busy. I must confess that I am having a whale of a time (apart from missing you, my sweet).

Another party came in here yesterday. They were from the World Congress on the Prevention of Accidents in Industry. Unfortunately one of them fell down the stairs on his way to the gents' and had to be rushed off to hospital with a broken leg.

Take care, my angel.

Your faithful,

Thomas xxx.

26th May 1958

Thomas my dear,

What a pleasure to hear from you again, and in a letter filled with such thrilling news. Fancy serving drinks to the London Symphony Orchestra! I have read a great deal in the newspapers about the Belgian hostesses and their role at the fair. They all seem to be very pretty girls. Does this Anneke speak good English or have you been learning to speak Belgian on her account? It must be very confusing there with everyone speaking in different languages all the time. It is certainly obliging of her to give you so much of her time. You and Tony B and Anneke and her friend must make up quite a cosy foursome. It is nice to know that you are not short of company.

For my own part, I have not been having nearly such a sociable time of it. Last weekend I had a little excursion, it's true, but it was more distressing than enjoyable. I had mentioned to Mr Sparks that I really felt guilty about not having visited cousin Beatrix since her accident. As you know she is presently in the Royal Free Hospital in Hampstead, and although it is not hard to reach by public transport, I have been put off by the difficulties of taking Baby Gill on a bus or the underground. That pram, as you know, sometimes seems to weigh as much as a small car! But Norman came to the rescue – his kindness never ceases to amaze me. We calculated that, if I used the Northern Line, I could do the whole round trip in less than three hours, and he gamely volunteered to babysit Gill for that time on Sunday afternoon. Wasn't that sweet of him? As it happens, he has been spending a good deal of time around her these last few weeks (last Tuesday evening he was here for a few hours, fixing that uneven shelf on the sitting-room bookcase – the one that has defeated you for so long) and Gill has become very comfortable with him. I suppose at that age they are just happy to have a masculine presence around the house, and scarcely notice whether the man happens to be their father or not. And I thought that if I gave her a good feed after lunch, the chances are that she would sleep through most of the afternoon, and Norman would not be put to much trouble. Which indeed turned out to be the case.

It was not a pleasant afternoon for me, however. Poor Beatrix is in a very bad way. Her neck is in one of those awful brace things and she cannot move in any direction. I thought she would at least be pleased to see me – I had brought her a large bunch of grapes, and a number of magazines – but as you know she has always been a fierce-tempered thing and her present situation seems to have plunged her into the darkest of moods. In the end I did not stay for much more than half an hour. At least when I got home everything was cheerful again. Gill had just woken up and she was playing with Norman very nicely. So we had a cup of tea and a very friendly chat.

I must go now, my love. Do try not to leave it so long before writing next time.

Your loving,
Sylvia x.

7th June 1958

Dear Sylvie,

Thank you for your last letter, even though the news about Beatrix was rather distressing. Do give her my best if you go to visit her again. It was decent of Sparks to babysit while you were making the call. Frankly I had not got him down as the sort of chap who was good with babies, but now that I think of it, I suppose there is something oddly feminine about him, so it probably makes a kind of sense.

The big news here . . . Well, there are two big pieces of news, really. One is that we had a visit from a bona fide VIP a couple of days ago. Of course, there are all sorts of famous people passing through the fair every day. A week or two ago they had a sort of mini-Cannes film gala here and it was wall-to-wall movie stars. Apparently in some parts of the site you couldn't move without bumping into Yves Montand or Gina Lollobrigida. Sadly, though, none of them ever made it as far as the dear old Britannia. Instead we have been graced by the presence of ... Mr Heathcoat-Amory! Yes, the Chancellor of the Exchequer in person. Second-in-command in Her Majesty's Government, no less. I would like to tell you that he was charm personified, put us all at our ease and treated us with that easy condescension which is apparently the mark of every well-bred Englishman. Instead, he was like a fish out of water. And a damned unfriendly fish at that. I don't know what else they teach you on the playing fields of Eton, but it's obviously not to tuck into a plate of fish and chips and a pint of bitter in a fake British pub and look as though you're enjoying it. Tony said he was probably disappointed that the menu didn't include Beluga caviar and roast swan (or whatever else it is they eat at Oxford High Table).

In fact Tony saw rather more of Mr H-A than I did, since he had the task of showing him over the scientific exhibits in the pavilion, and his impression, I have to say, was not at all favourable. I don't know if I mentioned it before, but my dear room-mate Mr B is a little bit of a radical, in his friendly way. Approves of CND, for one thing – and don't get him started on the subject of Suez. He's no great admirer of Mr Macmillan and his cabinet, that's for sure, and so after Heathcoat-Amory and his entourage had dispersed, he was pretty vocal and forthright about what he thought of them. Anneke, who happened to be with us at the time, was highly shocked – she hadn't realized we phlegmatic Brits were capable of such bluntness! Although, naturally, Tony too well brought up to say any of this to our guests' faces. We are all here to represent the best of Britain, after all, and nobody wants to create a scene.

The other news I mentioned relates to Tony as well. Because, after weeks of doing his best to give the hapless Clara the slip, he has suddenly landed on his feet, girl-wise. He has started knocking around with Emily, the girl from Wisconsin. Now, nobody can quite remember where she appeared from, or how she popped up in the Britannia one day. But pop up she certainly did – and how! She is, according to her own account, an actress by profession. Roles on Broadway being hard to come by, however, she has been sent over here to pose as an ordinary young housewife in one of the many impressive domestic displays in the American pavilion. Her job is to demonstrate – mainly to the awestruck Soviet bloc visitors – the myriad of labour-saving devices in common currency in the Land of the Free. Vacuum cleaners seem to be her speciality, and she spends her days in a dazzling mock-up American sitting room, cheerfully Hoovering mountains of dust which an accomplice has tipped onto the floor for this same purpose a few minutes earlier. Anyhow, she wandered into our little hostelry recently and attached herself to Tony B in a big way. So now he is walking around with a grin on his face like the cat that got the cream: for young Emily is quite a looker, if I haven't mentioned that already; on top of which, despite the fact that she comes from some little town in the back-woods which is probably called something like Diddly Squat, WN, she seems fearsomely cultivated and well-spoken and independent. These Yanks certainly don't lack confidence, I'll give them that.

Ah well – in the meantime Expo 58 rumbles on, as busy as ever. The Bolshoi Ballet are coming to town soon, and yesterday the Britannia was visited by a sizeable delegation from the impressively named 5th European Congress on Fluorisation and Prevention of Dental Decay. Unfortunately one of their members broke a tooth on the crust of one of our restaurant's speciality pork pies, and his colleagues had to perform an impromptu extraction.

With love as always,

Thomas x.

PS Just remembered – I did promise that I was going to tell you all about the enigmatic Mr Chersky in this letter, didn't I? Well, he must wait until the next one.

28th June 1958

Dear Thomas,

Thank you so much for your last. You cannot imagine how exciting it is, in the midst of my humdrum little domestic life, to receive these tantalizing little bulletins of yours. They are like dispatches from another world – a world of infinitely more interest than my own, sadly. I really don't know what I can tell you of the last few weeks that will not bore you to tears by comparison with your own account of a visit from the Chancellor of the Exchequer.

And not only are you spending your days hob-nobbing with the Great and the Good, it would seem, but Brussels is also a veritable hotbed of romantic entanglements! Your new friend Tony must be terribly good-looking – it sounds as though he is attracting women like flies. I'm sure that you, he, Emily and Anneke must make a most appealing foursome when you all go out together to sample the bright lights of an evening.

Back here, alas, I have nothing so glamorous to distract me. I live in a world bounded entirely by prams, nappies, feeds and gripe water. My only distraction this week was a trip to the cinema, and I wouldn't even have had that if it wasn't for the kindness of Norman, once again. I had mentioned to him, during one of our chats last week, that I had been dying to see the film *Peyton Place*. (You will remember this, because I asked you to take me to see it the weekend before you left, but you chose another film instead.) Well, I never thought it was anything but a pipedream, but then, the evening before last, just as I was about to put my supper on, Norman suddenly turned up on my doorstep with a young girl I did not recognize. He introduced her to me as Susan, one of the secretaries from his office, and said that she had kindly agreed to babysit while he took me out to the flicks! Well, I was absolutely dumbfounded as you can imagine. I started to protest but he insisted that it was all arranged and that I deserved a treat, and so before I knew what was happening I was upstairs putting my best dress and make-up on! Norman and I took the tube up to Oxford Circus and managed to catch the early-evening showing at the Prince Edward cinema. It was quite a long film and we did not come out until after nine o'clock but even then he insisted on taking me for dinner. We went to Jimmy's restaurant on Frith Street, which is a rather dingy place in a dark basement. The menu included some Greek dishes such as moussaka and Norman urged me to be adventurous and try something like that but I'm afraid I lost my nerve and ordered lamb chops and mashed potatoes instead. It was very tasty I must say. We also drank a whole half-bottle of red wine between the two of us! I am sure I was quite tipsy by the time we left. That is probably why I can't remember very much about the film or what we talked about afterwards, except that the subject of Norman's corns came up more than once. He is not what you would call a brilliant conversationalist – I am sure he could not hold his own in a conversation with you and your new friends about Atomic Energy or Nuclear Disarmament – but he has a good heart and is full of kindness. And that certainly counts for something – as far as I am concerned, anyway.

Well, this is not such a very long letter, but as I mentioned at the beginning, I really have very little of interest to tell you. Anyway it is time for me to feed Baby again so I had better put a stop to this.

With love from,

Sylvia.

2nd July 1958

Dearest Syllabub,

No word from you in a long time, so I can only hope that everything is well at home. I did try to telephone the other day but the line is obviously still playing up: all I got at the other end was a lot of crackle. I wonder what is going on

So, in the absence of any news from you, I will write you a few lines (as promised) about Mr Chersky.

Andrey (as I have come to call him) is a gentleman from Moscow who for many years has made his living editing magazines of a cultural or literary nature. He has been sent over to the Expo for six months to produce a weekly newspaper called *Sputnik*. I feel rather sorry for him, as he has been put in a very awkward position: what his bosses want him to produce, clearly, is a crude propaganda sheet, whereas Andrey's instincts are far more sophisticated than that. Consequently he has a very fine balancing act to perform.

Most pleasingly, he has decided to come to me for help. I don't think he knew my name as such, but word must have got around that someone from the COI was on site for the duration of the fair, because he came and sought me out at the Britannia on the night of our launch party. Since then, we have had a number of meetings, all of them at the pub. I was surprised at first that he would prefer this venue, but it turns out that Andrey has a deep love for all things British. He has an encyclopaedic knowledge of the Sherlock Holmes stories, seems to have committed the London Underground map to memory and has developed a passion for – of all things – Smith's *Salt'n'Shake* crisps, of which Mr Rossiter keeps a steady supply. He collects the little salt sachets, which he says he is going to show to his nieces and nephews when he returns to Moscow. That is one of the wonderful things about this fair – discovering the different (often very surprising) aspects of one's own culture that appeal to people from other countries. In return, in a few days' time Andrey has invited us to see the Bolshoi Ballet at the Monnaie Theatre in town, and to attend a private party afterwards. This is really very generous of him, considering that the advice I have given him so far has been pretty footling. Really just a question of 'toning down' the propaganda element of his paper, making it a bit less obvious and using rather more humour, which is always a good tactic in these circumstances.

I have just one bone of contention with Andrey. He has got it into his head that it would be interesting for the readers of *Sputnik* to learn something about the ZETA machine in the British pavilion, and last time he came round to the pub he did his best to get some information out of Tony about it. Tony – who is (in my humble opinion) rather naive when it comes to political matters – doesn't find anything wrong with this, but I have been trying to talk him out of it. In fact, I wonder whether Tony, Emily and Andrey are not becoming altogether too friendly. Did I mention that our Muscovite friend was a very handsome specimen? Sometimes I catch Emily looking at them both and it is hard to tell which one she seems to admire more.

To change the subject completely, last week there was another conference taking place here. This time it was the second annual congress of the Belgian Society of Urology. A selection of the delegates came to sample our beer on the Friday afternoon. Luckily nothing untoward happened in connection with their visit whatsoever.

With much love,
Thomas xxx.

PS I have reopened this envelope to add a line and to let you know that your last letter has arrived, finally. So, no diminution in the attentions of Mr Sparks, I see. A trip to the pictures, and dinner afterwards! It's a good job I'm not the jealous type.

Artificial stimulants

There are certain people, Thomas thought, who command attention; and there are others who blend into the background and become invisible, no matter how many interesting things they might have to say. It struck him, at the time, as an original reflection, being new to him, at any rate. And the person who had inspired it, sitting a few inches away from him at the glass-topped table, a small beaker of vodka raised to her lips, her eyes flitting evenly between Tony Buttress and Andrey Chersky as the latter tried to persuade the former of the many benefits of Soviet children's holiday camps, was Emily, the girl from Wisconsin.

The bar was crowded. Even though Andrey had told him that the dress code was not important, and that nobody would mind if he came in a lounge suit, Thomas still felt self-conscious, surrounded by so many impressive-looking figures in white tie. The air was buzzing with after-show conversation: much of it, but by no means all, in Russian. Thomas was only half-listening to his friends' conversation, however. He kept finding his eyes drawn back to Emily, and not just because she was so good-looking: there was an element of that, of course (why deny it?), but this had more to do with the strange quality he was struggling to define – he supposed that charisma would be the word for it, or magnetism. Or perhaps, thinking (as he so often did these days) in terms of atomic physics, what Emily gave off was a kind of energy. An energy concentrated in her eyes, and the brilliance of her smile, rather than her gracefully angular features, or slender but masculine frame.

Now she turned to look at him. She was laughing delightedly at some instance of the combative banter between Tony and Andrey.

Thomas joined in with her laughter weakly, half-heartedly, annoyed with himself for not following the conversation. He felt excluded, squeezed out: a feeling, it now occurred to him, which had recently become quite familiar when he was in the company of these three.

'Come on, Thomas, back me up on this,' she said. 'Mr Chersky is trying to tell us that these wonderful children's holiday camps on the Baltic Sea are havens of innocent fun and pleasure, and the thought of political indoctrination doesn't enter anybody's heads. And your friend is putting up a *very* feeble counter-argument, if I may say so.'

'All I'm saying,' Tony insisted, after a pause in which it became clear that Thomas was not going to intervene, 'is that Andrey has a point. After all, American children go to summer camps every year.'

'Yes,' said Emily, 'to learn how to be independent, and how to enjoy themselves in the wild.'

'And to have all the other American values drummed into them,' said Andrey. 'Don't they raise the flag every night, and sing patriotic songs? Of course they do. I keep telling you, in all its essentials, the West is no different to the East.'

'He has a point,' Tony repeated, draining his fourth or fifth vodka glass. 'There's propaganda on both sides. And personally, I think Artek sounds wonderful. I'd give anything to go there.'

'Darling, I'm beginning to think you're practically a Communist yourself,' said Emily, tickling him playfully under the chin. Thomas wondered if the endearment had any meaning, or if Emily was perhaps the kind of person who called everybody 'darling'. She was an actress, after all.

'My goal,' said Andrey, 'is to make Communists of you all. My weapons are ballet, and vodka.' To emphasize these two words, he gestured around the bar of the Monnaie Theatre, first of all, and then held up the three-quarters-empty bottle.

Tony and Emily laughed. After a moment Thomas joined in – again, rather faintly. He was beginning to feel that the others were somewhat too ready to accept Andrey's relentless outpourings of pro-Soviet sentiment as little more than a charming foible; whereas it was all intended, as far as he could see, in deadly earnest. None the less, he made no complaint when Andrey filled up his glass, along with all the others'. The man was persuasive, there was no denying that. And in any case, what were you supposed to do, other than drink vodka, after an evening of Russian ballet? He told himself that he should relax, and enjoy the moment.

'Mr Chersky, does this stuff contain much alcohol?' Emily asked, not so innocently. 'Because it sure tastes that way. In fact it tastes as though there's nothing much else in it.'

'Miss Parker, do you think that I would try to get you drunk?' the Russian responded, wide-eyed. 'Come on. We are all friends. We can all trust each other. *Budem zdorovy!*' At which words, the three men downed their vodkas in one draught, as they had been told to do. Emily took a careful sip and, as before, she winced when the bitter liquid caught her throat for the first time.

'I always thought that Russians said *Na zdorovie* when they were making a toast,' she said.

'A popular myth,' Andrey explained. 'We say it to foreigners, because – knowing no better – they say it to us, and we are too polite to embarrass them. But no Russian would ever say it to another Russian. We have an elaborate etiquette of toasts. Toasts for different occasions. Toasts which must be spoken in a certain order. Toasts which signal the start of a celebration, and those which signal the end. Come on now, drink up! I will help you on your way.' He spoke a few more words of Russian – an especially resonant, florid and musical phrase – in response to which Emily, holding his gaze in something between scepticism and adoration, drank down the rest of her vodka.

'It's a beautiful language,' she admitted. 'At least, the way you speak it. What did you just say?'

'That,' Andrey conceded, 'is a relatively new toast, from the more recent era of Soviet history. Loosely translated, it means, "May all your scheduled tasks be completed according to the designated timetable."'

Emily's eyes locked onto his again for a moment. 'How poetic,' she said, her mouth trembling slightly at the edges. And then, recovering herself, she rose to her feet. 'I must pay a short visit to the ladies' room,' she said, and disappeared in the direction of the cloak-rooms.

The men watched her retreating figure in silent admiration.

'Your companion is charming. Quite charming,' said Mr Chersky, turning to Tony.

'Thank you. I think so too.'

'With your permission, gentlemen, I will order another bottle. The music of Tchaikovsky has transported me to another world this evening, and I'm sure we would all like to remain there for as long as possible: with the aid of artificial stimulants if necessary.'

Andrey did not go to the bar, but walked over to one of the waiters and exchanged a few whispered words with him. It appeared that he was asking for a particular bottle to be obtained from some special quarter. While he was thus occupied, Tony noticed Thomas glancing at his watch.

'What's up, old boy?'

'Oh, nothing. I just thought that Anneke would be here by now. She promised she would drop by.'

Tony's face darkened at the mention of her name. Thomas was surprised.

'What's the frown for? I thought you liked her.'

'Oh, I like *her* well enough. What I don't like is the way you're behaving towards her.'

Thomas sighed. 'We've been through all this.'

'Yes, we have. And I've still never had a satisfactory explanation of what you think you're playing at.'

'There's nothing to explain.'

'Have you told her yet?

'Told her what?'

'About your wife. Your family.'

Thomas hesitated, and then said, without conviction: 'Why should I?'

Tony shook his head in exasperation. 'Thomas, I don't want to think you're a heel, because I like you. But that's the conclusion I'm rapidly coming to. Either that, or you're very, very confused. And naive. That girl is growing fonder and fonder of you, and sooner or later, she's going to want more than a chaste peck on the cheek at the end of an evening.'

Thomas thought about this, and could not come up with a suitable answer. So all he said, in the end, was: 'Oh, knock it off, can't you?'

'You're getting tight,' said Tony, surprised by the note of petulance in his friend's voice.

Emily returned and lightened the mood at once with a spontaneous change of subject. 'Darling,' she said to Tony, 'do you think that now would be a good time to talk to Mr Chersky about Angela's dresses?' Adding to Thomas, by way of explanation: 'Back in New York I have this college friend, Angela Thornbury. She's been working on the most *stunning* collection of evening wear, but what she really needs is a good shot of publicity. And I was thinking that Mr Chersky might be able to help.'

'I don't quite follow,' said Thomas.

'Well, he's an editor, isn't he? And he's looking for stories for *Sputnik*.'

'But he only wants stories about the Soviet Union.'

'Well, I think that's very narrow-minded of him. The whole point of this fair is to promote cultural exchange. What about an article comparing fashions in New York with fashions in Moscow? I'd be interested to read that, wouldn't you?'

'He'd put a slant on it – and your friend's dresses wouldn't come out well.'

'I'm going to raise it with him anyway.'

And raise it she did, although Andrey's response was more polite than anything else.

'You know, in some ways it's a good idea,' he said. 'Contrasting different ways of life in the East and the West. We could even extend it to all sorts of different subjects. Technology, for instance.'

At the sound of this word, Thomas looked across at him warily.

'As I believe I said to you before,' Andrey continued, addressing Tony now, 'we are already preparing an article about Soviet advances in nuclear fusion. What would be interesting would be to compare our discoveries with those of the British.'

'Well, you're at perfect liberty to do that,' said Tony. 'As you know, we're pretty transparent about our work. That's part of our culture. The ZETA machine is there for all to see in the British pavilion.'

Andrey laughed. 'A *facsimile* of the machine, yes. Very handsome to look at, but of limited interest to a real scientist.'

'Of course. Much like the model of the Sputnik in your display.'

'Precisely. Neither of us wants to give away too much. And why should we? That would be foolish. As always, West and East behave in exactly the same way. It's just that you always insist on claiming the moral high ground, by pretending that the West is different.'

'But we *are* different.'

'Then prove it.'

'How?'

'By sharing some new information about the ZETA machine with our readers.'

Tony looked at him intently. Something in Andrey's tone seemed to have rattled him.

'I've a good mind to do that,' he said. 'If only to prove you wrong.'

'Look, old man,' said Thomas, laying a warning hand on his arm, 'that's a silly way of thinking.'

He was about to say more, when Anneke appeared. He stood up to greet her and there was a long moment of embarrassment, while he aimed a kiss at her cheek and she (unless he was imagining it, under Tony's influence) offered her lips instead. As a result, the kiss landed somewhere in between.

'I'm so sorry I'm late,' said Anneke, blushing with pleasure to see him. 'It's been the busiest day . . .'

And she launched into a long explanation about a Dutch couple who had become separated from their six-year-old daughter at the fair, and how she and some of the other hostesses had spent two hours looking for the little girl, only to find her sitting outside – of all places – one of the straw huts in the pavilion of the Belgian Congo, staring as if hypnotized at one of the half-naked natives as he stood and shivered in the unaccustomed chill of a North European summer evening. Thomas nodded and smiled at every stage of the story, even though he was far more interested in what Tony and Andrey were saying, because the Russian would not drop the subject of the ZETA machine, and Tony seemed, if anything, to be encouraging him to pursue the matter further, and Emily was glancing from one to the other, looking increasingly concerned, and the more Thomas listened, or rather half-listened, through the curtain of Anneke's interminable guileless monologue, the less he liked what he heard, especially when he heard Tony saying that he had always wanted to visit Moscow, and Andrey saying that his home would always be open to him, and Emily saying how wonderful it was that two people from opposing countries could join together in friendship like this, and how it just showed that international politics was a lot of hogwash, and Tony agreeing, and saying that it proved what he had always thought, that the nuclear arms race was an expensive and dangerous waste of time, and he didn't believe the Soviet Union had any aggressive intentions towards the West at all, and anyway what was so great about the Western way of life, it was all based upon materialism and inequality, and Communism might not be perfect but neither was it the aberration that people made it out to be, and Andrey said, Yes, at last!, a Westerner who understands, and clasping him around the shoulder he declared that he was One of Us, and then all three of them drank more vodka, and poured some more for Thomas, and after another couple of glasses he realized that this stuff was strong, I mean *really* strong, much stronger than the stuff they had been drinking before, and he dimly realized that he didn't have much grasp on what was going on any more, but he did notice that Emily had her arm round Tony's waist, or rather – and this was odd – around Andrey's waist, and soon afterwards he felt the comforting touch of Sylvia's arm around his own waist, except that – and this was also odd – it was actually Anneke's, because Sylvia was hundreds of miles away in London, but then, what did it really matter, the whole evening was turning out to be so jolly, and these were all such lovely people, and here was yet another lovely person, that nice Mr Carter from the British Council, coming over to join them, and sitting down beside them, and saying something to him, only he never actually knew what he had said, because Mr Carter sitting down was the last thing he could remember, he could remember nothing at all after that: not until he woke up early the next afternoon, in a strange hotel room, with the worst headache he had ever experienced and a craving for cool water and a taste in his mouth that made him want to retch.

Wilkins

With a considerable effort of will, Thomas raised his aching body onto one elbow and looked blearily around the room.

The slightly moth-eaten velvet curtains were still drawn, and it took a few seconds for his eyes to become accustomed to the dark. Soon, enough shapes were visible to make him sure that he had no idea where he was. A wave of panic rushed through him and he sat up sharply. His head pounded with the sudden movement. Fumbling in the half-dark, he found the switch of a bedside light and turned it on.

The room was plainly furnished and far from luxurious. From the bathroom Thomas could hear the sound of a dripping tap. He was fully clothed. He swung his legs over the side of the bed and stood up, moving more carefully than before, aware that any sudden movements of his head would trigger more pain. He walked over to the window – a matter of only two or three steps – and drew back the curtains. But the view from the window did not tell him very much. He saw only a grey, rainswept back alley, separating him from a brick wall by just a few feet. Even now it was difficult, from the quality of the light, to judge what hour of the day it might be. He glanced at his watch. It was a quarter to three.

After running his head under the cold tap for a minute or two, checking in the pocket of his jacket (which was hanging in the wardrobe) to see if his wallet was still there, and taking a final glance around the room to make sure that none of his possessions had been left on any of the surfaces, Thomas quietly opened the door and stepped out into a narrow, thinly carpeted corridor. He pocketed the key and eased the door shut behind him. Everything was quite silent. There was no maid in the corridor, vacuuming the carpet or carrying clean sheets from one room to another while breezing past him with a cheerful 'Bonjour'. He had rarely experienced a silence so profound.

Not being able to find any lift, he descended three flights of stairs and finally came upon a mean, narrow little vestibule. The lighting was poor and there was nobody sitting behind the reception desk. Thomas rang the bell. Before long a lank, gangly-looking fellow with a sallow complexion emerged from a doorway at the rear. He was eating a sandwich.

'*Oui?*'

'*Bonjour, monsieur,*' said Thomas; then chided himself for sounding so deferential. He was about to adopt a far more authoritative tone when he realized that he had no idea what he wanted to ask. 'Erm, *je voudrais . . . le check-out?*' he concluded, with a feeble rising note of interrogation.

'Room number?' said the receptionist.

Thomas had to look at his key. 'Three-one-two.'

The man took the key and thumbed through a card index on his desk. Then he glanced up at Thomas and said: 'Nothing to pay.' He was about to disappear again into his rear doorway when Thomas – himself about to make for the front door and the street outside – turned, hesitated and said: 'You mean – my bill has been paid?'

'Yes.'

'By . . . by whom? – If you don't mind my asking.'

The man sighed, and looked again through his card index.

'Monsieur Wilkins.'

'Wilkins?'

'Wilkins.'

Thomas and the receptionist stared at each other for a few seconds in silence. There were many questions Thomas wanted to ask now, but he suspected that he would be wasting his time.

'Did you enjoy your stay?' the receptionist asked.

'Yes. Yes, it was . . . very comfortable.'

'*Bien.*'

The man took another bite of his sandwich, and withdrew. Thomas turned and walked out onto the street.

In the course of the last few weeks, he had paid very few visits to the centre of Brussels, which was where he now appeared to be. He didn't recognize his surroundings at all. A walk of a hundred yards or less brought him out on a wide boulevard, lined with shops and cafés, where two busy lanes of traffic were moving in both directions. The sun was by no means bright – in fact it was having trouble breaking through a wall of ashen clouds – but it was enough to make Thomas wince and close his eyes. Looking into the distance, he saw what seemed to be a taxi rank, and hurried towards it. He told the taxi driver to take him to the Motel Expo at Wemmel.

The taxi ride seemed to make his headache and nausea worse than ever. It was as much as he could do to raise himself out of the car and count out the notes for his fare. Once the car had gone, he slunk past the bored, inattentive figure of Joseph Stalin in the reception hut and began to trace the familiar path back to his temporary home. Threading his way between the breeze-block cabins, twice he had to stop, in order to lean against a wall, regather his strength and wait for a feeling of dizziness to pass. It took him several fumbling attempts to get the key to turn in his own lock.

Thomas had hoped to regain some sense of normality by returning to his cabin that afternoon. But soon after he stepped inside, he discovered something more disconcerting than anything he had experienced on this already disconcerting day.

The first sign that anything was amiss came when he went into the bathroom to run water over his head again. He noticed that Tony's toothbrush was gone. So was his toothpaste (the new, special stripey sort), his razor and shaving cream – in fact his entire sponge bag. Rushing back into the bedroom, Thomas flung open the wardrobe door and found that Tony's half of the wardrobe was entirely empty. Shirts, ties, jackets, underwear – all missing. He looked under the bed, where Tony kept his suitcases. They had been removed as well.

Thomas sat down on his own bed and ran a hand nervously through his hair. He realized that he was shaking, and breathing much too heavily. Something strange was going on here, and he didn't like the look or the feel of it. Not at all.

There was a knock on the door, and then it was pushed open (Thomas had left it ajar). And there stood the latest in today's series of surprises.

'Anneke!' he said. 'What are you doing here?'

'The man at the gate told me your cabin number,' she said. 'I thought I should come by before I started work.'

'But why?'

'I wanted to see that you were all right. I was worried about you.'

She came a few steps further inside. Thomas realized that there was nowhere for her to sit. Embarrassed, he cleared away the pile of dirty laundry that covered the only chair in the room: a plain, uncomfortable, wooden affair, not at all suitable for lounging in, or indeed receiving visitors.

'Here, please,' he said, gesturing towards the bed. Anneke sat down there, smiling secretly to herself, while he perched awkwardly on the chair.

'So,' she said, looking around with the same smile on her face, evidently enjoying the novelty of the situation, 'Now I see why you and Tony have been getting to know each other so well and so quickly. It's very . . . intimate. What happens when either of you wants to bring one of your romantic conquests back here?'

'But that's just the point,' said Thomas. 'I mean, that isn't the point . . . The point is that Tony seems to have gone. None of his things are here any more.'

'Gone?'

'Vanished. *Disparu.*'

Anneke reflected. 'Perhaps he has just gone to work?'

'With his toothbrush? And all his clothes? And two suitcases?'

'That is very strange,' she admitted, frowning.

'Look – exactly what happened last night?'

'To you? Or to Tony?'

'Both. Me, first of all, I suppose.'

'Well . . .' She leaned forward, and looked into his eyes. It was a look full of concern, and full of affection, which touched him deeply: although he did not realize this, or reflect upon it, until some time afterwards. 'I think . . . I had the impression . . . that you were very drunk.'

'Obviously. Did I do anything terrible, like stand on the table and start dancing to the strains of the balalaika, or anything like that?'

'Not at all. You fell asleep. On my lap. It was rather sweet, I have to say. Everybody thought so – not just me.'

'Everybody?'

'Yes. Tony, and Miss Parker, and Mr Chersky, and Mr Carter.'

'Carter? Was he there?'

'Yes, he was. Don't you remember him joining us? In fact he was the one who started to get concerned, when we couldn't wake you up.'

Anneke explained how Mr Chersky and Mr Carter had finally managed to half-carry, half-drag Thomas out onto the street. Mr Carter had then called a taxi and taken Thomas away – presumably to the hotel – while Mr Chersky had shortly afterwards returned and rejoined them in the bar.

'After that,' she said, 'I began to feel very tired. And now that you were gone, I did not really want to be there. I was going to stay the night in the hostel that some of the hostesses use in Laeken. So Tony and Miss Parker and Mr Chersky escorted me there. They were very loud and very happy. They were singing songs all the time. Children's songs, Mr Chersky said, from the Young Pioneers camp at Artek. And then when they had seen me to my door they all said goodnight and then Tony said to Mr Chersky, "Come on, we have to show you those designs." And off they went, into the night. The three of them.'

Thomas looked at her in horror.

'Designs? What designs?'

'I've no idea. I thought you might know.'

Thomas ran a hand through his hair again. Could this be as bad as it looked?

'Wait a minute!' he said. 'They *were* talking about designs earlier. Emily's friend is a dress designer. They were trying to get Andrey to feature some of her fashions in his paper.'

'Really?' said Anneke. 'When I was there, all they seemed to be talking about was that machine. The one that Tony's been working on.'

Thomas thought about this. It was true. He tried to recall again the details of last night's conversation, but everything was too blurred. *Why* had he allowed Andrey to ply him with drink like that? He should have known when to stop. His head was still aching, and his thoughts would not come into focus. He needed coffee, strong coffee.

Anneke was watching him still, her eyes brimming with sympathy. They looked at each other for a moment. The sun must have been struggling through the clouds, because her hair and her face were illuminated, briefly, by a passing, brighter glow admitted through the skylight in the roof of the cabin. She looked so beautiful. Thomas wanted to reach across and kiss her.

'We should go,' he said.

'Yes. I'm expected at work.'

'I'm going to stop by the British pavilion and make a few enquiries. There's bound to be some perfectly rational explanation for all this.'

But Thomas's confidence was misplaced. When he reached the British pavilion he found something even more alarming. One of the exhibits was missing.

'Excuse me,' he said to one of the assistant curators, in a voice which he could hardly stop from shaking, 'but . . . where's it gone? The ZETA machine?'

'It was removed this morning,' said the assistant.

'Removed? On whose orders?'

'Mr Buttress, sir. He came in and supervised the work himself. He and a couple of the lads took it all apart and loaded it into a van.'

'And then what? Where did they take it?'

'Couldn't tell you that, sir. Leaves a bit of a gap, though, doesn't it? We're going to have to fill it up with something else. Apparently there's some sort of big new computer thing arriving in a day or two.'

His mind reeling with the implications of all this, Thomas thanked the assistant and hurried off around the ornamental lake and towards the Britannia. Nodding the curtest of greetings at Mr Rossiter, he pushed his way through the crowd of patrons and squeezed behind the bar. He asked Shirley to make him a double-strength coffee as soon as she had a moment, and made straight for the telephone.

'Can I speak to Mr Carter, please?' he said, after dialling through to the British Council offices in Brussels. 'My name is Foley. Tell him that it's very urgent.'

Before long Mr Carter's reassuring cheerful drone came down the line.

'Afternoon, Foley. So you're still in the land of the living, then?'

'Yes, I am, just about. Largely thanks to you, by the sound of it.'

'Think nothing of it, old man. All in a day's work. Best go easy on the old potato juice next time, though. That stuff is deadly. How was the hotel, anyway? Sorry, we didn't exactly leave you in the lap of luxury. Was everything all right with the bill?'

'Yes, it was all paid for. Settled in the name of Wilkins – whoever that might be.' Mr Carter did not comment. It was unclear, from his silence, whether the name Wilkins meant anything to him or not. 'Well, anyway, you have my eternal thanks, however the thing was managed. But that's not really why I'm phoning. Listen, Carter, there've been some rum things going on today.' (He glanced around, but no one seemed to be listening, apart from Shirley, who was hovering at his elbow with the coffee.) 'Tony – Tony Buttress – has disappeared. Vanished. Packed up all his belongings and scarpered, without even leaving a note. And even worse than that . . .'

(Thomas's voice dropped to an even lower register) '. . . *the machine has gone as well.*'

There was another longish silence at the other end of the line.

'I'm not quite sure I'm with you, old man.'

'The machine. The ZETA machine.'

'Well, how can that have gone?'

'Apparently Tony himself came in first thing this morning and had it packed up. About eight hours after you and I *both* heard him telling Mr Chersky what a great thing it would be for international relations if the Russians knew all about it.'

Again, there was silence at Mr Carter's end. Thomas could tell that these revelations had shocked him.

'All right,' came the voice, finally. 'Situation understood. I think we might be getting into pretty deep waters here, Foley. I'm going to need to take some advice at my end. I'm just going to . . . ask around a little bit, and then I'll call you back. Or somebody will. Where are you? At the pub?'

'Yes.'

'Then don't go away. Stay where you can be reached, on this number. You'll hear something within the next hour or two.'

'Understood. But what I really wanted to –'

Thomas stared at the receiver. Mr Carter had already rung off, and the line had gone dead.

He busied himself for the remainder of the afternoon by rearranging the display of nautical prints in the Exhibitors' Club upstairs. When that was done, he polished the glasses and made a record of the quantities of liquid left in the spirit bottles above the bar, since Mr Rossiter did not seem to have undertaken this task for some time. He was still upstairs when he heard Shirley calling him from the hubbub of the main saloon bar.

'Mr Foley! Telephone!'

On taking the call, Thomas found himself being addressed by an unfamiliar voice, speaking with a neutral English accent.

'Foley?'

'Yes, speaking.'

'Good. Now listen carefully. We want you to come to Josaphat Park tonight. Nine p.m.'

'But look, when you say "we", what do you mean? Who am I talking to?'

'Find a bench in the north-western corner of the park. You must have a copy of a newspaper with you. *De Standaard*. You must have it open at page twenty-seven. Do you understand?'

'Well, I understand *that*, yes, but what I don't understand is who –'

It seemed to be a day on which people were resolved to hang up on him. Once again he found himself staring at an unresponsive receiver. Shirley laughed and offered him another coffee.

It was still light at nine o'clock that evening. None the less, there was a chill in the air, and the park was almost deserted. For the first few minutes, Thomas's only companion was an elderly woman exercising a pair of miniature poodles. At least, he assumed that it was an elderly woman. The day's events had become so surreal and inexplicable that it would not have surprised him if she had turned out to be his mysterious caller from earlier in the afternoon, carefully disguised. But no, it was fairly obvious when that particular figure appeared. He was wearing the regulation beige macintosh and trilby hat, and could be spotted from some distance, even in the encroaching twilight. Thomas sat forward on his bench and held up his copy of the newspaper at an angle which was not conducive to reading but would certainly make it visible to the advancing stranger. The ruse seemed to work, for the man sat down beside him and then stared intently at the newspaper for some little time, before switching his gaze to Thomas, and then back to the newspaper, then back to Thomas again, apparently in a state of some indecision. Finally he cleared his throat and spoke.

'Mr Foley?'

Thomas nodded. 'Of course I'm Mr Foley. Do we have to go through all this palaver? Do you see anybody else reading *De Standaard* in this corner of the park?'

'You're reading page twenty-three. I told you to have it open at page twenty-seven.'

'There are only twenty-four pages.'

'Oh. Really? I should have thought of that. Blast.' The oversight seemed to preoccupy him, for a moment or two, but then he dismissed it and rose briskly to his feet. 'Follow me, would you?'

He set off at a furious pace. Thomas rushed to fall in beside him.

'Yes, but look, where are we going? What the devil is this all about?'

'You'll find out.'

'When?'

'In the fullness of time.'

'You could at least tell me your name.'

'My name's Wilkins.'

They reached the edge of the park. Wilkins looked up and down the street, scrutinizing a row of parked cars, his indecision having evidently returned. After a few seconds, however, a pair of headlights flashed at them from one of the cars.

'Ah! There we are.'

He led Thomas towards the car, a green Volkswagen Beetle. The driver leaned over and opened the passenger door for them.

'What on earth did you bring this thing for?' Wilkins said to the driver, throwing an impatient gesture at the car. 'Couldn't you have chosen something a bit bigger?' The driver said nothing. Wilkins let out an exasperated sigh. 'Come on,' he said to Thomas, 'we're just going to have to squeeze in.'

It was easier said than done. Wilkins was a corpulent man, and Thomas himself was no featherweight. The first attempt, with Thomas going in first and Wilkins climbing in after him, was not successful: Wilkins ended up wedged fast between the front passenger seat and the door frame, and only managed to extricate himself after a prolonged, energetic struggle, accompanied by a chorus of ill-tempered grunts. Finally, when they were both settled on the back seat, they found themselves so tightly pressed up against each other that they could scarcely breathe, let alone move.

'Is this going to be a long drive?' said Thomas, 'because if so, I'd better take my coat off.'

This action also presented considerable difficulties. By the time he was halfway through it – after giving Wilkins at least one accidental poke in the eye with his elbow – both men's tempers were starting to fray even further.

'For God's sake, man,' said Wilkins, 'why couldn't you just keep your coat on and be done with it?'

'Nearly done,' said Thomas, tugging at his one remaining sleeve. 'And I must say, it would be a lot more comfortable if that . . . thing in your pocket wasn't sticking into me. What on earth is it?'

'My gun, of course.'

Thomas paused in the act of folding his coat on his lap and stared at Wilkins, aghast. 'Gun? What are you talking about? Are you pointing a gun at me?'

'Of course I am.'

'What for?'

'God damn it, man, I don't think you understand the gravity of the situation. Now put this on and pipe down.'

He handed Thomas a strip of black cloth.

'What's this?'

'What do you think it is? It's a blindfold. Now hold still while I tie it at the back.'

'What the . . .?'

Remembering the presence of the gun, Thomas decided that protest, let alone resistance, was useless. He waited in silence for the blindfold to be tied firmly at the back of his head.

'Right,' said Wilkins, emphatically. 'That should do. How many fingers am I holding up?'

'Three,' said Thomas.

'God damn it to hell, how did you know that? Can you see through the cloth?'

'No. It was a guess.'

'Well you're not supposed to guess. For crying out loud, I'm trying to make sure that you can't see where we're going. We're not here to play guessing games. How many fingers am I holding up?'

'I've no idea. I can't see a bloody thing.'

'Good. It was four, by the way. Not that it matters. Now shut up. We're going to be stuck together like this for a while, and I'm not in the mood for chit-chat.'

The driver started the engine and the car at last shuddered its way out onto the empty, quiescent, midsummer street.

A nice old pickle

The journey was long (about an hour and a quarter, Thomas guessed) and very uncomfortable. After twenty minutes or so he could tell that they were leaving the hum of the city traffic behind and entering the countryside, although still driving along straight main roads. There were enough right and left turns, in random succession, for him to suspect that they were being taken mainly to confuse him. It was only in the last quarter of an hour or so that the car slowed down, and the roads seemed to become narrower and less reliable. Thomas and Wilkins would have been violently thrown from side to side by some of the sudden turns, if they had not already been wedged so tightly together.

Eventually, after climbing a slight but steady incline for several minutes, the car came to a brief halt, with its engine still running; then it took a sharp right turn, and they were travelling along a dirt track, which lasted for perhaps half a mile, with many bumps and lurches. After that, the car swung to the left, and came to an abrupt, final stop. The engine was turned off and at once Thomas's suspicion was confirmed: they were in deep countryside. The silence around them was profound, and its profundity was emphasized by the regular hooting, no more than a few yards away it seemed, of a solitary owl.

'Right,' said Wilkins. 'Let's get out of this confounded vehicle.'

Getting out proved just as difficult, long-winded and bad-tempered a process as getting in; even more so, in Thomas's case, because he was still blindfolded. Freed from the confines of the tiny car at last, he stood in the fresh air for a moment or two, sensing loose gravel beneath his feet, until he felt the barrel of Wilkins's gun being thrust into his ribs again.

'Come on,' his abductor said. 'This way, and no funny business if you please.'

They walked perhaps fifteen or twenty yards across the gravel. Then someone – Wilkins, presumably – knocked loudly upon a heavy wooden door with an iron knocker. The door was opened and they stepped inside. No words were spoken.

They walked along a corridor which, from the sounds of Thomas's footsteps, was paved with flagstones. There was one shallow upwards step which he almost tripped over. The corridor was quite long, so Thomas imagined that the house – if this was indeed a house – must be a large one. At the end of the corridor another door was opened and he was pushed through it.

'Right you are,' said Wilkins. 'Made it. Home sweet home.'

He untied the blindfold and Thomas blinked in the sudden brilliant light from an overhead lamp. Still blinking, he looked around him. He was in a small ground-floor bedroom, plainly but comfortably furnished with heavy, dark furniture. The window was shuttered. The walls were painted a dirty mustard-yellow and decorated with reproduction (or were they original?) landscapes in the Flemish style. In addition to the single bed, there was a desk and an armchair. Altogether it looked considerably more inviting than Thomas's cabin at the Motel Expo.

'Very well,' he said, turning to Wilkins. 'I've been very patient. Now would you *kindly* tell me the purpose of this ludicrous rigmarole.'

'Someone's put some cocoa out for you, I see,' said Wilkins, nodding towards a mug on the bedside table. 'I should get it down if I were you. Help you to sleep.'

'Are you seriously telling me that –'

'Good night, old chap. Sweet dreams and all that. There'll be someone along in the morning. I dare say all will be made clear.'

And before Thomas could press him for any further explanation, he was gone – locking the door behind him. Thomas grabbed the doorknob and pulled on it with all his strength, but it was no use.

And the shutters on the window, he soon discovered, were firmly locked as well.

Despondent, he sat down on his new bed and picked up the mug of cocoa. He'd had nothing to eat all day – apart from one packet of Smith's *Salt'n'Shake* crisps at the Britannia – and was beginning to feel fierce pangs of hunger. He sniffed the cocoa gingerly a few times and then took two or three sips. It was lukewarm, so it was easy to drink it down in a few draughts. And the sedative it contained must have been powerful, for he did not wake up until late the next morning.

Even the noise of the key in the lock and the opening of the door did not wake him: instead it was the sudden invasion of light – cheerful morning sunlight – when the shutters were unlocked and thrown open. He sat up in bed and saw that an elderly woman was in the room. She was fussing around, dusting, emptying the waste-paper basket, straightening the furniture. She picked up his cocoa mug and looked at it with some distaste.

'*Waarom blijf je zo lang in bed liggen?*' she muttered. '*Ik heb werk te doen. Ik moet deze kamer schoonmaken en klaar maken. Er komt nog iemand vanavond is me gezegd.*'

Thomas got out of bed, rubbing his eyes. It was the second night in a row that he had slept in these clothes. He felt filthy and tired and his headache was worse than ever.

'Where am I?' he asked.

'*Naar buiten! Nu! Ontbijt!*' said the old woman.

Thomas walked over to the window. The view was a pleasant surprise, he had to admit. Outside his bedroom was a wooden verandah and, beyond that, a vast expanse of lawn. The grass was neatly trimmed for the first hundred yards or so, and beyond that, it had been allowed to grow long, and was scattered with wildflowers of every colour imaginable. There were sculptures in the modernist style placed at intervals amid the grass, and in the far distance, a line of oak trees rose up, silhouetted regally against a flawless blue summer sky. To the left, he could glimpse open cornfields; to the right, a paddock where three chestnut horses and a pony were nibbling contentedly on bales of hay.

'*Kom mee!*' said the woman, standing in the doorway and gesturing impatiently. '*Naar buiten! Volg me!*'

Thomas turned and followed her, back down the long corridor which he had walked through but not seen the night before. It was lined with books and more pictures, in dark oak frames. The overall impression was rather gloomy, but this mood did not last for long: after leading him through a bright and airy sitting room to the right, Thomas's elderly guide brought him out through some French windows and they emerged onto the terrace, into the full dazzle of the morning sunshine. And here was a large round table, already laid for breakfast: white tablecloth, silver cutlery, the lot. And sitting around it, clearly awaiting his appearance, were two familiar figures whose presence at this mysterious house at once struck him as wearily inevitable.

'Ah! Morning, Foley!' said Mr Radford.

'Good to see you again,' said Mr Wayne.

'Pull up a chair.'

'Take a pew.'

'Help yourself to coffee.'

'The cup that heals.'

'It's jolly good.'

'If you like the continental stuff.'

Thomas sat down without saying a word. Greetings on his part did not seem to be appropriate, given the manner of his arrival at this house. He allowed Mr Radford to pour him some coffee, and sipped at it eagerly. After this, there was a considerable silence. Mr Wayne was busy buttering his toast and spreading it with strawberry jam. Mr Radford applied himself to tapping open the top of a boiled egg with the back of his teaspoon.

'Beautiful morning,' said Mr Wayne, finally.

'Delightful,' said Mr Radford.

'Would you pass the sugar, old man?'

'Happy to. Some more milk?'

'Just the ticket. Thanks very much.'

Meanwhile, Thomas helped himself to toast and an egg. He was damned if he was going to open the conversation by asking them what he was doing here. For several minutes the three Englishmen continued to silently occupy themselves with breakfast, and admiration of the scenery.

'Well, Foley, it's very good of you to come all the way out here to join us,' said Mr Wayne at last.

'I wasn't aware,' said Thomas, 'that I had any choice in the matter.'

'My dear fellow,' said Mr Radford, 'whatever can you mean?'

'We thought Wilkins was bringing you out here.'

'He bundled me into a car and pointed a gun at me, yes.'

'A gun?'

At this, they both started to chortle.

'A gun! Dear me!'

'Poor old Wilkins!'

'Really, he's the end.'

'He's the absolute limit.'

'Lives in a fantasy world, poor fellow.'

'Reads far too many of those books. You know the ones I mean.'

'I know the ones. What's the author's name?'

'Fleming. Have you read them, Foley?'

'No, I can't say that I have.'

'Having a terrible influence, you know . . .'

'. . . on the chaps who work in our department.'

'Pure fiction, of course. Gadding around the world . . .'

'Bumping people off without so much as a by your leave . . .'

'Sleeping with a different woman every night . . .'

This detail, it seemed, struck both of them as especially implausible.

'I mean, dash it all, Radford, when was the last time you did that?'

'Bump someone off, you mean?'

'No – sleep with a different woman.'

'Well, depends what you mean. Different from whom?'

'Different from the last one you slept with, I suppose.'

'Oh, well, in that case, I couldn't possibly say.'

'Within living memory?'

'Hardly, old boy.'

'Well, there you are, then. Not the smallest basis of reality in it.'

'Well, we do, apologize, Foley, if you were made to feel at all uncomfortable.'

'Uncomfortable?' said Thomas. 'Not at all. I love to be driven blindfolded for hours at a time.'

'Driven blindfolded?' said Mr Wayne.

'You don't mean to tell us,' said Mr Radford, 'that Wilkins made the driver wear a blindfold while he was bringing you here?'

'Of course not.'

'Thank God for that.'

'There are limits, after all.'

'Basic safety procedures, that sort of thing.'

By now Thomas felt ready to ask: 'Where the hell am I, in any case?'

'Well, we can't very well tell you that, old man.'

'What would be the point of the blindfold?'

'But what *is* this place?'

Mr Radford and Mr Wayne glanced at each other; then nodded, and rose to their feet.

'Come on then, we'll give you the tour.'

They re-entered the house by the French windows, turned right into the gloomy corridor but almost immediately took a narrow wooden staircase to the upper floor. Here it had the feel of a long attic, running the full extent of the house, with doors leading off on either side of a central passageway. Some of the doors were open, and through these, as Thomas passed, he could see small rooms filled, for the most part, with a bewildering variety of electronic equipment: tape recorders, microphones, massive radio sets, even computers. Finally they came to a larger room which had all of this equipment and more; and contained, besides, the figures of three people – two women, and a man – who were wearing headphones and sitting at desks in front of radio sets, rapidly transcribing whatever it was that they heard. They looked up when Thomas, Mr Radford and Mr Wayne came in, but did not otherwise deviate from their tasks in hand.

'Well, here you are,' said Mr Wayne. 'Welcome to the nerve centre.'

'The heart of the operation, as it were,' said Mr Radford.

'Rather impressive, isn't it?'

A man in a dark suit materialized behind them.

'Everything OK, gents?'

'Yes, yes, absolutely.'

'Just giving our friend here an idea what you're up to.'

'Fine. Well, if he's seen everything that he needs to see . . .'

The man's tone was polite, but there was no mistaking his note of authority. The three of them were being dismissed. Mr Radford and Mr Wayne turned and shuffled out. Thomas, following them back down the staircase, could not remember ever having seen them so cowed.

'Who was that?' he asked as they walked out again on to the terrace.

'That,' said Mr Radford, 'was the gentleman from whom we take our orders.' He did not sound too happy about it.

'Notice anything about him?' Mr Wayne asked.

'American, wasn't he?'

'Precisely,' they said in unison; and began to lead him across the well-tended lawn towards the wilder reaches of the grounds.

After a few paces, Thomas turned to look back at the house. It was the first time he had really taken it in. In this setting – nestling amid woodland, ivy twining itself around the wooden pillars of the verandah, a brace of doves settled at the apex of the roof at one end

– it looked rather like an illustration from a children's picture-book. (That, at least, was how he might one day have described it to Sylvia – had he ever felt free to do so.) The warm reddish tint of the brick, and the thatched roof with its four dormer windows peeping out sleepily over the garden added to this effect. It was certainly hard to reconcile the house's enchanted, fairy-tale aspect with the nature of the work that seemed to be carried on inside.

Mr Radford and Mr Wayne sat down on one of the wooden benches at the edge of the first cluster of oak trees, and invited Thomas to sit between them. Mr Radford took out three cigarettes and passed them along. Mr Wayne took out his matchbox.

'Nice place, isn't it?' said Mr Wayne.

'Shame it has to be used for something like this,' said Mr Radford. 'Doesn't seem right, somehow.'

'Still,' said his colleague, 'these are desperate times.'

'Absolutely.' Mr Radford sighed, in contemplation of this sentiment, and turned to Thomas. 'So, what's your reading of it all?'

'My reading?'

'The situation, as it's developed, over the last couple of days. What do you think's been going on?'

'We'd be interested to know what you make of it.'

Thomas looked at them both in turn. It seemed they were genuinely curious to know what he thought. 'Well,' he said. 'This is how it appears to me.' He drew deeply on his cigarette, then plunged on: 'Tony – Mr Buttress – has been working at the British pavilion, giving technical advice on the replica ZETA machine and other exhibits. Increasingly, he's been getting friendly with Mr Chersky of the newspaper *Sputnik*. I dare say you people have somehow been listening to their conversations and getting concerned about it. Tony is a bit of a radical, in his unassuming British way. Supports CND, votes Labour, that sort of thing. And now, it would seem, his socialist instincts have got the better of him, and Mr Chersky has persuaded him to go over to the other side. He's taken the designs of the machine, and for all I know the replica itself, and handed them over to the Soviets and right now he's quite probably sitting in their embassy telling them everything he knows.' Thomas paused for breath, and looked to them both for confirmation. 'Well, am I right?'

Mr Radford glanced at his colleague. 'What do you think, Wayne?'

'I'd say he's had a pretty good shot at it. I'd give him two out of ten for effort.'

'Plus another point for ingenuity, would you say?'

'Why not, old man? No harm in being generous.'

'What do you mean?' said Thomas. 'Are you saying that I've got it all wrong?'

'From start to finish, I'm afraid.'

'Not even close.'

Thomas let out an impatient sigh. 'So what *is* going on? Could you please tell me why I've been dragged out here?'

'Well,' said Mr Wayne, pausing only to tap a morsel of ash from the end of his cigarette onto the wild grass at his feet, 'let's start with your friend Tony. Mr Buttress and his famous machine. Where to begin, with that one? As I'm sure he's told you – or you read in the papers – a few months ago the head of the ZETA programme in the UK, Sir John Cockroft, announced a huge breakthrough. I'm no scientist – I don't know the details – maybe Mr Radford can help out on this point . . .'

'Not me, old man,' said Mr Radford, shaking his head sadly. 'Wouldn't have a clue.'

'Well – apparently – I don't know – but back in January Sir John claimed that his team had been observing these things – what are they called? – neutron bursts, and they'd been happening in the sort of numbers you might expect when there was a thermonuclear reaction. Would that be fair, would you say?'

'Search me. Didn't even get School Certificate in science.'

'Well, that's my spin on things, anyway. Nuclear fusion. Announced to the press in January, and generally considered to be the biggest feather in the cap of British science since the Lord knows when.

Three cheers for brave Sir John, and yah boo sucks to the Russians, while we're at it. And so your mob in Baker Street suggest they mock up a replica of the machine and show it off at the British pavilion. Jewel in the crown of British research, and so on. Which is all done, with a certain amount of secrecy – enough to make sure that nobody gives away the finer points of how the thing actually works. With me so far?'

Thomas nodded.

'All right. So here we all are in Brussels, having a jolly good time at the fair, pulling together, selling Britain to the rest of the world as hard as we can, and all the rest, and meanwhile back at home Sir John and his team of eggheads are still hard at it, tinkering away with their beloved machine and carrying out more and more tests. And earlier this week – guess what? Another discovery. Another breakthrough. Only it's not quite so exciting this time. They've found out something new about the ZETA machine, something no one was expecting.'

'Yes?' said Thomas.

'Unfortunately, it doesn't work.'

Mr Wayne allowed these words to sink in, while he lit himself another cigarette. Neither Thomas nor Mr Radford was inclined to say anything.

'Seems the announcement in January had been much too optimistic, and this burst of neutrons, or whatever it was, was just some sort of coincidence, just a perfectly ordinary by-product of the experiments. Egg on face all round, of course. And there was the offending machine on display, in the middle of the British pavilion in Brussels, with your pal Mr Buttress on hand to tell all and sundry what a terrific invention it was and how it was going to solve mankind's energy problems for the next few centuries. Well, the chaps at home weren't going to put up with that for long. Yesterday morning an urgent call came through from Whitehall telling him to pack the whole thing up and bring it home, pronto. Which is exactly what he did.'

'So he's gone? Back to London? And he's not coming back?'

'Afraid not,' said Mr Wayne. 'Still, look on the bright side. You've got that cabin to yourself now.'

'Every cloud has a silver lining, and all that,' Mr Radford agreed.

Thomas was silent for a long while. He was so confused that it became difficult, now, to phrase even the simplest question.

'So . . . I don't follow . . . if none of this has anything to do with Tony, or Mr Chersky . . . what does it have to do with me?'

'It has everything to do with Mr Chersky,' said Mr Radford. 'Mr Chersky, and Miss Parker.'

'Emily?' said Thomas, more surprised than ever.

'Yes indeed.'

'The girl from Wisconsin.'

Mr Radford leaned towards him. 'What do you *know* about her, exactly?'

'What's your impression?'

'What do you make of her?'

'How does she strike you?'

Thomas blew out his cheeks. 'I don't really know. Lovely girl, of course. Highly attractive. Apart from that, I hadn't given her much thought.'

'Well, it's about time you did.'

'It's about time you started giving a bit more thought to her, and a bit less thought to Anneke Hoskens.'

Thomas stared from one man to the other, utterly out of his depth.

'Emily Parker,' Mr Wayne explained slowly and emphatically, 'is in love with Andrey Chersky.'

'How on earth do you know that?'

'Oh, for goodness' sake, you've seen all the equipment we've got up there. We know everything that's going on at the fair.'

'But she's Tony's girl. At least she has been for the last few weeks.'

'That might be what you think. And it might be what *he* thinks. But we know differently. She's been meeting Chersky in secret. Much more often than she's been seeing Mr Buttress.'

'All right,' said Thomas, taking this in slowly. 'What of it? A young American girl falls for a handsome Russian journalist. They have a . . . fling in Brussels. So what? What difference does it make?'

'Andrey Chersky is not a journalist,' said Mr Radford. 'He's a high-ranking officer in the KGB.'

'And Emily Parker,' Mr Wayne continued, even before Thomas had properly been able to absorb this new information, 'is not just any American girl. Her father, Professor Frederick Parker, is one of the world's foremost experts in the field of nuclear research.'

'Nuclear weapons research, that is.'

After a moment, Thomas stood up. He walked away from the bench and towards the shade of the oak trees. Mr Wayne and Mr Radford watched him, wordless and impassive. He paced between the trees for a minute or two, until he had finished his cigarette, the stub of which he then crushed under his foot. When he came back to join them, he had a new note of resistance in his voice.

'Even if what you tell me is true,' he said, 'I don't see why it has anything to do with us.'

'Us?' said Mr Wayne.

'Us. The British. This is a matter for the Americans and the Russians, surely. The best thing would be for us to keep well out of it.'

Mr Wayne and Mr Radford looked at each other, and then both laughed.

'My dear fellow, it isn't as simple as that.'

'Things don't work like that any more.'

'We're all in it together, these days.'

'You have to take sides.'

'Look at it this way.' Mr Radford stood beside Thomas, and gestured towards the quaint old house in the distance. 'You've seen what's going on here. Who do you imagine is paying for all that? Whose equipment do you think we're using? We don't get it for nothing, you know. They expect something in return.'

'They expect favours.'

'You scratch my back, I'll scratch yours.'

'Share and share alike.'

'All right,' said Thomas, after giving this some thought. 'But why me? Where do I come into it?'

Now it was Mr Wayne's turn to stand up and start pacing.

'Miss Parker,' he explained, 'is a very emotional girl. As I'm sure you've noticed. Excessively romantic, you might say. Highly strung.'

'She is an actress, after all,' Mr Radford chipped in.

'She's come to Belgium, it seems, hell-bent on having a European romance. First it was your friend Tony. Then she lost interest in him and set her sights on Chersky. The point is . . . well, we think she can easily be diverted.'

'Diverted?'

'Yes. All she needs is someone to take her mind off this Russian chap. Another object for her affections.'

'A good-looking fellow, preferably – like yourself.'

'Me?' said Thomas. 'Good-looking?'

'Oh, come on, don't be modest.'

'Don't try to deny it.'

'There's a touch of the Gary Coopers about you, you know.'

'A spot of the Dirk Bogardes, I would have said.'

'So, do you see what we're driving at?'

'Do you get our drift?'

Thomas saw what they were driving at, at last. He didn't know whether to be horrified or flattered. At the moment, indeed, he felt a combination of the two.

'You're proposing,' he faltered, 'that I . . . that I, as it were, should attempt to *lure* Miss Parker away from Mr Chersky?'

'In a nutshell, yes.'

'As a matter of some urgency.'

'Urgency? Aren't you being a tad over-dramatic? I mean, I assume you wouldn't have gone to all this trouble if it wasn't important to you, but . . .'

Mr Wayne took his arm. 'Look, old boy, we don't bandy words

like that around without any reason. We've got to do something about this.'

'Our information,' said Mr Radford, 'is that this silly girl is ready to follow her Soviet sweetheart to Moscow just as soon as he says the word.'

'Really?'

'Yes, really.' Mr Wayne snorted, in a way which suggested to Thomas that his response to the predicament was, chiefly, one of resigned irritation. 'And you know where that would leave us, don't you? In a nice old pickle!'

A private room

SMERSH is the official murder organization of the Soviet government. It operates both at home and abroad and, in 1955, it employed
a total of 40,000 men and women. SMERSH is a contraction of
'Smiert Spionam', which means 'Death to Spies'. It is a name used
only among its staff and among Soviet officials. No sane member of
the public would dream of allowing the word to pass his lips.

The headquarters of SMERSH is a very large and ugly modern
building on the Sretenka Ulitsa. It is No. 13 on this wide, dull
street . . .

Thomas was reading these words two days later, sitting up on his
bed in the cabin at the Motel Expo, killing the half-hour before he
was due to go for dinner with Anneke. He had bought his hardback
copy of *From Russia with Love* the day before, at an English-language
bookshop on Sint-Katelijnestraat in central Brussels.

He found the passage troubling, to say the least. Were things
really so ruthless in the Soviet Union? He could hardly believe that
anyone as witty, ingratiating and hospitable as Mr Chersky could be
party to such matters. It was tempting to dismiss Ian Fleming's novels
– which were beginning to enjoy a considerable vogue in Britain –
as pure fantasy. And yet, at the same time, he appeared to be writing
with great authority. Hadn't he worked in military intelligence
himself? Thomas seemed to remember an article about him in one
of the newspapers which had gone into his background. Quite a
considerable personal experience of espionage, apparently. So there
was a good chance that the man knew what he was talking about.

He had read enough, for now. There was no point worrying, or
even thinking too hard, about what he was getting himself into,

because he had committed himself to helping Mr Wayne and Mr Radford in their tortuous scheme, and there could be no backing down. Why he'd agreed to it was difficult to say. There had been an appeal to his vanity, certainly: it was pretty flattering, after all, that someone should want to cast him as the bait in a romantic mouse-trap. If they really saw him as that sort of fellow – the irresistible romantic hero type – who was he to argue? But he was also, to some extent, acting upon a residual, unexpected sense of patriotism: Thomas had been more than dimly conscious, these last two days, of a certain heroic glow at the thought that he was stepping up to the wicket now that his name had been called, and doing his bit for Queen and country. And then there was also the bonus (although he would never have admitted this to himself) that a number of hours, or perhaps even days (or perhaps even nights) spent in Miss Parker's company was far from being an unpleasant prospect.

He put the book face down on his continental quilt and contin-ued to think, staring up through the skylight at the idly drifting summer clouds. Altogether it was going to be a very delicate affair. First of all, he would have to choose his words carefully when tell-ing Anneke what he had been asked to do.

Mr Radford and Mr Wayne had, to his surprise, shown consider-able tact when approaching this side of things. They fully understood the difficulties of his situation. Thomas must, they said, explain everything to Anneke fully and clearly. She was a lovely girl: naive, guileless and entirely trustworthy. They had given her a careful vet-ting, of course, but there was nothing in her family background to cause any alarm. Given the closeness of the friendship (they put it no stronger) that had developed between Thomas and Miss Hoskens over the last few weeks, they felt that he only had one honourable course of action: to tell her the whole truth about Mr Chersky, Miss Parker, and the important task he had agreed to undertake, so that she might understand why, for the time being, he would be spend-ing so much time in the American girl's company. It was not going to be an easy conversation, they realized that: but they implored him to be candid, to answer all her questions, to conceal nothing from her. To behave like a gentleman, in other words. They suggested that he talk to her over dinner; and made a booking in Thomas's name, for this purpose, at Praha, the restaurant of the Czechoslovakian pavilion – generally considered to be the best restaurant on the Expo site, and one which Anneke herself had expressed a special interest in visiting.

So much for Miss Hoskens. Mr Wayne and Mr Radford had been less tactful, he thought, in dealing with the other matter he had raised: the question of Sylvia. At first they had misunderstood him. On no account, they cautioned, should he mention to Miss Parker that he had a wife and child back in London. That would be a grave mistake. And if she already knew about this, through her conversations with Mr Buttress, Thomas should invent a pretty convincing story to explain it away. Tell her that you're separated, they said. Tell her that the marriage broke down some time ago, that you never see her, that there isn't the smallest prospect of a reconciliation. Thomas listened to this advice, and agreed that he would follow it, but then explained that he had been thinking of a different problem altogether. He was a married man, after all, and was not sure that, even in the execution of this important mission, he would be prepared to betray his wife, physically, with another woman.

Mr Radford and Mr Wayne had exchanged embarrassed glances. This question, it seemed, lay well outside their area of expertise.

'Well, look, that's entirely down to you, you know.'

'We can't very well help you with that one.'

'These are deep waters, after all.'

'Deep waters. Dangerous currents.'

'All we would say is . . .'

'Well, the pleasures of married life . . .'

'. . . which we know you are awfully keen on . . .'

'. . . they haven't exactly held you back, so far, have they? . . .'

'. . . they haven't seemed to weigh very heavily with you . . .'

'. . . in your relations . . .'

'. . . your dealings, we should probably say . . .'

'. . . with Miss Hoskens.'

'Don't misunderstand us, of course . . .'

'. . . don't take offence . . .'

'. . . but our impression is . . .'

'. . . that you seem to play . . . pretty fast and loose . . .'

'. . . have a fairly flexible interpretation, as it were . . .'

'. . . of the rules and regulations, and all that.'

'On top of which . . .'

'. . . moreover . . .'

'. . . your good little woman back in Tooting . . .'

'. . . from what we understand . . .'

'. . . not that we want to spread gossip, or anything like that . . .'

'. . . or sow the seeds of mistrust, Heaven forbid . . .'

'. . . but there does seem to be a small possibility . . .'

'. . . if our information is correct . . .'

'. . . that she and your next-door neighbour . . .'

'. . . are becoming pretty . . . intimate . . .'

'. . . taking that word in its broadest sense, of course . . .'

'. . . in your absence.'

Mr Radford and Mr Wayne had delivered themselves of these sentiments with an air of great discomfort, and then left Thomas alone for several minutes to ponder them. At the end of which, his feelings on the subject were no less conflicted than before. And even now, he found himself quite unable to see his way out of the moral labyrinth into which the bizarre developments of the last few days seemed to have led him.

He picked up the book again. How would James Bond have acted in this situation, he wondered? It seemed to Thomas, from everything he already knew about him, that the differences between himself and Fleming's hero were probably too great for any meaningful comparison. There was no way that Bond, for instance, would ever have got himself tied down to married life in

Tooting, with a nine-to-five office job and a baby daughter, up to his ears in bills, domestic chores, nappies and gripe water . . .

He sighed and got up from the bed. In just a few days' time he was supposed to be going back to London for the weekend: his first trip home, away from the fair. He already sensed that it was not going to be an easy visit. No wonder that he looked forward, with a certain nervous pleasure, to tonight's dinner with Anneke, and after that the rendezvous with Emily Parker that had been arranged for two evenings' time.

The last two days at Expo 58 had been declared Czech National Days: Czech films had been shown in the cinemas, Czech music performed in the concert halls, and bookings at the already popular Restaurant Praha had reached a record high. When the doorman admitted Thomas and Anneke at nine o'clock that evening, the buzz of conversation in the restaurant was uncomfortably loud, and there did not seem to be a single place free at any of the thirty or forty tables.

This, however, was merely the less exclusive of the two main dining areas: the Restaurant Pilzen. A waiter escorted them briskly between the crowded tables towards a door at the rear. Perhaps, then, Thomas thought, we have been booked a table in the Restaurant De Luxe: in which case, Radford and Wayne were really pushing the boat out on their behalf. But even on this point he was mistaken: for he and Anneke were ushered reverently into a private room, containing only one table, dominated by an enormous silver vase filled to overflowing with flowers, and laid out with a variety and volume of cutlery which suggested that this was going to be a very long meal.

'Sir – madame,' said the waiter, showing them to their seats. He then presented them with two menus, in stiff white card thickly embossed with gold lettering, and withdrew from the room discreetly, leaving them in a situation of far closer intimacy than either of them had been expecting.

Anneke looked at Thomas shyly, her eyes round with surprise, and the first thing she said was: 'Can you afford all this?'

Now, perhaps, would have been a good moment to say that the bill was in fact being picked up by a little-known department of the British government; information which would have led on, naturally enough, to the difficult subject which Thomas was obliged to broach with her this evening. And indeed, he almost said it. Almost, but not quite. Instead he gave a worldly smile – one might almost have called it a smirk – and murmured: 'Of course.'

Neither of them had ever had a meal quite like this before. Finding themselves unable to choose from the menu, even using the English translations, they asked the *maître d'* to make a selection for them. The courses came in rapid succession, in dauntingly large portions: but every taste sensation was so unfamiliar, and so delightful, that they made much better headway than they would have thought possible. There was beef tartare Kolkovna, served with garlic toast; a clear beef soup called *hovězí polévka*; wonderfully savoury pancakes (*bramboráky*); a lamb hock braised in red wine, served with rosemary potatoes; a beef stroganoff; chocolate soufflé; apple strudel; and more pancakes to finish – this time with cream yoghurt and blueberries. They began the meal with a bottle of sparkling Bohemian Sekt, and were then offered a deliciously sweet Gewürztraminer, followed by a rich, plummy Pinot Noir from Moravia. Finally, they drank brandy from giant snifter glasses, which had been specially designed, the waiter told them, to commemorate the hundredth anniversary of the famous Moser glassworks. The designer, he said, had classified humanity into six different types and created six unique snifters to express them. Thomas's was called the Long Face; Anneke's, the Slim Lady. The brandy warmed them both with a deep, satisfying liquid flame.

As for the conversation which accompanied their meal, that too was free-flowing, if a little one-sided. Thomas did not have a huge experience of talking to women. A meal out with Sylvia, for instance, would typically be punctuated by long, difficult silences, as the two of them quickly exhausted every topic and struggled to dredge up new ones. And at work, there was a strict but unspoken orthodoxy which required that Thomas took lunch with his male counterparts rather than the secretaries. It was a new experience for him, that evening, to be addressed by someone like Anneke in such a spontaneous, confiding way: telling him stories of her family life, her wayward elder brother and over-protective father; explaining how, from a very early age at school, it had become obvious to everybody that she had a gift for learning languages; how as an infant, she used to pore over the leather-bound atlas they kept at home, and how she had never lost her fascination for foreign countries or eagerness to travel, although so far she had been no further south than Paris, or further north than Amsterdam. Thomas chipped in occasionally, usually to make more general remarks: wasn't it interesting, he observed, that despite the acknowledged excellence of Britain's public schools and grammar schools, it was still hard to find an Englishman capable of speaking a foreign language when he went abroad for a holiday? But he could not help noticing, at such moments, that Anneke was not really concerned to discuss what he would have called the broader picture. She liked to talk about things from a personal, subjective point of view, so for the most part all he could do was listen; drifting off, occasionally, to wonder how and when he was going to broach the sensitive topic of Emily, and his strange new assignment.

Still on the subject of her yearning for travel, Anneke at one point asked him: 'So, you never got to see the pavilion of the Belgian Congo?'

'Not yet, no. I was planning to visit some time in the next few days.'

'But you can't,' she said. 'They've gone home.'

'Who's gone home?'

'The natives from Africa. Hadn't you heard?'

'What happened?'

'Well, I read in the newspaper that they were complaining about the way that some of the visitors were treating them. They were sitting all day in their straw huts, working on their . . . native crafts, and so on, and apparently some of the people were shouting bad things at them, and sometimes they were trying to –' (she giggled) '– feed them bananas, and things like that. They said they were made to feel like animals in a zoo. So now most of them have gone home and the huts are empty.' Anneke frowned. 'I thought there was something wrong about it, the first time I went there. It felt somehow . . . not kind, making them sit and work like that while all the Europeans just stood and watched.'

'Yes,' said Thomas, 'I thought so too, when I heard about it. On the other hand – perhaps it's not so different from what Emily has to do in the American pavilion.'

'Perhaps not,' said Anneke, doubtfully. 'Only it doesn't seem *quite* the same . . .'

'Talking of Emily . . .' Thomas began, taking this opportunity to engineer a smoothish change of subject, 'there was something I wanted to tell you.'

'Oh?'

'Yes. I'm going to be taking her to a concert on Thursday night. Tomorrow is the start of the Swiss National Days and their orchestra is giving a performance in the Grand Auditorium on Thursday. I've managed to get myself a pair of tickets.'

'Oh,' said Anneke. She drew back, visibly surprised. 'And you're taking Miss Parker?'

'Yes.'

So now there was nothing for it but to plough on. He drew a deep breath, and explained to her, in detail – just as Mr Radford and Mr Wayne had insisted that he should – the nature of the difficulty he had been called upon to resolve. He told her that, for the next few weeks, he would be spending a good deal of time in Emily's company. He told her that, despite the impression she gave, Emily was actually a very naive and politically unsophisticated person. He told her that the American secret services had been monitoring her friendship with Mr Chersky, and were terrified that she was soon going to succumb to his persuasive charms, and follow him back to Russia; and that they had called in their British colleagues to find a way of obstructing the burgeoning romance; and that he, Thomas, was the person chosen to attempt the task. He told her that he had no choice, as far as he could see, but to do whatever he could to help.

How had he been expecting Anneke to respond, exactly? Somewhere deep in his psyche, he had imagined something like the wide-eyed, trusting, admiring gaze that Tatiana Romanova, the girlish young Soviet spy, was forever fixing upon James Bond in the pages of *From Russia with Love*. He'd been quietly convinced that she would be impressed by his self-sacrifice and unassuming heroism. But, oddly enough, it wasn't really like that at all. She looked more and more downcast as the explanation went on.

'It's not what I would have chosen to happen, of course,' he insisted, and began to wonder if it would make things easier if he tried to make light of the situation, turn it into a joke. 'Really, the entire rigmarole seems rather absurd. But these are the sorts of games that these people like to play, so I suppose . . . Well, anyway, I've agreed to go along with it.'

'It doesn't sound absurd to me,' said Anneke. 'It all sounds rather dangerous.'

'Oh, I don't know. It's hard to take it all that seriously. I mean, you've met Mr Radford and Mr Wayne, haven't you?'

'Yes.'

'Well, didn't they strike you as somewhat comical? With their trench coats and their trilby hats. Like something out of a cheap novel. The way they talk . . .'

'How do they talk?'

'Well, for instance, whenever they've finished saying their piece and putting me in my place, do you know what they always say? "This conversation never took place." I didn't think *anybody* really used that phrase. Smacks a little of . . . too much theatricality, don't you think?'

Anneke nodded, but without much conviction, and for the next few minutes she was very quiet. Before long she announced that the hostel where once again she would be staying the night closed its doors at midnight, and she would have to rush back if she was not going to find herself locked out. She thanked Thomas very much for a lovely evening. It was something she would remember for a long time. And she hoped that they might run into each other again before long – certainly before the Expo was over.

After that, she excused herself and went to the ladies' room for some little time. Thomas checked with the *maître d'* that the bill had already been settled, and then, when Anneke returned, he walked her to the Porte des Attractions. It was a close summer evening, and the crowds were still thronging La Belgique Joyeuse and the Parc des Attractions. Thomas and Anneke said goodbye at the gate, with a quick, functional kiss on the cheek.

He stood and watched her retreating figure as she receded into the darkness. Then he sighed and scratched his head. Well, that had been awkward. Decidedly awkward. Perhaps Tony had been right, and the girl had rather been more stuck on him than he'd thought. But he had this one consolation, at any rate: there had been no deception. At least he had told her the truth.

The trouble with happiness

On the evening of Thursday, 31 July 1958, Thomas waited for Emily outside the Grand Auditorium, at the north-western end of the Expo site. In his jacket pocket he carried the two tickets – dress circle, front row – that had been provided for him by Mr Radford and Mr Wayne.

Emily arrived slightly late, at four minutes past seven. She was wearing a light-grey cape, secured at the base of her throat by a single button, and beneath it, a black velvet evening gown. Her strange, angular grace momentarily took Thomas's breath away. But he recovered in time to take her hand, and bring his lips to it in a gentle kiss.

'Miss Parker,' he said.

'Mr Foley,' she answered. 'How very delightful to see you.'

'The pleasure is all mine. Would you care to step into the bar for a glass of champagne?'

'I can think of nothing more heavenly.'

The bar, like everything at Expo 58, was crowded. But Thomas was lucky enough to secure one of the last available tables, by a big picture window overlooking the Place de Belgique. He left Emily there for a few minutes and returned with two glasses of champagne. She took the glass from his outstretched hand but before drinking, she gazed for a few moments at the surface of the pale, effervescent liquid. Her eyes sparkled and her cheeks dimpled into a smile.

'I just adore champagne,' she said. 'I love to watch the way the bubbles dance in the glass.'

'That's why they make the bowl of the glasses so wide,' said Thomas, with a worldly, knowledgeable air; then realized that he was dredging up some half-forgotten piece of information which he had never really understood anyway. 'So that . . . so that all the bubbles don't escape at once . . .'

'Really?' said Emily. 'How fascinating.'

Thomas raised his glass. 'Cheers,' he said, and silently reminded himself to be a bit more careful next time, when trying to impress her.

'Cheers,' Emily answered, and they touched glasses.

'I can't thank you enough,' she continued, 'for asking me here tonight. It was inexpressibly thoughtful of you.'

'Well, I'm afraid that Tony was supposed to be your date. But he left the two tickets with me, so I thought that to invite you to a concert which you might otherwise have missed was the very least I could do.'

'It was a charming gesture. Absolutely charming. Of course, I was rather shocked to hear that Tony had left so suddenly like that. I'm sure it's foolish of me, but I'm surprised he didn't say goodbye. We'd seen a lot of each other, and we were getting on so easily.'

'He'll write to you, I'm sure. Tony's nothing if not a perfect gentleman.'

'That had been my impression, yes. Anyway . . .' Wishing to divert herself from this train of thought, perhaps, she began to study the concert programme she had picked up in the entrance hall. 'Who and what are we hearing tonight? L'Orchestre de la Suisse Romande. Conducted by Ernest Ansermet. Are you any the wiser?'

'They have quite a reputation, I believe. For twentieth-century music, in particular.'

'Really? Well, the words "twentieth-century music" send a shiver down my spine. Most of today's composers have forgotten how to write a tune – if they ever knew. Let's see what they're proposing to inflict on us.' She glanced down at the programme notes. 'Hmm . . . Beethoven's Fifth. Well, I guess we can all handle that. Debussy's *La*

Mer . . . Not too alarming, though I should probably have brought my seasickness pills. Now who's this fellow? *Arthur Honegger* . . .'

Thomas shrugged. 'New to me.'

'"Arthur Honegger",' Emily read aloud, '"is generally considered to be one of the most important Swiss composers of the twentieth century." Talk about damning with faint praise . . . "His magnificent cycle of five symphonies offers a musical narrative of some of the most brutal and savage years in recent human history, a cry from the depths of despair which culminates . . ." Oh Lord, one of those. Rubbing the audience's noses in the misery when he should really be trying to help us forget about it.'

'One shouldn't make premature judgements, I suppose . . .'

'Indeed not, but doesn't this kind of thing get your goat? It certainly does mine. What is an artist for, anyway? What use is he, if he doesn't . . . elevate us, somehow? Perhaps I have a narrow view of things, but to me, an artist is someone who adds to the beauty in the world, he shouldn't take away from it. Music that sounds like two cats fighting in a scrapyard, sculptures that look like someone's accidentally dropped a heap of clay on the floor, paintings that give you a headache, with a couple of eyes on one side of the face and three noses on the other . . . ' She checked herself and took a sip of champagne. 'I'm sorry. Perhaps you don't like an opinionated woman. I do have a habit of speaking my mind. That's one of the things you'll find out about me if we . . . start to know each other a little better.' Before Thomas had a chance to reply, a bell rang, signalling that the concert was about to start. They hastily emptied their glasses and rose to their feet.

'Well, into the field of battle, then,' said Emily, taking Thomas by the arm in a companionable sort of way. 'Let's see what Mr Honegger has to throw at us.'

Honegger's tone poem of 1920, *Pastorale d'Eté*, was the first item on the programme. As the celebrated Monsieur Ansermet raised his baton, Emily watched with a steely look of suspicion and disapproval in her eye, but after hearing only a few bars of the music, her resistance melted away.

It began with a low, gently rocking figure played – or rather whispered – by the cellos. Very soon, above this, the central melody began to rise up on the French horn. Its long, slow, leisurely phrases were answered by high and subtly dissonant chords from the violins. Then the tune was taken up by the oboe, while a flute added floating, birdlike interjections: the whole tapestry of strings, horn and woodwind gradually knitting together into a complex, seamless whole which, even without the programmatic title, would inevitably have evoked the hazy timelessness of a summer afternoon. The main tune reappeared, and became even more insistent and seductive when it was taken up by the first violins, but the languorous atmosphere was then interrupted by a boisterous interlude in which a sprightly, instantly memorable tune – a folk tune, surely – was introduced by the solo clarinet, and for a few minutes the tone shifted to one of fleet-footed gaiety. After reaching the gentlest of climaxes this interlude was wafted away by the reappearance of the main theme, which by now was beginning to take on the character of an old friend: once again, it rose and fell, rose and fell, a soft, endlessly renewable conversation between the different sections of the orchestra; until it too faded into nothingness, amid the dying flourishes of gossamer-bowed violins, the last twilit birdcalls of flute and clarinet. As the musical distillation of a time, and a mood, it was perfection; or, as Emily said herself later that evening, as she and Thomas stood close beside each other in the Parc d'Osseghem, on the footbridge overlooking the lake which glimmered beneath the light of the yellow summer moon: 'It was the sort of music that makes you think of all your childhood summers, don't you agree? It took me back twenty years or more, when we used to visit a house belonging to friends of my parents. It was on the shores of Tomahawk Lake. Such splendid times we had there . . . It was uncanny, how he . . . *evoked* that place for me, while all the time I suppose he was thinking of his own summers in Switzerland. Paints a pretty nice picture of it, I must say. Have you ever been?'

'Yes, I spent a summer there myself. Four years ago. Near Basle. I was thinking of that time, of course, while the piece was playing.'

'Well, really, I take my hat off to Mr Honegger for that composition. I should never have been so rude about him. It was the most delicious thing I've ever heard. Now it makes me long to get out into the countryside, to sit beneath the sun, with a bottle of good wine and a basket of good food, and to lie on my back and watch the clouds floating across the sky, with someone special sitting next to me, someone I could talk to all afternoon about nothing and everything . . .'

After thinking about this for a moment or two, Thomas said, daringly: 'Well, of course, we could easily do that.'

Emily looked at him eagerly. 'Meaning?'

'We're surrounded by countryside here. And it's the height of summer. Why don't we drive out somewhere – the next time you have a day off – and take some food, and take something to drink, and . . . make a proper occasion of it?'

Her eyes gleamed with delight at the prospect.

'Could we really, do you think? That would be just wonderful. Such a treat. This place is a blast, all right, but it also gets to you after a while. I could do with a day out. Do you have a car?'

'No,' Thomas admitted. 'But I can . . . try to arrange something.'

She clapped her hands together. 'Oh, I'm looking forward to it already.' And then, when Thomas had only just begun to savour the pleasure of having excited her so much, her next words snatched it away: 'We could make a real party of it. Invite the whole gang along.'

'The gang?'

'From the night at the ballet. Perhaps Mr Chersky would like to come. And that exquisite little Belgian girl you're such good friends with. I forget her name.'

'Anneke?'

'Anneke. And anyone else who wants to come. The more the merrier! Don't you agree?'

'Well . . . of course. The more the merrier, indeed.'

He had said what was expected of him; but the lack of conviction in his voice, he knew, was obvious. Emily said nothing in response, directly. But after a few seconds' uncomfortable silence she said: 'Look, Mr Foley, I know what I'm proposing is not quite the same as a picnic for two, but . . . I don't want you to feel any sense of obligation towards me, just because your friend Tony has left me in the lurch, as it were. You've already done your duty, and I appreciate it very, very much. It's been the loveliest of evenings, one I shall remember for a long time.'

'I don't consider it has anything to do with duty. I don't see it that way at all.'

'Well then, let me put it another way. You can consider your mission accomplished.'

Thomas thought, as soon as he heard it, that this was an odd phrase to use. Too clinical for words. But he brushed the thought aside; assumed it had something to do with American phraseology. The Yanks and the Brits barely spoke the same language, after all.

'Anyway, it's getting late,' said Emily. 'I need my beauty sleep. The *hausfraus* of Belgium will be turning out in their droves tomorrow to learn from my Hoovering skills, and I can't turn up looking like a fright. That would earn me the sack.'

'I really don't know how you stand it,' said Thomas, as they began to walk alongside the lake, in the direction of the Porte du Parc. 'Demonstrating the same thing, day in, day out. Fielding the same questions from the public. Doesn't it drive you mad?'

'Oh, it's no worse than getting a part in a Broadway thriller as the second maid, and having two lines, "Tea will be ready presently" and "I found this parcel in the front porch, madam", and having to say them six nights a week, plus matinees on Wednesdays and Saturdays, for the whole of a four-month run. Of course, if I was ever offered another part like that, I'd leave Belgium and take it like a shot . . .'

'Is that likely to happen?'

'Well, none of us really knows how long we're going to be here, do we? What about you? Are you in Brussels for the duration?'

'I suppose so. Though the Britannia does seem to be running rather smoothly at the moment. More or less taking care of itself. I haven't had very much to do, these last few weeks.'

'Well then.' She turned and looked him directly in the eye. 'We must all savour our time here, while we can. Because it could all come to an end at any moment, and none of us can ever know when, or how.' She reached up and kissed him on the cheek. 'That's the trouble with happiness.'

Tooting Common

Thomas stood beside the dark oak table in his dining room, looking out over the back garden, a cup of sweet, milky coffee in his hand. It seemed unreal to him that he was back at home. His memories of the last few days were so vivid that they gave the suburban normality of Tooting the quality of a daydream. The drunken night at the Bolshoi ballet; the blindfold trip into the countryside in Wilkins's car; the incredible revelations of Mr Radford and Mr Wayne; his evenings out at the Restaurant Praha, with Anneke, and the Grand Auditorium, with Emily: how could these bizarre adventures exist in the same universe as this neat vegetable patch, this disused air-raid shelter, this spectacularly tasteless goldfish pond now decorated (courtesy of Mr Sparks) with a fake bronze statue of an overweight cherub pouring water out of an urn?

It was eleven o'clock on Saturday morning, and Sparks had already paid a visit, to nose around and find out how he was getting on.

'Morning, Foley,' he had said, coming into the sitting room, where Thomas had been reading the newspaper, and plonking himself down on the sofa without even being asked. 'How's Belgium been treating you, then?'

'Very nicely, thank you,' Thomas answered, without putting the newspaper down.

'Been reading about the Expo in the newspapers from time to time,' Sparks continued. 'Sounds like it's all happening over there. Royal visits one day, movie stars dropping by the next. Sometimes I show the clippings around at work and say, "My next-door neighbour's over there in the middle of that lot, you know." Bit of reflected glory. Never did anybody any harm.'

'Yes,' said Thomas, drily and non-commitally, as he flicked through a few more pages. The British news stories he was reading – nothing but party politics, labour disputes and petty crime – seemed trivial beyond belief. Did he really live in this country?

'Of course, it's been very quiet here in the meantime. I dare say you consider it quite a backwater now, compared to Brussels. When are you going back? Tomorrow evening, is it?'

'Monday morning.'

'Really? Well, I'm sure Sylvia will be happy to have you for the extra day.'

'Look, Sparks,' said Thomas, putting his paper down at last and leaning forward emphatically. 'I'm very grateful for the attention you've been showing to my wife. I'm sure you've been a great comfort to her. But please don't worry yourself on her account, or indeed mine. She told me only this morning that she's been coping perfectly well on her own. So kindly attend to your own concerns – looking after your sister, for instance, who I'm sure needs your company much more than Sylvia does.'

Thinking about the conversation now, he wondered why he had felt compelled to be so rude. Really, Mr Sparks was not such a bad sort, and besides, it was the sheerest hypocrisy to be worried about what Sylvia was getting up to at home, while Thomas himself had been spending so much time (however innocently) in the company of other women. If only he could talk to her about his Belgian adventures; if only he could tell her of the strange turn things had taken lately, and the delicate role he had been chosen to play. But the whole business was shrouded in such secrecy, and it was this, he was sure – this inability to discuss with Sylvia the most important things that were preying on his mind – that created this confounded distance between them. This coldness and lack of communication that had been evident since the moment he had crossed the threshold.

'Did you have plans for today?' Sylvia asked. She had entered the dining room silently behind him, and was now standing at his side.

'Not really.' He made an effort, and mustered a smile. 'Perhaps there are some odd jobs you'd like me to do, while I'm here?'

'There's no need,' she answered. 'Your time is your own.'

The day dragged on, solemn and interminable. Thomas's mother arrived at about five o'clock. She had an overnight bag with her, and was also carrying, rather to his puzzlement, a small leather satchel which was battered around the edges and worn with age. He took the overnight bag upstairs and then showed her into the sitting room. She refused his offer of a glass of sherry (five o'clock was far too early to be drinking alcohol, in her book) and watched in disapproval as he drained his own glass in two large gulps.

Unable to bear the thought of a dinner consumed in silence, Thomas brought the wireless in from the kitchen, set it up on the sideboard, and tuned it in to an orchestral concert on the Light Programme. Gill was awake, by now, so Sylvia sat her up in a high chair at the table, opposite Mrs Foley. She served out helpings of steak and kidney pudding, mashed potato and runner beans for the adults. Thomas poured himself a glass of red wine, but the women would not join him, and drank water instead. While they ate dinner and listened to the music, Sylvia fed Gill mouthfuls of mashed potato and gravy with a teaspoon.

Afterwards Sylvia drew the curtains in the sitting room, to keep out the evening sunlight as they all started to watch *Television Music Hall* on the BBC. Thomas would once have allowed himself to be mildly amused by the antics of Richard Hearne as Mr Pastry, but this evening he was feeling less tolerant. And after a few minutes watching Jack Billings (*'With the dancing feet'*) and Claudio Venturelli (*'Italy's singing star'*) he found he could not bear the inane cheerfulness of the programme any longer, and left the sitting room without saying anything. He stood out in the garden and smoked two cigarettes, tipping the ash vengefully into the urn carried by the overweight cherub at the edge of the goldfish pond. Then he went back into the hall, picked up the telephone receiver and dialled a number he had been keeping with him on a folded scrap of paper.

'Ealing four-double-nine-three,' a familiar voice answered.

'Tony?'

'Yes?'

'It's Thomas here. Thomas Foley!'

'Thomas! By Jove, it's a clear line from Brussels, if that's where you're calling from.'

'I wish that I was, old man. But I'm in Tooting.'

'Tooting? What the devil are you doing there?'

'Home for the weekend. Come to see how Sylvia and the baby are getting on.'

'So the prison authorities at the Motel Expo gave you compassionate leave, did they?'

'Something like that. But look, what happened to you? Why did you just up and leave?'

'Got my marching orders. You heard about the ZETA fiasco, did you? They couldn't get that replica home fast enough.'

'But aren't you coming back?'

'No. They terminated my contract. Two days later I was back at the Royal Institution, pushing papers around my desk. I say, though, how's Emily shaping up? Have you seen her?'

'Yes, I saw her the other night. Took her to a concert as a matter of fact.'

'Did you, begad? Well, you haven't wasted much time. You could have allowed a bit of a cooling-off period, you know.'

'Oh, it's not like that at all. She's pretty sorry you've gone, if you ask me.'

'Ah, she's a nice girl all right. But there was no future in it anyhow. I've no intention of upping sticks to the United States. And besides, in my absence, this new secretary has arrived at the RI, and she's an absolute corker! In fact I'm taking her to the flicks tonight.'

'Really? Well, it doesn't sound as though you've wasted much time either.'

'Oh, you know me – easy come, easy go.'

'Ah well, I was going to ask you out for a pint tonight, but it sounds like your hands are full.'

'I hope they will be, before the evening's over, yes. Sorry, that would have been nice, but – on this occasion, no can do.'

'Oh well. Keep in touch, won't you?'

'Of course I will, old man. Of course I will.'

After he had replaced the receiver, Thomas sat at the telephone table in thoughtful silence, until he became aware that someone was standing in the gloom of the hallway behind him. He turned round. It was his mother. Beneath her arm she was clutching the old leather satchel.

'Can we speak for a few minutes?' she asked.

'Of course. Weren't you enjoying the programme?'

Without answering, she led him back into the dining room. They sat down opposite each other at the table.

'Your wife is not happy,' said Mrs Foley bluntly.

Thomas, taken very much aback, could think of nothing to say.

'She is lonely, she misses you, and now that you are home for a short time, you behave badly towards her. Don't try to deny it.' (He had been about to protest.) 'What is going on? Why are you treating her this way?'

'I don't know . . . It's nothing, I'm just finding it hard to adjust. Everything at the Expo is so different, so much . . . *bigger* than here.'

'You're running around with other women in Brussels?'

'No. Not really.'

'Not really?' She reached out and touched his hand. 'Tommy, you're a good boy. Always have been. Everybody likes you. Don't turn into your father.'

'I won't, Mother. Is that what you brought me in here to tell me?'

'No. I brought you in here to show you something.' She began to open the satchel, while Thomas looked on curiously. It was made of smooth light-brown leather, but this had clearly become very worn over the years: it was scored with scratch-marks and mottled with darker stains. Given that it appeared to be many years old, it surprised him that he could not remember ever having seen it before.

'Is that yours?' he asked.

'Of course it's mine,' she said. 'This is the bag in which I used to take my books to school when I was just a child. I never showed it to you before. Grandma kept it until she died, and since then, it's been in my bedroom all these years.'

Opening the satchel, she revealed that its contents were sparse: just a handful of papers, postcards and photographs. Thomas reached across and picked up one of the postcards. It showed an impressive cathedral-like building in the Late Gothic style, with highly detailed corbels and statues in canopied niches. The photograph had been taken in black-and-white, clearly, but then colourized by an artist. There was no handwriting on the back of the postcard: just a printed caption which said 'LEUVEN, STADHUIS'.

'That is the famous town hall,' said Mrs Foley. 'I don't know how we came to have that postcard. These were the few things that my mother managed to collect from the house and take with her on the night that we escaped. Here.' Now she handed him a tiny, creased and indistinct monochrome photograph. 'This was our house. The house where I grew up.'

Thomas looked closely at the picture. It was hard to make out much detail. He could see a farmhouse and a number of other farm buildings clustered neatly around a central courtyard. The roof of the main farmhouse appeared to be thatched. Behind the farm buildings could be seen a row of trees, beneath a grey sky which loomed heavily over the steeply sloping roofs: the picture had been taken from a low angle. To the far left of the photograph was what appeared to be the edge of a field, in which you could just about glimpse the heads of two cows.

'It looks . . . not how I've always imagined it,' he said. 'It looks tidy. Well kept. Prosperous.'

'Of course,' said Mrs Foley. 'My father was a successful man. He made a lot of money from that farm. He worked hard and employed many people in the area. You cannot see it,' she continued, pointing at the photograph, 'but just behind these trees was the river. The Dijle. It was not a big river, at that point, more like a brook or a canal, but it was where we used to go and play, when we were children. Come on, I'll show you.'

She unfolded another piece of paper. It was an old map, the colours so faded, and the creases and folds untouched for so long, that it could barely be read. Mrs Foley started to trace a path along the paper with her finger, following the ribbon of light blue that curled and wound its way through the centre of the map.

'So,' she said. 'This is Wijgmaal, which in those days was just a small village. Maybe it is much bigger now, I don't know. This village was where I used to go to school. There is a bridge . . . *here*, and from that bridge, you used to be able to walk down to the footpath beside the river. I used to walk along this path every day, to school in the morning and back home again in the afternoon. Coming home, you would follow the path for about ten minutes, about half a mile, and then you saw these trees – the ones in the picture, these great big sycamores, you see them? – on your right. Just after those trees, there was a beautiful field, which in the summer was full of buttercups – tall ones, meadow buttercups, I think they are called. A whole field of brilliant yellow. All you had to do was walk across this field and that brought you to the back of the farm.' Her forefinger rested on a point on the map where someone had marked a cross in pencil. 'Right there. This was where we used to live.

'I came to London with my mother – Grandma – in 1914. I think it was late in September when we got here, when we started to feel safe again. We left my father and my two brothers behind at the farm in Wijgmaal. I did not learn what had become of them for some months. Every day Grandma used to tell me that Papa would be joining us soon, and that Marc and Stefan would be with him, and we would be all together again. But I waited and waited and nothing happened. It was Papa's brother Paul who came and told us in the end. Mama sent me out into the street to play – we were living in the East End in those days, in Shadwell – and she heard the whole story from Uncle Paul that afternoon but she didn't tell me everything. Not then. I was only ten years old. But I did learn that I wouldn't be seeing my father and brothers again. It seems the Germans were closer than we thought when Mama and I made our escape. Another few hours and we would have been too late. They killed Papa and they killed Stefan. Marc managed to escape but he died too, later in the War. They looted the farm and took every-thing of any value, and anything they could eat or drink, and after that they burned it to the ground. Uncle Paul said there was noth-ing left of it any more. Not a single beam or a single brick.'

Mrs Foley fell silent. Thomas thought about what she had told him, but he could not turn it into a mental picture: when he tried to imagine his grandfather and his uncles being gunned down by German soldiers, the blazing thatched roof of the farm in the background, nothing vivid or real would come into his mind. Instead, he found himself presented with a memory, a memory from his own childhood, something he had not thought about for many years: the little flat in East London, two or three storeys above a butcher's shop, where his grandmother used to live, and where he used to visit her, sometimes, with his mother, when he was only five or six years old. After that he remembered one visit, one visit only, to some sort of hospital or nursing home where she was staying and where she had seemed much younger than all the other patients. She had smelled strongly of some violet-scented perfume and when she had leaned in to kiss and hug him he had recoiled slightly and tried to avoid contact with the enormous, prominent mole on her left cheek . . .

The door to the dining room opened and Sylvia came in.

'Wouldn't you like the light on in here?' she said, turning on the overhead lamp. 'You can hardly see what you're doing.' She came forward and peered with interest at the map spread out on the table. 'What's this? Looking for buried treasure?'

'Mother was just showing me where her parents' farm used to

be,' said Thomas. 'Here – this is what it looked like.' And he passed his wife the tiny, blurred square of black-and-white photograph.

'I want Tommy to go there while he is in Belgium,' Mrs Foley now announced, with her characteristic brusqueness and emphasis.

'Really?' said Thomas. 'I thought you specifically said . . .'

'I know. But I've been thinking about it, and I've changed my mind.'

Thomas nodded slowly. 'All right. But why don't you come with me?'

'No. I don't want to come. But it would mean something to me, to know that you have been there, and stood on the same ground where the farm used to stand. I would like a photograph of you, standing there. Taken in the yellow field – if there is still a yellow field.' There was a pleading look in her eyes, now, which was entirely new to him. 'Will you do that for me?'

'Of course I will, Mother.'

'I think it's a lovely idea,' said Sylvia. 'Now – does anybody want coffee?'

While Sylvia was in the kitchen, putting the kettle on to boil, Mrs Foley gathered up the map and the papers from the table and put them back in her old school satchel, saying to her son as she did so: 'Don't forget what I told you.'

'I won't. You'll get your photograph.'

'Not about that. Remember: Grandma and I never saw my father again. I grew up without him. She grew old without him. Life was more difficult for both of us. Don't make your wife and daughter go through anything like that.'

And with those words, she finished securing the buckles on the satchel and handed it across the table to him, in a manner that was almost sacramental.

The morning of Sunday, 3 August 1958 opened in a blaze of sunshine. In London, it was the first really warm day of the summer. Thomas and Sylvia decided that it was too hot to cook a roast lunch, so they put the lamb joint aside until the evening, and prepared a green salad, with ham and pickles, which they ate with Mrs Foley in the garden, while Baby Gill played contentedly in the sandpit which Mr Sparks had finished building just a few weeks earlier. Mr Sparks and his sister Judith were out in their own back garden, eating a simple lunch of cold beef sandwiches. It was rare to see Judith out of doors: even today, she had covered her legs with a thick woollen blanket. Such was the benign influence of the good weather, Thomas had forgotten yesterday's fit of animosity towards his neighbour, and they chatted for a few minutes in a friendly, casual sort of way, while Sylvia enquired most solicitously after Judith's health. After that, it was time to walk Mrs Foley to her bus stop.

When they had seen her safely onto the Leatherhead bus, they continued on to Tooting Common, with Thomas behind the push-chair and Sylvia, after a while, taking him by the arm. Sylvia was concerned that, even with the hood of the chair pulled up, Gill would become grumpy under the heat of the afternoon sun; but it seemed that nothing was destined to spoil their mood that day. The baby behaved herself perfectly. They bought ice creams from the van parked on the Common and sat on the grass to eat them, watch-ing the hordes of younger people passing by, towels and swimming costumes tucked under their arms, on their way to the Lido in self-absorbed pairs and excited, giggling groups.

If only every Sunday, every day, in London, could be like this, Thomas thought. For half an hour or more he and Sylvia lay down together on the grass, holding hands, their eyes closed against the sun as it shone down on them benignly and uninterruptedly from a pale-blue sky. To Thomas, Brussels seemed further away than ever before, and he realized with a shock that he had no desire to return to Belgium tomorrow. Now, suddenly, it was the Expo, and every-thing that had been happening there, that seemed distant and unreal, and his life at home – his life with Sylvia and Gill – was what he wanted to cling onto.

That night, lying awake in bed beside Sylvia, he rested a tentative hand on her hip, and then, in a slow, supplicating sort of movement, he began to slide her nightdress up to expose the lower half of her body. When he had attempted this manoeuvre the night before, Sylvia had turned away and rebuffed him coldly. Tonight, although she made no immediate gesture of acquiescence, neither did she resist. When the nightdress was rolled up around her waist, Thomas eased his hand gently between her legs and felt the hot, expectant wet-ness. She turned towards him, and they kissed. Eagerly, but not wanting to repulse her with a display of undue haste, he wriggled out of his pyjama jacket and trousers. Dropping them to the floor on his side of the bed, he switched on the bedside lamp, and made as if to kiss her again. But she drew back.

'What are you doing?' she asked.

'Can we not have the light on? I'd like to see you.'

'Please,' Sylvia said, 'I'd rather not.'

Thomas smiled, and kissed her forehead.

'So modest,' he whispered. 'So well brought up!'

He turned off the light and then Sylvia, as if roused to unex-pected passion by his teasing, pulled her nightdress roughly over her head and wrapped herself around him, her arms and her legs cling-ing to him in a tight, almost desperate embrace. He entered her swiftly and their lovemaking, accompanied by deep, furious, hun-gry kisses, was soon over. Thomas reached his climax in less than a minute, Sylvia soon afterwards. But even when they were done, she continued to cling to him, and they lay closely entwined for all the time it took her to drift off into sleep. Only when Thomas heard her breathing grow slower and more regular, until it evolved into a familiar, very soothing and very gentle kind of snore, did he dare to ease the weight of her head carefully from his shoulder, and slide his arm free from the place where it had been sweetly trapped beneath her neck.

Slightly disturbed by the movement, Sylvia murmured some-thing indistinguishable through her drowsy breath and then quickly sank down into an even deeper and more contented sleep. But

Thomas was not so lucky. He lay awake for a few minutes and soon realized, with a sense of weary acceptance, that he probably had several wakeful hours ahead of him. Every position that he tried to adopt felt awkward. His mind raced with fleeting impressions of all his strange experiences from recent days, and he felt weighed down with dread at the thought of leaving for Brussels early in the morning. He rolled over and lay on his front but could still not get settled. To compound his discomfort, there was something at the bottom of the bed that was annoying him. With his big toe he could feel something – something small and unidentifiable, a little pellet of soft and sponge-like matter. He could not for the life of him think what it was. After brushing it backwards and forwards with the tip of his toes for a minute or two, he finally reached down and retrieved it with his hand. But he was none the wiser for exploring it with his fingers. What on earth could it be?

Wide awake now, and impelled by a nagging curiosity, he swung his legs out of bed, put his pyjamas and slippers on and went to the bathroom, taking the foreign object with him. Once there he yawned, turned the overhead light on, and examined it in horror.

Too many statistics!

'Are you all right, Mr Foley?' Shirley said. 'You look as though you've seen a ghost.'

She placed a pint of Britannia on the table in front of him and Thomas turned away from the window – through which he'd been staring sightlessly – to nod his thanks.

'You've been looking strange ever since you got back from London,' she added.

'Really? Oh, it's nothing. Think I might have picked up a bit of a bug on the plane or something.'

'Well, you be careful – summer colds, they're the worst.'

He took his first sip of the beer as she walked away, back to the bar, and reflected that her turn of phrase, unoriginal though it was, might contain a germ of truth. Had he been seeing ghosts? Where was the reality in these surroundings, after all? The Britannia was a fake: it was a fake pub, projecting a fake vision of England, transported into a fake setting where every other country was projecting fake visions of their national identity. Belgique Joyeuse, indeed! Fake! Just like the Oberbayern! Fake! He was living in a world constructed entirely out of simulacra. And the more he thought about this, the more ghostly and unstable everything around him began to appear. These people waiting to be served at the bar, and sitting at the tables: were they real, or were they fake? Were any of them as they seemed? A few days ago he had believed that Mr Chersky, whose arrival he was awaiting now, was a friendly young Muscovite writer and journalist who wanted his editorial advice; now, apparently, he was supposed to accept that he was a top-ranking officer in the KGB. Which was the truth, and which the lie? Maybe Shirley *was* a ghost. Even Emily was playing a part, now that he thought of it: she too was nothing more than an actress, pretending to be an ordinary suburban housewife for the benefit of visitors to the American pavilion. Maybe every single person in the Britannia this Tuesday lunchtime was an actor, too, hired by Mr Radford and Mr Wayne as part of some elaborate, insane masterplan to confuse and disorientate him.

There was only one thing that he knew for sure: at the foot of his marital bed, on Sunday night, he had found a used corn plaster. A Calloway's Corn Cushion, no less. Which meant that Norman Sparks had been in that bed, perhaps only a day or two before. That was the only reality in his life at the moment, and everything else, for all he knew, might be a figment of his or the British security services' or for that matter Baron Moens de Fernig's vivid imagination. No wonder Shirley thought that he looked strange. He felt as though he was beginning to go mad. Having a nervous breakdown, or something.

He looked across at Shirley. She was talking to that American, Ed Longman, again. Thick as thieves, nowadays, those two. Nice to see at least one of these Expo romances flourishing, he supposed, in a relatively uncomplicated way. He wondered how many of the love affairs taking shape at this fair would stand the test of time: how many of the couplings begun in its heady, unnatural atmosphere would lead to anything substantial: to marriage, or to children. Shirley and Longman seemed pretty tight together, at any rate. He was looking into her eyes and pressing something into her hand. She saw Thomas looking at them and winked at him.

Thomas sighed, drank more beer, and looked at his watch. Chersky was late. He did not much care for being made to wait here, alone with his thoughts. The more he contemplated his wife's betrayal, the more depressed he felt, and the less he could decide what to do about it. He had promised to wake her before leaving the house on Monday morning, but in the event he had not done so: unable to talk to her, look at her or even be close to her, he had spent the rest of the night in the spare bedroom and then sneaked out of the house at six in the morning after looking in on the sleeping Gill. Since arriving back in Brussels he had not phoned Sylvia, let alone begun writing the letter he knew would finally have to be written. In fact, apart from calling on Emily in the American pavilion earlier that morning, he had done nothing apart from sitting in his cabin, and at various bars and cafés around the Expo site, in a daze of indecision and inertia.

'My dear Mr Foley,' a familiar voice now said, 'I'm so sorry for being late.'

It was Mr Chersky, looking somewhat flustered and out of breath. He had his briefcase with him, filled with the usual sheafs of papers. Thomas already had the latest issue of *Sputnik* open on the table. He stood up and shook Chersky by the hand, hoping that his eyes did not give any indication of the new wariness he felt towards him.

'Sit down, sit down,' he said. 'Can I get you a drink?'

'Miss Knott saw me come in, I believe. I'm sure she will bring me my usual, without me having to ask. This is the sign of a good English pub, isn't it? Knowing your "regulars", as I believe they are called.'

'You'll be returning to Moscow a veritable expert on the British way of life,' said Thomas, flatly.

'I hope so. That is certainly my intention. Now – did you get the chance to read our last number? I would welcome your thoughts.'

'Yes, I did read it,' said Thomas, casting his eye across the large sheet of cheap newsprint, folded in half as always to make up a four-page issue. 'I have to say that I don't think you've made much progress. It has all the same faults as the earlier ones.'

'Namely?'

'Well, I've told you all of this before. First of all, it's the statistics. There are too many statistics!' He started to read aloud from an article extolling the triumphs of the Russian childcare system. 'Listen to this: "In the Soviet Union there are 106,000 accommodations in children's sanatoriums, 965,000 accomodations in permanent, over 2 million in seasonal crèches, and 2.5 million accomodations in kindergartens and children's summer playgrounds."'

'Well?' said Andrey. 'Don't you think that's impressive?'

'Of course it's impressive. But this is hardly the way to make your readers –'

'Sorry to interrupt, gentlemen.' It was Shirley, carrying another pint of bitter and a packet of crisps. 'Here you are, Mr Chersky. I don't have to ask what you want any more, do I?'

'Indeed you don't, Miss Knott.'

'I'm going to buy shares in Smith's crisps when I get home,' she said, putting the drink carefully down on the table. 'In a year's time I reckon the whole of Russia will be eating them, if you have anything to do with it.'

'You might be right.' And as she walked away, he called after her, laughing, 'But not with the salt on! Salt is bad for you, remember?'

Shirley laughed too. 'Oh, Mr Chersky, you are a card!'

Andrey was still chuckling to himself as he took his first sip of the beer. 'Ah, the English sense of humour. Finally I think I'm beginning to get the hang of it. And, as I hope you noticed, there is also more humour in the paper now than before. That's your influence, Mr Foley.'

'Yes, I was going to mention that. This collection of "humorous" sayings from Russian children.'

'Charming, aren't they?'

'Baffling, would be my own way of putting it. What about this one? "Is the knife the fork's husband?"'

Andrey laughed long and hard at this. Thomas stared at him.

'I don't get it,' he said, and Andrey turned off his laugh abruptly.

'Neither do I,' he admitted. 'I was hoping you could explain it to me. What about this: "What if a rooster forgets he's a rooster and lays an egg?" Isn't that funny?'

'Not especially.'

'Hm!' He snorted with displeasure. 'The writer assured me that these were hilarious. I thought I just wasn't clever enough to understand them.'

'I think you should forget about humour for a while.'

'Very well. That sounds like a good idea. Especially as our next issue will be devoted entirely to science. And the main feature is an *excellent* piece of work. Even you, Mr Foley – even you who are so hard to impress – you are going to enjoy this article.'

'Why, what's it about?'

Mr Chersky had opened his packet of crisps and was munching through them, as usual, with an expression like that of a gourmet enjoying an especially fine example of *haute cuisine*.

'It's about the man of the future,' he said, between mouthfuls. 'A very eminent Soviet scientist has written an article explaining how mankind will have evolved one hundred years from now.'

'And . . .?'

'Well, of course you will have to read it. But it will be one of many things in this particular issue to interest you, I think. We also have a good article about Russian advances in nuclear fusion. Of course, in the interests of journalistic truth and impartiality, we had to report – with great sorrow, naturally – that the British scientists who have been working in this area seem to have greatly overestimated their own achievements. Which reminds me . . . there was one fact I wanted to check with you. Is it true, as I have heard, that the replica ZETA machine has been removed from the British pavilion to save embarrassment?'

This question was accompanied by a smile but also by an insolent, challenging look. Thomas's own smile barely concealed his distaste. Honesty, however, compelled him to say: 'Yes, it's true.'

'Good. We will mention it in the article. Only, it's always best to check the facts first, don't you agree?' He finished the last of his crisps, folded up the empty bag carefully and put it into the side pocket of his jacket. 'And in the next issue but one, you'll be pleased to hear, we will be talking about Soviet ladies' fashions, and contrasting them with their American counterparts. Miss Parker has been most helpful in supplying us with some designs. And talking of Emily –' (his smile became even more charming, and at the same time – Thomas thought – even less sincere) '– I understand that you are planning an excursion with her in the next few days. Is that correct?'

'Yes,' said Thomas, carefully, wondering how Andrey could have heard of this already, and realizing at once that there were hundreds of ways.

'It sounds a delightful idea. A summer picnic, in the Belgian countryside! This Saturday, I believe.'

'That's right.'

'She told me that you know of a most attractive location. A field of golden buttercups, she said, by the banks of a river, not far from Leuven.'

'Something like that,' said Thomas – who had seen Emily, and shared his imagined impression of this scene, only a few hours before.

'Then only one question remains.' Andrey gathered his papers and shuffled them together into a neat pile. 'What time shall I pick you both up?'

Pastorale d'Eté

Early in the afternoon of Saturday, 9 August 1958, Andrey and Emily came to collect Thomas from the gateway of the Motel Expo Wemmel. As he might have predicted, they were travelling in some style. Andrey was driving a 1956 ZiS 110 convertible sedan, in pale blue: the very pinnacle of Soviet car production. The weather promised to be perfect and Andrey had folded the roof of the car all the way back to allow maximum exposure to the sunshine. His eyes were shielded by cobalt-blue polarized sunglasses and he was wearing a light-cream sports blazer, with a silk neckerchief tucked into the open collar of his white shirt. Emily, for her part, wore a white linen shirt, navy-blue slacks, a navy-blue patterned paisley headscarf, and cat-eye sunglasses. They looked like a pair of movie stars. Climbing into his allotted space on the back seat, Thomas felt scruffy and self-conscious by comparison.

It took little more than half an hour to drive the thirty-five kilometres to Wijgmaal, where the arrival of the Russian car caused something of a sensation. It was a sleepy, suburban town, split in two by the narrow strip of green water that was the river Dijle. Half a dozen children were playing on the grassy recreation ground near to the bridge, but they abandoned their game and came running when the visitors appeared. 'Kom kijken! Kom kijken!' they shouted to all their friends, trotting along in the wake of the car and running their hands along its bodywork, treating it as though it were a cat that did not particularly want to be stroked. Andrey waved back at them and maintained the fixed, white-toothed grin that, to Thomas at least, was beginning to look more and more calculated and sinister. Look at him, he thought: he's loving this attention, even though he would probably run these kids over at the drop of a hat if it suited his purposes.

'Beautiful car,' was all he said, however, as they unloaded the picnic things from the boot.

'Not bad, is it?' Andrey agreed. 'You see, even we Russians know something about design.'

'And yet, I would have thought,' Thomas said, lifting up one of the two heavy wicker baskets, 'that the use of cars like this would be restricted. To people high up in the Party, I mean.'

Was it just his imagination, or did Andrey seem to bridle for a moment, before resuming his usual air of slightly menacing *bonhomie*?

'You have a very inaccurate idea of how things work in my country,' he said. 'This car belongs to the Soviet Embassy in Brussels. All I had to do was ask.'

'I had no idea that magazine editors were granted such privileges.'

'We are a nation that loves literature.'

'And is that why they give you so much freedom of movement?'

'Freedom of movement?'

'It's just that somebody told me most of the Soviet pavilion staff were confined to a hotel when they weren't working. And they were taken to and from the pavilion every day by bus. They've not seen anything of Brussels itself at all. Whereas you seem to have more or less the run of the place.'

'The "somebody" who told you these things was misinformed,' said Andrey, shortly. 'Now – which way shall we go? I think we are sure to find a pleasant spot in that direction.'

He pointed roughly south, upstream along the Dijle, back towards Leuven. But Thomas shook his head.

'No, we have to go this way,' he said, and gestured northwards from the bridge. 'It doesn't look as nice, but once we've followed the curve of the river for a few minutes, you'll see. It will be much prettier.'

Emily could sense the tension between the two men and did her best to defuse it, by saying: 'Thomas has very definite ideas about where we should be having this picnic. He seems to be quite the expert on this part of Belgium.'

'Very well,' said Andrey, grimly. 'Let's follow the expert.'

The river, as Thomas's mother had told him, was not very wide at this point, and the bridge they were standing on crossed it without rising or falling at all. Although there was no clear path to be seen, it was easy enough to scramble down to the water's edge, and from there they started to pick their way through the long grass, Thomas and Andrey carrying a basket each, Emily a rolled-up picnic rug under each arm.

The sky was deep-blue, almost azure, and there was a wonderful stillness all around them. To their left, the river meandered, a pale, mysterious green, opaque and cloudy in the afternoon sunlight; to their right, after two minutes' walk from the bridge, a broad meadow opened out, dotted here and there with thistles, its grass bleached to grey-brown by weeks of dry weather. Thomas carried his mother's map with him and led the way, looking back occasionally at Emily and Andrey, who were walking too close together for his liking, and talking in a way which seemed to be far too murmuringly familiar.

Soon they had reached a place where the river curved languidly to the west, and at the point of the curve there was a wide expanse of long grass – partly shaded by a nearby cluster of sycamores – which positively insisted that passers-by throw down their picnic rugs and linger there. So that was what they did. And after only a few minutes they heard voices, and the sound of approaching bicycles: Thomas looked back towards the bridge and saw that the others had arrived. After Andrey had derailed his plans for a quiet afternoon with Emily *à deux*, he had admitted defeat and, falling in with her original suggestion, given her free rein to invite as many people as she liked. So now Anneke was here, along with her friend Clara and a dark-haired young man he didn't recognize. The three of them dismounted from their bicycles and began to push them along the riverbank towards the picnic spot. Thomas and Emily went to meet them halfway; Andrey stayed where he was.

'My, my!' said Emily to Anneke, admiringly. 'Now that's a sensible mode of transport, if ever I saw one. Did you ride them all the way from Brussels?'

'It wasn't so far,' said Anneke. 'About an hour and a half. And as you know, there are no hills in Belgium.'

She looked flushed and healthy from her morning's exercise: her skin, which had already been sporting an even tan for the last few weeks, glowed with new vitality, and her eyes were shining brightly. Clara was sweating and gave off a faint, not displeasing animal smell. But Thomas was more interested in the third member of their party. He was tall and thickset and carried himself well. He looked to be roughly in his mid-twenties. He had a neatly trimmed black moustache and dark, enquiring brown eyes which returned Thomas's stare with challenging but friendly curiosity.

'Oh – this is my friend,' Anneke explained. 'His name is Federico. I hope you don't mind that I brought him along.'

'Of course not, my dear,' said Emily. 'An Italian gentleman – how exotic! Could this little gathering *be* any more cosmopolitan?'

Federico nodded at her and smiled.

'Federico is a waiter at the Italian pavilion,' said Anneke. 'We met for the first time a few days ago. I'm afraid he doesn't speak much English.'

'Well, never mind that, dear. He's awfully ornamental, at least. Now come along and spread yourselves out. We were just about to dive into the food. We worked up an appetite just driving here, so Lord knows what you must be feeling like.'

Andrey stood up when the ladies approached and offered Anneke and Clara each a gracious kiss on the hand. He shook hands briefly and formally with Federico, and then poured glasses of wine for everyone. When they were all seated, with their glasses poised, he said: 'Allow me, if I may, to propose a short toast. We live in a world in which political barriers are constantly being erected between people of the different nations. Many of these barriers, in my view, are needless. The fact that we can sit down together like this – six people, from five different countries – proves that they are needless. Expo 58 proves that they are needless. So let us raise a glass to our generous and forward-thinking hosts, the people of Belgium, and to Expo 58!'

'To Expo 58!' everyone echoed.

'I would also like to thank Mr Foley,' Andrey continued, 'for bringing us to this truly delightful spot. Tell me, Thomas, how did you hear of it? Where did you obtain your information?'

'It was my mother's suggestion,' said Thomas.

'Your mother?'

'Yes. My mother is Belgian.'

'Really? You've kept that a very closely guarded secret from the rest of us.'

'We're all entitled to our secrets, Mr Chersky,' said Thomas. Andrey gazed back at him coolly. 'And as for my mother, she used to live near here. Very close to where we're sitting right now.' But he realized, at that moment, that he would very much rather keep the rest of his mother's story to himself. There were at least two people present with whom he preferred not to share it. 'She told me about this river. She used to come here herself, I believe, when she was a young girl. Perhaps even on days like this.'

Breaking the reflective pause that followed, Emily said: 'Well, who could blame her? It's quite heavenly here.' She rested her wine glass carefully on the grass and sat back, reclining on her elbows, tilting her face towards the sun. 'Look at that sky. Listen to that stillness. This is one of those places – one of those days – that just makes you wish time could stand still. Don't you agree?'

'Today, I suppose, we might allow ourselves the luxury of thinking like that,' said Andrey. 'Although it strikes me as a somewhat decadent viewpoint. We are not typical people, after all, and the situation in which we find ourselves this afternoon is not typical. To be sitting here as we are, in these circumstances, marks us out as privileged. None of us lives in extreme poverty, or want. Yet there are workers all around the world whose lives are a daily fight for survival. They would not want time to stand still, even on a day like this. They are hungry for progress. Which reminds me . . .' (he reached into the jacket of his pocket and pulled out the latest issue of *Sputnik*, carefully folded) '. . . have you seen this yet, Thomas? It contains the essay I was telling you about.'

'Ah! The famous essay,' said Thomas, taking the paper from him.

'Thanks for the lecture on workers' living conditions,' said Emily, allowing Andrey a smile which was at once fond and challenging. 'And what essay is this, exactly?'

'I have commissioned one of our most eminent scientists to gaze into a crystal ball, as it were, and tell us what life will be like for us all in one hundred years from now. I think the results will impress you.'

Thomas had found the relevant page and was scanning the opening paragraphs of the article with interest.

'Well, come on, then,' said Emily. 'Read it out loud. I'm sure everybody here would like to know what it says.'

'Very well.' Thomas folded the paper in half for easier reading, cleared his throat, and announced: '"*The Man of the Twenty-first Century*.

'"The science which deals with man's life, his development and nutrition is progressing year after year.

'"*What will man be like 100 years hence?*

'"This was the question put by our correspondent" – Mr Chersky, in other words – "to Honoured Worker of Science" – very impressive! – "Prof. Yuri Frolov. The substance of the answer is as follows.

'"Imagine that we are living in the year 2058. The boundaries between manual and mental labour have been obliterated throughout the century. All the necessary conditions exist for the normal and harmonious physical and psychological development of man. Although people are already using atomic energy in every sphere of the national economy, and have tamed the forces of nature, they have not grown weaker; on the contrary, they look stronger than 100 years ago. They are always cheerful, they feel at ease everywhere and . . . pray, let this not trouble you, they eat and drink comparatively little."'

'That doesn't trouble me at all,' said Emily. 'But do carry on.'

'"Biochemists of the 21st century have succeeded in synthesising carbohydrates and even proteins, with the result that new foods have been produced; although their nutritive value is good and they taste as nice as bread or meat for instance, they are not as bulky. The internal organs are performing entirely new functions connected with the special qualities of deuterium. Taken in minute quantities instead of ordinary water, this isotope of hydrogen is performing a formerly unknown function; it is inhibiting the processes of dissimilation, i.e. decomposition of substances in the organism."'

'Hmm. So what is he saying, exactly? That a hundred years from now, we're all going to be spared the embarrassment of having to queue for the ladies' room?'

'Possibly. But more importantly – listen: "That is why the height of people in the 21st century will be much above average. They will all be healthy, irrespective of their age, though some of them will be over 100. Together with fruit juices they will drink heavy water in prescribed doses.

'"Physical culture and sport are popular among the young and old. All the cities have been converted into garden cities, and every city has stadiums, swimming pools and other athletic facilities. And most interesting of all, one does not meet any grey-haired or senile people in these cities. They all walk proudly erect, with a springy step, their complexion is healthy and their eyes shine with vigour and happiness."'

'It sounds wonderful,' said Anneke. 'What a shame that none of us will be alive to see it.'

'Well,' said Emily, 'if we all manage to stagger on until, say, 130 or 140, then there's hope for us yet . . .'

'"This rejuvenation has not come at once,"' Thomas continued. '"It was a gradual process, and it is the result of the measures taken by the state" – ah yes, I was wondering when we were going to get around to that – "to improve the health of the people, with special stress on the investigation and elimination of the causes of ageing.

'"Even more astonishing than the appearance of the people, are the novel features of life and work connected with the inordinate development of the sense organs. The organ of sight has become much more powerful and complex. At the end of the 20th century, scientists were gradually expanding the range of electromagnetic vibrations detected by the eye and raised its potentialities by means of electronic and other instruments.

'"With the aid of electronic instruments the human eye is now able to 'see' not only in impenetrable darkness, in infra-red light, but also in the shortest ultraviolet light. All mysteries have been pierced. Man has learned to see through all obstacles, his vision penetrating even the inner structure of matter, as we can see on X-ray pictures, for example."'

'Goodness, what a frightful prospect!' said Emily. 'I don't want any man using his electromagnetic vision to see through my clothes, thank you very much. Never mind casting his eye over my internal organs.'

'"Thanks to electromagnetic reduction of the frequency of sound vibrations, the man of the 21st century can easily hear what he cannot see: how grass is growing, how liquid is moving in a glass, how broken bones are growing together, and much else."'

'Hmm, that's more like it . . .' Emily sipped some more wine, and stared into the distance, contemplating this prospect. 'I like the idea of being able to hear the grass grow. I'm sorry, Andrey, I know this is a serious piece of scientific research, but this is the sort of thing that appeals to my poetic nature.'

Andrey smiled at her and took her hand. 'Don't apologize,' he said. 'There is a place for science, and there is also a place for poetry. Your response is . . . charmingly feminine.'

Thomas flashed him a disbelieving look, and continued: '"It is now possible even to trace by hearing all the processes at work in the nerves and nervous centres upon which man's health and life depend.

'"Greater knowledge of nature has made it possible to improve the sense of smell. Man is now able not only to recognise thousands of scents, but also to determine the dimensions and shapes of one or another object by means of his sense of smell amplified by the new technique.

'"The discovery of the ultra-short wave nature of smells has made it possible to transmit them over distances by means of a new 'tele-scenting' unit. The air in the theatres, homes, factories and laboratories is now kept not only pure and fresh; it is filled with fragrant scents which have a soothing effect on the nervous system.

'"Much else could be told about the man of 2058, about his life and work. And there is nothing unusual in all that. Much of what we are dreaming of is already becoming part of daily life."'

Thomas laid down the newspaper and looked around at the circle of faces, each one, it seemed, preoccupied with some aspect or other of these unlikely predictions.

'Well,' said Clara. 'I find that all very interesting.'

'Me too,' said Anneke. 'I love this idea, that we will be able to transmit smells over a long distance.'

'True,' said Emily. 'We will have a lot to thank the state for, if that comes to pass. As soon as someone finds a way of taking the air from this place and broadcasting it live to New York, believe me, I'll be the first to tune in. Just take a mouthful of it! Feel how clean it is! So clean and sweet-smelling.'

She breathed in deeply, and the others followed her lead. There was an appreciative silence.

'Cigarette, anyone?' Thomas asked.

He handed round the packet, and they all helped themselves.

Now Thomas and Emily were alone.

Emily was lying in the grass, on her side, turned towards him.

Her ear was to the ground and her eyes were closed, although behind the lids could be sensed traces of quick, flickering life.

Thomas had taken out his mother's map and was examining it closely, looking around him and trying to match the features of the landscape with this cartographer's approximation from more than fifty years ago. Closing in on a particular area, he attempted to fold the map down to a more manageable size. The noise made Emily open her eyes.

'Ssh!'

'Why, what's the matter?'

'I almost heard it then. I swear that I did.'

'Heard what?'

'The sound of the grass growing.'

Thomas smiled, put the map down and stretched himself out beside her. They lay side by side, facing one another. It felt, suddenly, like a very intimate situation.

'Can you hear it?' she asked.

'I'm not sure.'

Thomas rested his ear close to the ground and tried to concentrate. But he found himself distracted, alarmingly distracted, by the proximity of Emily. Her face was just a few inches away from his. He could see freckles, pores, wrinkles, that he had never noticed before. The freckles, in particular, were adorable. There was a tiny patch of them on either side of her nose. Her pearl-grey eyes stared back at him, with unnerving directness.

'I can hear something,' he said. 'A kind of rustling.'

'Maybe that's it.'

'Well, how do you account for it? The man who wrote that article –'

'The "Honoured Worker of Science", you mean?'

'Yes – he said that we wouldn't be able to do this for another hundred years.'

'Well, I don't know quite how I account for it. Perhaps this place has … special properties.'

'Special properties?'

'Perhaps, you know, it has a high concentration of those electro-magnetic vibrations we were told about.'

'That could be it.'

'You think?'

'I think you've solved it.'

Was it Thomas's imagination, or had they inched a fraction closer to one another during this curious, affectionate exchange of whispered frivolities?

'Mr Foley?' Emily said now.

'Yes, Miss Parker?'

'Do you mind if I ask you rather a dangerous question?'

'I suppose not,' he said, bracing himself. 'What is it?'

'My question is this . . . What is your impression – your truthful impression – of Mr Chersky?'

Thomas did not know, exactly, what sort of question he had been expecting. But it wasn't this one.

'Well . . .' he said. 'I shall have to give that a certain amount of thought.'

'Don't hurry yourself. Take your time.'

'I suppose . . . Well, if I might make a particular observation, rather than a general one . . .'

'By all means.'

'I would say that he did not seem especially pleased, just now, when you decided to stay behind here, with me, instead of returning to Brussels, with him.'

'Oh, you noticed that, did you?'

'I could hardly fail to.'

A few minutes earlier, Andrey had announced that he was leaving. The car had to be returned to the embassy in Brussels, he said, by four o'clock, and he seemed to assume that Thomas and Emily would accompany him, as before. But Emily had demurred. She was having such a wonderful time, she said, and they had only been here for a couple of hours, and today was her day off, and she saw no reason why she had to go back to Brussels right away. Andrey had been unable to conceal his disapproval; but, at the same time, he was in no position to put obstacles in her path, apart from raising an obvious question: How did she and Thomas propose to get back to Brussels, without his help? To which, eventually, an answer was found: Clara and Federico (both of whom were required to work at the Expo that evening) would come with him in the car, leaving their bicycles behind so that Emily, Thomas and Anneke could all cycle home together whenever the mood took them. To say that Andrey disliked this suggestion would be a gross understatement. But he had agreed to it, through gritted teeth, at Emily's insistence. And so he, Clara and Federico had set off together, back along the path towards the bridge; and Anneke had gone with them, presumably to say a fond, temporary goodbye to her new friend; although, just before they left, Clara had leaned in confidentially towards Thomas, and whispered in his ear, 'He means nothing to her, you know. You're the one that she cares for' – after which she had turned and left, hastening to catch up with the others, leaving Thomas to chew over these befuddling words as he watched the four retreating figures dwindling into the heat-hazed distance.

'I would go so far as to suggest,' Thomas now went on, aware that he was about to say something audacious, 'that Mr Chersky is beginning to grow fond of you.'

'Really?' said Emily. 'That's your impression?'

'Yes.'

'Well, that is very surprising, I must say. What would you advise me to do about it?'

'Nothing. To be perfectly frank – I don't trust the man. Emily, you won't do anything stupid, will you? You won't throw yourself at him?'

The words had burst out before he could stop them. But Emily, to his relief, did not seem offended.

'Of course not.' She raised herself up on one elbow and said to him, earnestly: 'You know, whatever anyone else may think of me,

I don't need protecting. Do remember that, Thomas. I'm a big girl, and I can look after myself. It's not your job to protect me and, to speak truthfully, I wouldn't thank you for it.'

Thomas nodded. There was something in her words, and her manner of speaking, that he found wounding, but none the less, there was no doubting that she meant it.

'And as a matter of fact,' she added, 'I happen to agree with you. I don't entirely trust him either.'

That seemed to bring an end to the discussion, for once again she lay full-length on the grass and closed her eyes against the sun. After a few moments Thomas lay back as well, and they rested like that for some while in silence.

'Have you ever thought of marrying?' she then asked him, without preamble.

He sat up again and looked at her in surprise.

'Yes,' he answered. 'In fact I have been married. In fact, technically speaking, I still am.'

'Technically speaking?' said Emily. 'You have an odd way of expressing yourself.'

'Back in London I have a wife, and a daughter,' said Thomas. 'But my marriage is over.' It was strange, saying these words. If he had spoken them to Emily at the Grand Auditorium concert, as he had half-intended to do, he would have been lying to her; but now, nine days later, he could make this statement, and know that he was telling the truth. Still, there was something final and irrevocable in the act of speaking it aloud. 'It happened a long time ago,' he said (which was a lie, but a necessary one), 'and yet the wound is still very fresh' (which was true).

'What went wrong?' Emily ventured. 'If you'll permit me to ask, that is.'

'My wife was unfaithful,' said Thomas.

'Ah. I'm very sorry. I didn't mean to drag up something so painful.'

'It's all right. I've never spoken about it to anyone. I'm happy –

that is, I don't mind talking about it with you. I'm beginning to feel a . . . sympathy between us.'

'Don't get carried away,' said Emily, 'with those electromagnetic vibrations. Did you know the fellow involved?'

'Yes. He was our neighbour. Perhaps I was to blame. I neglected her.'

'To my mind, that hardly excuses –'

'Of course, you're right. But she can't have been happy. If you saw the man, you would know … It could only have been an act of desperation.'

'How did you deal with it? What did you do?'

'Nothing,' said Thomas. 'In a situation like that, what can you do?'

'I would have thought a punch on the nose, for one thing. For him, that is.'

Thomas laughed bitterly. 'What would that have achieved?'

'Well, it might have made you feel better. It might have made your wife realize how much she meant to you. And it might have stopped him from behaving like a louse again, the next time he took a fancy to the married woman next door. I doubt if any court would have convicted you. Not in the state of Wisconsin they wouldn't, anyway.'

Thomas shook his head. 'It's not really . . . my style.'

'Then perhaps you should change your style.' She sat up, now, and wrapped her arms around her knees, hugging them tightly to herself. She frowned in thought for a second or two, choosing her next words carefully: 'Besides, sometimes we don't really understand our own natures. We don't really know who we are, until a new circumstance comes along to reveal it to us.

'Take my father, for instance. He's the sweetest, gentlest, most placid kind of man you could imagine. A scientist. The only time he ever gets really passionate about something is when he's inside a laboratory. Now, many years ago – I suppose I would have been ten or eleven years old – he took us hiking in the woods. Me and my younger sister, Joanna. It was a steep, rocky sort of area – beautiful to look at, all right, but kind of tough going for two little kids. Well, early in the afternoon we stopped to eat the food that he'd brought. I settled down on a rock, and was tucking into a ham sandwich or something, and Joanna – who was only eight at the time – sat down on the ground right next to a tree trunk that had fallen over. A hollow trunk. And there we both were, eating happily away, when my father, very slowly, started walking towards Joanna. In his hand he was carrying a thick, heavy, straight piece of wood he'd just picked up, about the size of a baseball bat. And there's a look in his eyes I've never seen before. He's staring right at the end of the tree trunk, just next to where Joanna is sitting. And all of a sudden, he raises the piece of wood and he brings it down – thwack! – on the ground right next to her. And there's a terrible sound, a sound like you can't imagine only once you've heard it you can never forget it. A kind of reptilian howl, if that makes any sense. But my father hasn't stopped. He raises the weapon again and again and he brings it down again and again, smashing it to a pulp, whatever this thing is that's been sitting next to Joanna. She's already screamed her head off by now and has run over to where I'm sitting, and she's clinging on to me for dear life. And we're both looking at my father and I swear to you that neither of us can even recognize him. This is a man we have literally never seen before. His face is twisted and contorted and he's breathing faster and more heavily than you would have thought possible but he also looks – and you may think this is an odd word to use, but I can picture him, even now, and it's the only one that fits – he also looks … *ecstatic*. Do you know what I mean? He was sort of transported, to another level, a place I don't believe he'd ever been before. And he didn't stop until he could be sure the creature was dead.'

There was a long silence.

'What was it?' Thomas asked, hoarsely.

'It was a timber rattler. One of our only two deadly species. A big one, too, more than five feet long.'

'And was it going to bite your sister?'

'Who knows? It certainly wasn't a risk my father was going to take. If it had chosen to bite her, she would have died, so he did what anybody would have done in that situation – he killed, in order to protect the thing that he loved. He . . .' She hesitated, searching for the right phrase, and when she found it, she pronounced it with a rhythmic, melancholy clarity: '. . . *He did the necessary thing.*' More reflectively, she added: 'I don't believe he knew that he was capable of it, actually. In any case, he changed after that day. Everything about him changed. He'd learned the truth about himself, you see. And my sister and I had learned something as well. We knew now what he was capable of.'

Emily held Thomas's eyes with a steady, questioning gaze, until he felt obliged to look away.

'Ever since then, it's been my belief,' she said, 'that when it comes to safeguarding the things that are most precious to you – your children, your family, your country if it comes to that – there can't be any limit on what you're prepared to do.' She smiled at Thomas – a somewhat alarming smile, he thought – and concluded: 'You should really have punched him on the nose.'

Just after those trees, there was a beautiful field, which in the summer was full of buttercups – tall ones, meadow buttercups, I think they are called. A whole field of brilliant yellow. All you had to do was walk across this field and that brought you to the back of the farm.'

The buttercups were almost waist-high. Thomas walked slowly through them, alone, leaving the river and Emily behind. He had the map in his hands and was walking towards the point where somebody, more than a half a century ago, had marked a thick cross in pencil.

At the edge of the meadow, there was a fence consisting only of a single thread of wire stretched between wooden posts. Thomas ducked under the wire and continued walking. The ground underfoot was ridged, now, as if it had once been ploughed. According to the map this was once a wide, open space, but now the surrounding woodland was beginning to encroach upon it. He knew that he was very close to the place where his grandfather's farm had once stood.

He heard footsteps behind him and turned around. It was Anneke.

'Hello,' he said.

'Hello. Do you mind if I join you?'

'Of course not.'

Actually he would have preferred to be alone. Too many impressions were starting to crowd his mind, that afternoon. Emily's story had taken him by surprise – it was the last thing he had been expecting to hear – and shaken him profoundly. He needed time to process it, but he could no longer put off the task of exploring these surroundings, combing them over for those buried traces of his family history he was sure they must contain. And now, on top of all that – Anneke. She was wearing the same pale-blue summer dress she had been wearing the night they had visited the Parc des Attractions and the Oberbayern, and she was standing close beside him (very close) in a way which made him feel that she expected something of him. Something he was not sure he could give, at this moment. Even without Clara's parting words, Thomas could have guessed that the sudden appearance of Federico at the picnic had been nothing more than a smokescreen, a distraction. Anneke's desire for him had never been more obvious, and everything about her – her youth, her beauty, her eagerness – should have made him realize that he was being offered a priceless gift. But something still held him back.

'Bringing us here,' she said, finally. 'You had a reason, didn't you? Something to do with your family.'

'Yes. This was where she lived. My mother.'

'Here?'

'I think we're standing on the very spot.' He looked around. 'Could there have been a farmhouse here, do you think? Even though there's nothing left?'

'I don't know. I suppose so. What happened to it?'

'It was burned down by the Germans.' He began walking towards the nearest thicket of trees, his eyes fixed on the ground, searching for clues. Anneke followed him. 'They were here in 1914. August 1914. There were two towns they almost destroyed, near to here – Aarschot and Leuven. In Aarschot they assassinated many people, including the burgomaster and his son and other members of his family. In Leuven –'

'I know. They destroyed the library. Hundreds of thousands of volumes. It's a famous story in Belgium.'

'One day, during that first round of attacks, they rounded up the people of Aarschot and decided to march them all the way south to Leuven. It was a completely pointless thing to do. I suppose they were just doing it to terrorize them. They must have passed very close to here. My mother's family knew they were coming. And they knew exactly what to expect. The German soldiers had been behaving with no shame, no remorse. The young Belgian men were being shot and killed, again for no reason except that the Germans suspected them of resisting. The women were . . . attacked as well. A ghastly business, absolutely ghastly. It was decided that my mother and my grandmother should try to get away, although they hated to leave the others behind. They thought their best chance of safety was probably to reach England. They left on bicycles, believe it or not, in the middle of the night. I don't know anything about their journey – my mother has never told me that story. I know they reached London a few weeks later.'

'And your grandfather? Did he escape?'

'No. They never saw him again. Nor her brothers.'

Thomas sighed, and looked around helplessly. What was there to see here? What traces were left?

'Has your mother talked much about those days – when she used to live here?'

'Not really. She was only a little girl. I know she was very happy. Her father was wealthy, successful. She went to the village school in Wijgmaal, along the river. She remembers going to Leuven on market days. Somewhere here –' (he gestured at the field) '– there used to be a barn where the hay was stored, where she used to play with a friend of hers from the village, a little boy called Lucas. She doesn't know what became of him, either.'

'Maybe we can find something under here,' Anneke said, kneeling down and tugging at the long grass. 'There must be something . . . Some bricks, some foundations.'

'No.' Thomas shook his head. He reached down to take her by the arm and pulled her gently to her feet. The feel of her warm bare skin beneath his fingers gave him a sudden thrill – fleeting, inappropriate, to be shaken away. 'There's nothing to see. Come on. Let's go. This is a sad place, now.'

On the way back to the river, they stopped in the field of meadow buttercups. He handed Anneke his camera and asked her to take a photograph, as his mother had wanted. The sun was behind her, turning her hair to a halo of light, throwing her face into shadow. The tranquillity of the scene was ruptured, briefly, as a plane flew low overhead, approaching its landing at Melsbroek. He did his best to smile for the camera.

Thomas had not ridden a bicycle for years, not since he used to cycle all by himself (he had no brothers or sisters, and his whole childhood had been solitary) along the country lanes around Leatherhead, back in the old days, the days before the War. He was worried, at first, that he might be out of condition, and that his two companions would humiliatingly outpace him; but these fears proved groundless. The roads were level, the going was easy, and as they approached the outskirts of Brussels from the north at about seven o'clock, he still felt that he had plenty of energy left.

There was something, too, that he had forgotten about cycling: it was a great stimulus to thought. He barely noticed the countryside rolling by: it was quite bland and featureless anyway. Instead, the complex events of the last few hours, the fragments of conversation, the looks, the gestures, the shifting relationships, all slowly began to swim into focus. He thought about the simple declaration he had made to Emily – 'my marriage is over' – and how its bald, incontrovertible truth could no longer be ignored. But at the same time, a surprising thing had happened this afternoon: the depression that had been weighing down on him all week seemed to have lifted. Hurt and dismayed though he was by Sylvia's betrayal, he no longer felt flattened by it. Instead, in a curious, unlooked-for, almost shocking way, he felt … liberated. Was it not possible to see this development, perhaps, as an opportunity rather than a setback? For months, privately, secretly, he had been railing against the shackles of married life; he had begun to feel like a prisoner in his own self-constructed, suburban cell. Well, here was a chance to get away from that: an opportunity to start again. Yes, it would be painful. He had emotional ties – strong emotional ties – to Sylvia, and to his daughter, of course. And divorce was an awful stigma: he would have to carry the shame and the embarrassment around with him for some time. And yet there could be no going back to how things were before. Today's visit to the site of his grandfather's farm had taught him that, at least: it was pointless trying to recapture the past, returning to scenes of long-lost happiness in search of relics, consoling souvenirs. As his mother had said – 'What's gone is gone.'

Just then Thomas turned a bend in the road and it came into view: the Atomium. Emily and Anneke were cycling together, side by side, about twenty yards ahead of him, and the gleaming aluminium globes of André Waterkeyn's surreal monument were between them, framed by them. The evening sun shimmered and bounced off the structure's sleek, massive curves and ellipses, as it reared arrogantly above the treetops of the Expo park. Thomas stopped pedalling and freewheeled onward, his mouth open; in no doubt, now, as to what this tableau represented: it was his own future: seductive, beckoning, previously unimaginable in its shapes and outlines, illuminated on all sides by glimmering, clairvoyant shafts of light, and above all, modern: irresistibly, unprecedentedly modern. A future which he now had the opportunity to share either here in Europe, with Anneke, or perhaps in far-off America, in the wilder, more mercurial company of Emily.

And so it was settled. And all that remained was for him to make a simple choice.

Excellent work, Foley

On Monday afternoon, Thomas was at work in the office towards the rear of the British pavilion. When Manchester University's large transistor-based computer had arrived more than a week ago – replacing the ill-fated replica ZETA machine as the most prominent scientific item on display – it had been accompanied by a lengthy booklet written in impenetrable scientific jargon. His job was to reduce the contents of this booklet to four or five hundred words of plain English, which could then be printed on a large display card for the enlightenment of the general public. He would also have to arrange for the card's translation into three or four different languages.

The telephone rang. Thomas sighed, and thought about ignoring it. This was not his desk, the call would not be for him, and the chances were that he would end up having to scurry around the pavilion for five minutes or more, trying to deliver a message. He did not like to have his concentration broken in this way. But after ten rings or so, his resolve crumbled.

'Hello? British pavilion, Brussels.'

'Good afternoon. Might I speak to Mr Foley, please? Thomas Foley.'

Thomas did not recognize the voice at first, but he recognized the tone of authority, and involuntarily sat up and straightened his tie before answering:

'Erm . . . yes, this is Mr Foley speaking.'

'Ah! Splendid! It's Mr Cooke here.'

'Mr Cooke? Oh, good afternoon, sir. This is a surprise. How's . . . how's the weather in London?'

'I wouldn't know, Foley. I'm in Brussels.'

'In Brussels?'

'That's right. And so is Mr Swaine. In fact we're partaking of the hospitality of the Britannia at this very moment. Are you anywhere in the vicinity? We need to have a word.'

Thomas abandoned his work at once and took the short, now familiar route around the ornamental lake towards the pub. For some reason his heart was thumping. Perhaps he had not realized, until now, that one of the many things he had been most enjoying about Expo 58 was the hundreds of miles of distance it had put between him and his superiors at the COI. But what would they be doing here now? Just carrying out a spot-check, he supposed. He prayed to God that Mr Rossiter was relatively sober this afternoon, and that Shirley was being her usual reliable self, keeping things running smoothly.

Mr Cooke and Mr Swaine were seated at a table for two, and seemed to be in the middle of a late lunch. Mr Cooke was tucking into his steak and chips with some gusto, while Mr Swaine was toying listlessly with a piece of battered cod. His brow, Thomas noticed, was beaded with sweat.

'Ah, Foley!' said Mr Cooke. 'Do come and join us. Pull up a chair. Perhaps that attractive lady behind the bar can bring you a drink.'

'That's all right, sir. I don't drink in the afternoons, as a rule.'

'Very wise. Glad to hear it, Foley. Well, it's very exciting to see everything here at last, in the flesh. The Britannia certainly seems to be packing them in.'

'Yes, sir, we've been doing exceptional business, for the last few weeks. When did you both arrive in Brussels?'

'We flew in yesterday. Mrs Cooke is here as well. And Mrs Swaine, of course. I believe they're sampling the pleasures of Gay Belgium, even as we speak. Combining business with pleasure, as it were.'

'Jolly good.'

'Yes, the four of us took a ride in one of those cable car things a little while ago. Gave us quite an overview. That's why Mr Swaine is looking somewhat green about the gills, I'm afraid. No head for heights, as it turns out. Think we might give the top of the Atomium a wide berth. Have you been up?'

'Yes, I have. Several times.'

'Queer sort of structure, if you ask me. But some people seem to like it. Each to their own, and all that.'

'Quite.'

'Anyway, we had a good look around the British pavilion this morning. Everything seems to be in good shape. That Mr Gardner may be a queer fish, but he's got a good eye, I'll give him that. The building stands out a treat, and all the displays seem to be ticking over nicely. Shame about ZETA, but I think we managed to wriggle out of it without too much embarrassment. Apparently there's a rather withering reference to it in the Soviets' news rag this week. Is that right?'

'I believe so, yes.'

'Well, can't be helped, I suppose. At least the papers have been nice about our pavilion. Hit of the fair, in some people's eyes. You know what they like about us? They say we don't take ourselves too seriously. Know how to laugh at ourselves, how to take a joke. Odd, isn't it? All that science, and technology, and culture, and history, and it's the good old British sense of humour that sees us through in the end. I'd say there was a lesson to be learned from that, young Foley.'

'I'm sure you're right, sir.'

'Wouldn't you agree, Mr Swaine? Dear me, I must apologize for my colleague, he looks as though he could do with a breath of fresh air and a good strong cup of tea. Come on, Ernest, give up on that fish, for goodness' sake.'

Mr Swaine laid down his knife and fork and mopped his brow with one of the Britannia's paper napkins.

'Terribly sorry,' he said. 'It's the heat at this place – the crowds – that blasted cable car.'

'And as for this pub,' Mr Cooke continued, with a disapproving look in Mr Swaine's direction, 'I've just been reading some of the comments in the guest book. Very impressive. Full marks for service and atmosphere. The place is clean, it looks good, the food is by all accounts . . . adequate, and the staff certainly seem to know their onions. And since you're the one who's been keeping an eye on the operation, I think you should have your share of the credit. You've been doing excellent work, Foley.'

'Thank you, sir,' said Thomas, blushing with pleasure.

'In the light of which, Mr Swaine and I are confident that we've reached the right decision.'

After an expectant pause, Thomas said: 'Decision, sir?'

'Exactly. There've been a few changes in personnel back in London recently. Last week Tracepurcel was poached by the Foreign Office. It's left us rather short-staffed and right now, we think we can make much better use of you back in Baker Street than here.'

Thomas looked from one man to the other, panic beginning to seize him. It was obvious what Mr Cooke was trying to say, but somehow his brain refused to process the information.

'We're sending you home, Foley,' Mr Cooke said, finally spelling it out. 'At the end of the week. Back to the bosom of your family – where you belong.'

Like a princess

Dear Miss Hoskens, Thomas wrote.

After considering the phrase for a few moments, he crossed it out and wrote *Dear Anneke* instead. Yes, that was better. Much more appropriate. He must try not to come across as cold. It was a frequent failing on his part, he knew.

Dear Anneke, By the time you read this letter, I will probably have returned to London. My employers at the Central Office of Information have decided that there is not much more work for me to do at the Britannia, or at Expo 58.

I would like to take this opportunity to thank you for all the . . .

For all the what? Thomas laid down his notebook and looked around the cabin, his mind scrambling for inspiration. He was sitting up on one of the beds. It was Friday evening, and he was due to meet Emily at the Britannia in just over an hour. His flight from Brussels was booked for nine o'clock in the morning. It was his last night. Was it cowardly of him, in the first place, to say goodbye to Anneke in writing, rather than in person? Not really. His conscience was clear on this point. He would be sparing them both an awkward scene.

I would like to take this opportunity to thank you for all the many happy hours I have spent in your company.

Not bad. 'Happy' hours, though? Could he not improve upon that?

Wonderful hours.

Memorable hours.

Hours of which I shall treasure the fondest memories for many years to come.

Terrible. And to think that he earned his living by writing for the public!

I do hope that if ever you get the opportunity to come to London . . .

No, definitely not. There was no point in prolonging the agony. And besides, in his newly lovestruck state (because he was suddenly and hopelessly in love, Thomas realized, with all things American) he did not envisage living in London for very much longer. New horizons were beckoning.

Best to keep the letter simple, and concise. But at the same time affectionate. After all, nothing much had really happened between them. The phrase he had used to Tony all those months ago – 'serious friendship' – still seemed a good way to describe it. He was sure that Anneke saw things the same way. The fleeting, charged moment of intimacy he had imagined between them last Saturday, as they had stood together in the buttercup field, must have been precisely that: the product of his own imagination.

Thomas ran a finger between his neck and the collar of his shirt. It was getting devilishly hot. All week the atmosphere had been growing more humid, and it wouldn't surprise him if there was a thunderstorm soon. Perhaps even tonight. In the meantime, wanting some fresh air, he took the wooden pole from the corner of his cabin and used it to open the skylight to its fullest extent. But it didn't make much difference to the temperature.

He picked up his notepad again and started writing. No point in agonizing over this letter any longer. He should treat it like any other piece of writing, composed to a deadline and targeted at a particular audience. He was experienced at this sort of thing. And besides, it was more important that he started to think about what he was going to say to Emily.

Entering the Britannia that evening, Thomas realized that it was the last time he would ever set foot in the place. In two months' time, when the Expo was over, it would cease to exist: at least, he assumed so. If there were any plans to preserve or relocate it, nobody had told him about them. He took a good look around the main saloon bar. It was crowded and noisy, as usual, and although most of the conversation was in English, he could make out at least three other languages being spoken at different tables. Mr Rossiter was behind the main bar, counting out change at the till while taking a none-too-surreptitious sip from the glass of whisky standing next to it. Shirley was doing her best to serve customers while reciprocating the attentions of Ed Longman, who never seemed to leave her alone these days. The scale model of the Britannia aeroplane was still suspended from the ceiling, threatening a knock on the head to anybody over six foot four who happened to pass beneath it. This had been Thomas's home for the last four months but tonight he was conscious, more than ever before, of its evanescence, its strange fragility. How could his life have been changed so profoundly by experiences which had taken place inside what was, essentially, a mirage? A place which would shortly be closed down, dismantled and finally unmasked for the chimera it most certainly was?

In the grip, once again, of the bizarre feeling that he was the only real person walking through a room thronged by ghosts, Thomas made straight for the bar, asked Shirley to prepare a couple of dry Martinis, and then managed to find a suitably secluded table for two in a corner near the main entrance. After only a few minutes, Emily appeared in the doorway and looked around for him. Thomas waved and beckoned and, as she came over, her face at once lit up by its habitual gleaming, immutable smile, he thought to himself: *Well, she looks real enough.* (Until he remembered, of course, that this was the same smile she turned on and off every day for the benefit of spectators to her *faux*-domestic activities at the American pavilion.)

'There you are, darling,' she said, kissing him on the cheek and pulling up her chair to sit close beside him. 'I don't suppose you had the foresight to order me a drink?'

'I did indeed,' said Thomas. 'Shirley will bring it over in a moment.'

'What an angel you are. I'm positively gasping for one.' She settled herself more comfortably in her chair, and quickly launched into a long story about the party of West German scientists who had come to the pavilion that day, asking a series of increasingly technical and complicated questions about the motor that powered her vacuum cleaner, and had then got very offended when she insisted that she didn't know the answers. 'They ended up complaining to my supervisor,' she said. 'Honestly, it's days like this that make me wish I was back in Manhattan. Even unemployment seems preferable, somehow.'

'Have a cigarette,' said Thomas. 'It'll help you relax.'

'Thanks. You're an angel. Did I say that before?'

'You did. But it bears repetition.'

As they were lighting their cigarettes, Shirley approached with a silver tray upon which two cocktail glasses were balanced.

'Here you are,' she said. 'On the house, naturally, Mr Foley. You can drink as much as you like tonight.'

'Thank you, Shirley, that's very kind.'

'I couldn't believe it when Mr Rossiter told me you weren't going to be here any more. The Britannia won't be the same without you!'

'What's this?' said Emily, turning to him sharply. 'You're leaving?'

Thomas sighed. 'I'm afraid so. The powers-that-be at the COI have given me my marching orders.'

'But when?'

'Tomorrow morning.'

Thomas was very slightly deflated by the impact his words had on Emily. She seemed only to have half-absorbed them. Her eyes, for some reason, were following Shirley as she walked back to the bar with the silver tray.

'So now you see,' he continued, 'why I was so anxious to have a drink with you here tonight.'

'Mm? Yes, quite. But this is shocking news, Thomas, quite shocking. Just when we were getting to know each other so well.'

'I know. The timing is wretched, from that point of view.'

'I shall miss you terribly, darling. I mean, the Lord knows, there are few enough friendly faces around here . . .'

Thomas took a sip of his Martini, and stirred it thoughtfully with the olive on the end of his cocktail stick. He knew that he would have to choose his next words carefully: they were among the most important he would ever speak in his life. It was not just his personal happiness at stake – although that was certainly, at the moment, the consideration uppermost in his mind. But there was also the not entirely negligible matter of the job he was supposed to be doing for Mr Radford and Mr Wayne. He opened his mouth and was just about to speak when he realized that Emily's eyes, once again, were elsewhere. Now she was watching Mr Longman as he left the Britannia and hurried away in the direction of the ornamental lake.

'Miss Parker . . .' he pressed on, regardless. 'Emily . . . I wonder if our . . . friendship has now become so advanced, that I might ask you a question that might in other circumstances appear presumptuous?'

'Excuse me?' said Emily, turning towards him with her glossiest and most disarming smile. 'I mean, I caught most of that but I'm not sure that I understood it. It sounded like something you might read in a Henry James novel.'

'Yes, perhaps I could express myself . . . more directly. Very well. Last Saturday, on our little excursion –'

'Which I enjoyed *very* much indeed.'

'– I shared with you some small details about my personal life. I was wondering, now, if you might – well, reciprocate?'

'Reciprocate?'

'Yes. I was wondering if you might . . . Well, I shall put this as bluntly as I can, Miss Parker, and damn the consequences. What I wanted to know was – are you a free agent, as it were? Is there a man in your life?'

But even now, it seemed, he did not have Emily's full attention. She had spotted yet another familiar figure, who was on the point of sitting down at a nearby table by himself: Mr Chersky.

'Oh look, Thomas, it's Andrey!'

She waved across at him, and called out a note of greeting. 'Coo-ee! Mr Chersky!' He looked up and gave them a smile and a politely questioning glance, in response to which Emily beckoned him over, only asking Thomas as an afterthought: 'You won't mind if he joins us, will you, darling?'

He had not had time to answer before Mr Chersky was already approaching the table, beaming with pleasure at this unexpected encounter.

'Well, well, well,' he said, drawing up a chair. 'Doesn't this demonstrate all that is good about the British way of doing things? Isn't this exactly what should happen when you walk into a British pub? The first thing you see is a couple of old friends. You'll permit me to sit with you, I hope, for a few minutes?'

'Of course,' said Thomas, making the words sound as frosty as he could. 'Would you care for a drink?'

'Martini!' said Andrey. 'How very metropolitan and sophisticated you both are. Myself, as a man of the people, I have rather more proletarian tastes. I'm sure Shirley will bring me my usual, just as soon as she's noticed I've arrived.'

He turned towards the bar, and caught Shirley's eye. She nodded back.

'Now then, Thomas, what's this I hear about you planning to desert us?'

'How could you possibly know that?' Emily asked. 'He's only just told me.'

'Oh, news travels fast at Expo 58,' said Andrey. 'Especially important news like this. You're leaving tomorrow, is that correct?'

'Perfectly correct.'

'Well, you will be sorely missed, I assure you. Your advice over the last few weeks has been invaluable, quite invaluable. I was just saying only the other day –'

He broke off as Shirley returned to their table, carrying a pint of Britannia bitter and the inevitable packet of Smith's *Salt'n'Shake* crisps.

'Miss Knott, you are the bringer of all that is good in my life,' said Andrey, putting his arm around her waist. 'Tell me that when the Expo is over, you will come back to Moscow to live with me as my wife, and devote yourself to my needs, supplying me with British delicacies on a silver platter whenever I ask for them.'

'Oh, Mr Chersky! You'll be the death of me, you will.'

'Tell me,' said Andrey, picking up the crisps. 'Is it just my imagination, or are these packets getting bigger?'

'No, you're quite right,' said Shirley. 'We've just had a special delivery in. These are the new jumbo-sized packets.'

'Jumbo-sized!' repeated Mr Chersky, marvelling. 'Astonishing. And I thought that life could not possibly get any better. Isn't there an English phrase, "Good things come in large packages"?'

'Small packages,' said Thomas.

'Ah. Thank you.'

'Well, just let me know if you need anything more,' Shirley said to them all. 'As I said, everything tonight is on the house.'

Thomas watched her leave, and took another, disgruntled sip of his Martini. He was already annoyed that Andrey had joined their table, rupturing the blossoming mood of intimacy between himself and Emily. He was even more annoyed that Emily herself did not seem to mind; or, indeed, even seem to be aware that anything had been blossoming between them at all. But what happened next was even worse: subtly, but unmistakeably, Emily shifted her chair away from him and towards Mr Chersky. She turned in his direction, too. She was actually turning her back on Thomas! She was leaning in towards the handsome Russian, her chin cradled in her hands, smiling at him, looking directly into his eyes. Thomas could not believe what he was seeing or hearing.

'Andrey,' she was murmuring, with a quite uncharacteristic girlish pout, 'I always thought it was *me* who was going to come to Moscow with you?'

'Of course,' he answered. 'You didn't take any of that seriously, did you? You know me by now. I'm a terrible flirt.'

'Yes, but sometimes you mean it, and sometimes you don't, and how's a girl supposed to tell the difference?'

'The difference,' he answered, 'is quite simple. When I say it to *you*, I mean it.'

Emily blushed and giggled.

'But then again,' he continued, 'in reality, *you* are the one who is teasing *me*. I know that you would never come with me. When you go home at the end of the Expo, you will forget all about me. The pull of your own country, and your own culture, is much too strong.'

'Not true.' Emily helped herself to a crisp and nibbled at it in a dreamy, preoccupied sort of way, her eyes still locked onto Andrey's. Thomas looked on in disbelief. It was the first time he had seen a packet of crisps used as an instrument of seduction. 'I'm dying to see your country. The wonderful buildings – Red Square, the Bolshoi Theatre, the Winter Palace at St Petersburg –'

'Leningrad, please,' Andrey corrected.

'Of course, I know it's not all like that. I know I probably have a romantic view of the place . . .'

'Most Westerners have a view of it which is not romantic enough, in my view. We don't all live in squalor.'

'Really? Well, what about your apartment, for instance? Is it comfortable?'

'I live very modestly, as befits my status as a humble worker in the newspaper industry.'

Thomas snorted. Emily and Andrey turned to look at him, momentarily, then resumed their conversation.

'Well, modest living has its virtues, of course,' Emily said. 'But personally, I think a little luxury doesn't come amiss, every now and again – wouldn't you agree?'

'Up to a point,' Andrey conceded. 'Up to a point, yes, I would agree.'

'For instance . . .' said Emily. She glanced over her shoulder, to see if Thomas was listening; and since it was obvious that he was, she moved in even closer to Andrey, as if purposely to exclude Thomas from this particular exchange. 'The accommodation they've found for me here is terribly shabby. So, do you know what I do, every so often, when it all begins to get me down?'

'No,' said Andrey, who seemed to grow more entranced by her with every second. 'What do you do?'

Emily took a handful of crisps and stuffed them into her mouth. Surprised, Andrey did the same.

'Well . . . I get in touch with my father, and he wires me some money over from home, and I use it to . . . pamper myself.'

'Pamper?'

'Yes, I book myself into the Astoria Hotel – into one of the honeymoon suites, actually – and I run myself a hot bath, and I order myself some caviar and champagne from room service, and for a few hours, I live . . . like a princess.'

'Like a princess . . . It sounds wonderful.' He took another mouthful of crisps. 'And you are all by yourself, when you do this?'

'Yes. All alone,' she said, thrusting her fingers into the packet again.

'And when,' said Andrey, finishing off the few remaining crisps, folding up the packet (as was his peculiar habit) and putting it into an inside pocket of his blazer, 'when do you next plan to spoil yourself in this extravagant way?'

'Tonight,' said Emily. 'In fact, I have the key to the honeymoon suite right here.'

From her handbag she produced a key, attached to the heavy brass tag of an expensive hotel. She held it up and dangled it before Andrey's eyes. Thomas looked on, his incredulity and outrage on the point of bursting forth in words when he was stopped short by a recognizably jovial English voice:

'Hello there, Foley! I was rather hoping to run into you here.'

Thomas wheeled around. It was Mr Carter, of the British Council.

'Would you care to join me at the bar for a moment? There are a few of us chaps from the Council. We'd like to wish you a fond fare-well, *bon voyage*, all that sort of malarkey.'

'Oh, well . . .'

Thomas looked helplessly at Emily and Andrey. It was clear that neither of them had any objection to him leaving.

'Fine. Yes. Jolly decent of you. Just a quick one, though . . .'

'Of course, old man.'

Mr Carter patted him on the back and steered him towards the bar, where for the next ten minutes Thomas was obliged to join a conversation in which he had no interest, with a group of British Council functionaries with whom he had nothing in common, while drinking beer for which he had no appetite. At the end of those ten minutes he glanced across at the table near the doorway – the table which he had believed, not so long ago, would be the set-ting for his own romantic evening with Emily – and was appalled, but by this stage not especially surprised, to see her leaving the Brit-annia in Andrey's company.

'Bloody hell . . .' he muttered, quite audibly. He put his half-empty glass back on top of the bar and, without even apologizing to the man who was in the middle of talking to him, slid off his bar stool. He was about to follow them when Mr Carter placed a gentle but authoritative hand on his shoulder.

'I say, Foley, don't go just yet. You haven't finished your drink.'

'Never mind that,' said Thomas. 'Did you see what just hap-pened? Did you see Mr Chersky and Miss Parker leaving together?'

Mr Carter nodded. 'Look, I'm dreadfully sorry. That's one in the eye for you, I'm afraid.'

'Yes, but it's not just that. We can't let him – I mean, he mustn't be allowed . . .' It was too complicated to explain. 'The point is, Carter, there's more to this than meets the eye.'

But Mr Carter was unflappable, as usual. He always seemed to know more than Thomas gave him credit for.

'Well, don't worry about that. Leave it with me. I'll make sure that . . . the right people are aware of what's going on.'

Thomas wavered, irresolute, as a group of four boisterous Portuguese tourists jostled past him on the way to the bar. Mr Carter stood aside for them, and then offered Thomas some final, well-intentioned advice.

'I should go home and pack,' he said. 'Or stay here with us, and get thoroughly sloshed. It's up to you – but I'd certainly know which one I'd do, if I was in your shoes.'

The easiest thing

In the event, Thomas realized that he did not want anything more to drink. For an hour or two, he took a solitary walk around the Expo park, saying goodbye to some of the familiar sights. Then he remembered that he still had a letter to deliver to Anneke.

There were distant rumbles of thunder in the air as he walked up the Avenue de Belgique towards the Grand Palais; but the rain was yet to come. For the last time (as he glumly reminded himself) Thomas crossed the Place de Belgique in the direction of the Hall d'Accueil.

The hall was still open; the overhead lights shone brightly and through the glass doors Thomas could see plenty of people passing back and forth across the lobby's vast floor space. Truly, this had become the city that never slept. At the entrance to the hall he paused and looked back down the Avenue de Belgique towards the Atomium, with its nine spheres brilliantly illuminated, like nine twinkling promises of a better future. It was the symbol of everything he had hoped to find at Expo 58. He couldn't believe that the adventure was now over; or that it had ended in such a bitter, unthinkable way. Emily and Andrey! Together after all! And in the end, Andrey had not even needed to do anything – not even click his fingers – to make Emily come running. The woman had literally thrown herself at him. Incredible. She had been transformed, within a few minutes, before Thomas's very eyes, from an intelligent, independent woman into a simpering floozy (yes, that was a good word – an American word, which made it even better) who brazenly whipped out the keys to a hotel room and more or less dropped them in her loved-one's lap.

Thomas's stomach tightened when he considered the possible

implications of tonight's disaster, the possible consequences of Emily's choice. His attempt to keep her away from Andrey had failed. He had let down his country. He had let down their American allies as well. What would happen next? It was beyond his understanding. Right now, it horrified him simply to think what a dreadful judge of character he had proved himself to be, and how many absurd, escapist fantasies he had built around this woman in the last few days. Images of them living together in a loft apartment in New York, a log fire burning in the grate and the crisp white snowflakes clinging to the windowpanes as winter swept over Manhattan . . . long summers spent in a log cabin on the shores of Tomahawk Lake, watching the sun go down as they cooked the day's catch over the grill, ochre sunbeams dancing off the waters of the lake . . . All of these visions, and many others, had been passing through his fevered mind this week, usually in the dark hours past midnight when he still lay poised between wakefulness and sleep, the fact of Sylvia's betrayal continuing to hammer at his unresponsive brain, demanding to be recognized, to be let in . . .

'Thomas?'

He turned. 'Anneke?'

She must have gone into the Hall d'Accueil to get changed out of her uniform, and was now walking down the steps, on her way to the Porte des Attractions, just as he would soon be. She was wearing that blue summer dress again (it was becoming more and more obvious that it was the only dress she owned) and was carrying a grey raincoat over her arm. She smiled at him and offered her cheek for a kiss. He gave it automatically, without even thinking.

'What are you doing here?' she asked.

'Well, actually, I was just coming to leave you a letter.'

'Really? You've written me a letter?'

'Yes.'

He took it out of his jacket pocket. It was quite crumpled by now.

'What does it say?'

Thomas was on the point of handing it to her. Then he thought better of it, and replaced the envelope in his pocket.

'I should probably tell you in person,' he said; and, taking her arm, he began to walk slowly beside her along the Avenue des Attractions, the gloomy bulk of the Heysel Stadium rising up to their left.

'What I wanted to tell you,' he began, 'is that I'm going home.'

'Back to London? When?'

'Tomorrow morning.'

Anneke stopped walking and drew back from him. She was shocked.

'I know,' said Thomas, 'it's very sudden, isn't it?'

But this was not what had shocked her. 'You were going to tell me this in a letter?'

Thomas nodded.

'That,' said Anneke, with quiet understatement, 'would not have been a pleasant thing to read.'

'I know. I see that now. It's a good thing I ran into you.'

He moved on, and Anneke followed him, but she did not take his arm this time.

'Shall I tell you something about myself?' Thomas said. 'I believe that I'm . . . a very confused individual.'

'I believe so too,' Anneke said. 'I've often found . . .' And then she hesitated. She was about to say something bold, and this did not come naturally to her. 'I've often found your behaviour towards me very hard to understand. In fact, it has been starting to make me angry.'

'Angry?'

'Yes. I have been angry with you. You never make your intentions clear. You invite me to your party, you come out with me and my friend, we have a lovely evening together – we have lots of lovely evenings together – but then I never know what you are going to do or say next. And then you start to take an interest in Emily, which of course I can understand, because she's very beautiful, but you can't be honest about it, you have to take me out for an expensive dinner and tell me this stupid story about how Mr Chersky is a spy and two strange men in raincoats and hats have asked you to look after her and protect her from him. At least Federico would never make up a story like that. At least with him, the intentions are always clear. I only met him two weeks ago and already he has asked me to marry him twice.'

'Really?'

Thomas could not help smiling. They looked at each other and laughed. The tension between them dissolved momentarily, but Thomas soon felt it begin to re-establish itself.

'Look,' he said, 'a lot of that is true. I do owe you an apology. But when I get back to London I'm going to start sorting things out. A lot of things in my life are going to change. I might even leave my job, move to another place, maybe even to a different country . . .'

They came to a halt, having reached the Porte des Attractions.

Anneke said: 'Why do you always talk about the future? What about now?'

He didn't answer.

'I'm not a shy young thing,' she continued. 'I wish you wouldn't treat me like one.'

They stared at each other. Then Anneke took Thomas's face between her hands and kissed him, full on the lips. It was a long, tender, melting kiss; and when, after a few moments, it came to an end, they continued to cling tightly to one another as the last remaining visitors to Expo 58 drifted past them on their way back to the outside world. Anneke stroked Thomas's hair and smiled up at him, her lovely, wide, open smile, and said: 'You see? It's not so complicated after all. It's the easiest thing in the world.'

Thomas was worried that they might be stopped by the Joseph Stalin lookalike in the reception hut, but Anneke had the solution: apparently there was a hole in the wire fence leading to the grounds of the Motel Expo, which was well known to many of the hostesses. They found it without too much difficulty, and squeezed through without being seen.

In the cabin, while Thomas was drawing the curtains, Anneke turned on the bedside lamp. The light was harsh and unforgiving, so she pulled her dress off over her head, and draped it over the lampshade, suffusing the room with a cool, pale-blue glow.

When this was done, Thomas stood and gazed at her, while she sat on his bed, half-naked in the turquoise light, waiting for him to come closer. They looked at each other for a long time, savouring the moment, the electric joy of anticipation.

The storm was coming closer. They could hear the thunder, and glimpse flashes of lightning, but there was still no rain over the Motel Expo. The heat, however, was stifling. The duvet had long since been swept to the floor. Thomas and Anneke lay on the bed together, uncovered, hotly entangled.

Thomas was wakeful, as usual. Anneke was breathing softly and regularly beside him. He had often imagined what it would be like to lie next to Sylvia in this way: not in a room shrouded in respectable darkness, not with their nakedness hidden from the disapproving gaze of non-existent spectators by layers of sheets and blankets, but glorying, without shame or embarrassment, in the fact of their intimacy. And now it was happening – but not with Sylvia: with another woman altogether: a woman who was not his wife. To Thomas, it was a shocking as well as glorious realization. Frankly, he would not have believed himself capable of this. He turned his head to look again at Anneke, feeling a wave of affection for the woman who had made it so easy, who had given herself to him tonight with such freedom and generosity. His lips brushed against her hair. It was only a tiny movement, but the warmth of his breath must have been enough to wake her, for she looked up, and her eyes flickered open, and she smiled a drowsy smile, and pressed herself against him even more closely.

'Not sleepy yet?' she asked.

'Not yet,' he said. 'Very happy, though.'

'Me too,' said Anneke, and planted a gentle kiss on his mouth.

In a few moments, she was asleep again. Thomas lay holding her for a while longer, enjoying the steady rise and fall of her breathing, the soft pressure of her breast against his ribs, and then carefully released himself from her embrace and rose to his feet. He went into the bathroom, cleaned his teeth and sat on the toilet for some minutes. More than ever, it felt unusual – and liberating – to be performing these actions in the nude.

Suddenly there was a bang from somewhere – a clap of thunder, possibly – and a small but unmistakeable scream from next door. Thomas ran into the bedroom and found Anneke sitting up on the bed. She was clutching her dress so that it covered most of her body, and the glare from the bedside lamp was painful to the eye.

'What's the matter?' said Thomas.

'I saw a flash,' said Anneke. 'Up there.' She pointed to the skylight.

'Lightning?'

'I don't know. Maybe. But then there was a noise as well – as if something was falling off the roof.'

Thomas pulled on his trousers, opened the door to the cabin and stood, bare-chested, in the doorway, looking up and down the pathway between the rows of buildings. For a moment he thought that Anneke might have been right, and that he could hear a faint noise: something like distant footsteps. But the sound was soon gone, and there was not enough light to see anything clearly.

He stood there for a few more minutes, breathing heavily, until he felt the first drops of rain on the palm of his outstretched hand.

He locked the door and climbed back into bed. Beneath the duvet, Thomas and Anneke finally drifted into an uneasy sleep at around four o'clock, just three hours before his alarm was due to go off. In his dreams, hearing the thick summer rain slap tirelessly against the skylight, Thomas mistook it for the sound of

The easiest thing

the audience at the Grand Auditorium, giving a prolonged round of applause as Ernest Ansermet stepped forward in front of the Suisse Romande Orchestra to take yet another triumphant bow.

Well and truly over

Thanks to the time difference between Belgium and England, Thomas's nine o'clock plane landed at London Airport promptly at 8.45 – fifteen minutes before it had taken off.

It was shortly after eleven o'clock when he arrived home, weighed down by his two over-filled suitcases. He knocked on the front door but there was no answer. He let himself in.

Inside the house, everything was silent. He left his suitcases in the hallway and sat at the kitchen table for a few minutes, listening to the gurgling of the water pipes and the intermittent hum of the new fridge switching itself on and off.

Thomas soon became impatient. The task which awaited him next door was not a pleasant one, and he wanted to get it over with as soon as possible. There was nothing to be gained by waiting a minute longer.

He left the house and marched up the garden path to the Sparks' front door. For once – perhaps because he was light-headed from lack of sleep, or still swooning from the thrill of the night he had spent with Anneke – Thomas was not troubled by any traces of doubt as to his next course of action. His blood was up, and he was going to do exactly what Emily had urged him to do: give Norman Sparks a punch on the nose. It was nothing more nor less than the swine deserved.

He rang the bell, and then had to wait a long time before it was answered. Finally, through the frosted glass of the front door, he could see a figure coming slowly towards him. It was Judith, Mr Sparks's invalid sister. She was wrapped up in a thin cotton dressing gown with a floral pattern, and her face wore its habitual blotchy pallor. She blinked at him as if her eyes were not accustomed to the daylight.

'Good morning, Miss Sparks. I was wondering if your brother was available for a few minutes' conversation?'

'I'm sorry, Mr Foley, he's down at the garage. The car's having its service. I'm sure he'll be back before long. Would you care to wait?'

'No, thank you. I've only just returned from Brussels, and I haven't even spoken to my wife yet.'

'Well then, I'll ask him to call on you, shall I?'

'If you would, yes.'

Deflated, Thomas wandered back to his own house – with a last, lingering, futile glance at the Sparks' front door – and went into the kitchen to put the kettle on. He had only been there a few minutes when he heard the door being unlocked and pushed open. It was Sylvia, struggling to manoeuvre Gill's pushchair over the doorstep and into the hallway while carrying a heavy wicker shopping basket. The two suitcases in her path didn't help.

Thomas emerged from the kitchen and there was a moment of stillness and wariness as their eyes met for the first time. It was almost two weeks since Thomas had discovered his wife's infidelity and in that time they had exchanged only a few words, over the telephone on Wednesday night when he had called to tell her, briefly and politely, that he would be coming home at the weekend. Doubtless she was offended, Thomas thought, at what she must perceive as inexplicable remoteness on his part: whereas he was feeling something far worse than offence; and with a good deal more reason.

'Hello darling,' she said. 'You're back already.'

'Yes. Couldn't you have waited in for me?'

'I didn't think you'd be home for another half-hour at least.'

She unstrapped Gill from the pushchair and set her down on the floor. The little girl began to waddle unsteadily towards her father, looking up at him with no obvious signs of recognition on her face. Thomas scooped her into his arms and gave her a kiss.

'Hello, little one,' he said. 'How have you been keeping?'

Sylvia squeezed past her husband as he cradled their daughter in the doorway of the kitchen, and put her shopping basket down on the table with a sigh of effort.

'Where've you been?' Thomas asked.

'Shops.'

'I can see that.'

'If you're making a pot of tea I'll have one.'

Without looking at him, she began to empty the shopping basket: tins of vegetables, tins of soup, some slices of ham from the counter at the supermarket, some packets of sausages. Thomas's heart sank when he saw them, at the thought of resuming a British diet. Sank, too, at the coldness of this homecoming. He really could not stand this atmosphere a moment longer. It was time to start the long, painful process of resolving the issue.

'Sylvia,' he said, placing Gill gently back down on the floor, 'we have something to discuss. Something very important.'

'Do we now?' said Sylvia, still absorbed in her unpacking. It seemed she had been to the chemist's as well, for now she was taking out baby powder, headache tablets and milk of magnesia.

'There is no easy way for me to say this,' Thomas began. 'So I shall be honest and direct. I know that, while I've been away, things have not always been easy for you. It was perhaps a selfish decision on my part, to –'

He broke off abruptly, and, stepping over to the kitchen table, snatched a small box from Sylvia's basket and glared at it, holding it at arm's length as though it were a foreign object.

'Good God, woman, what's this?' he said. 'Are you even doing Sparks's shopping for him now?'

Sylvia seemed to have no idea what he was talking about. Thomas lifted up the offending item – a box of Calloway's Corn Cushions – and brandished it under her nose.

'What do you mean?' she said. 'Those aren't for Norman. They're for me.'

Thomas fell suddenly silent. It took him almost half a minute to recover his power of speech.

'You? Since when have you suffered from corns?'

'Just in the last couple of months. I'm sure I told you once that they run in my family. Norman recommended these, because he has the same problem. In fact – weren't you there, the morning we talked about it?'

Thomas sat down at the table, and gazed vacantly into space.

'Yes,' he said. 'Yes, I was there.'

'I've been using them since . . . May or June, I suppose.'

There was a knock at the door.

'It's on the latch!' Sylvia called, and a few seconds later – inevitably – the amiable, ingratiating face of their next-door neighbour popped itself around the kitchen door.

'Good morning!' Mr Sparks trilled. 'And welcome back, Thomas! Sylvia told me you'd been given your marching orders. Dear me! Goodbye Brussels, hello Tooting. No more gallivanting around with *les belles dames de Belgique* for you. That's going to take a bit of getting used to, I should think. Now, what was it you wanted to see me about?'

Thomas raised his eyes slowly, and stared at his neighbour for a long time, without malice, without anger, without jealousy, without irritation, without anything except the sensation of a deadly numbness creeping all over him. It was true, he thought, that Sparks's nose still looked eminently punchable. But there was nothing much he could do about that.

'Do you know,' he said, speaking in a careful, laboured, measured tone. 'I've completely forgotten why I wanted to see you. It's gone clean out of my head. All I know is that I suddenly feel . . . very tired.'

'Ah,' said Mr Sparks, chortling in his usual offensively conspiratorial manner. 'No wonder you do. The morning after the night before, eh? Well, I'm afraid it's back to reality for you now, old man. Back to the marital grindstone. Back to the deadly old nine-to-five. Good grief, no wonder you look so glum! The party's well and truly over.'

*

The English summer had not lasted for long. Thomas and his mother sat on a bench at the top of Box Hill, close to the viewpoint at Salomons Memorial, and shivered in the wet afternoon air. It was a grey, misty Sunday, and there was no view across the weald today.

They both continued to stare fixedly into the distance, none the less. Since Thomas had made his revelations, and asked for his mother's advice, neither of them had looked the other directly in the eye.

Finally, Martha spoke. Her voice, always rather flat and toneless, sounded drier and more coldly emphatic than ever.

'I'm sorry,' she said, 'but to me it's obvious what you must do. You have a wife. You have a child. That means that you have duties, and responsibilities. It was a very stupid thing that you did in Belgium. Stupid in many different ways. To start with, anyone could see that Sylvia would never behave like that. She is completely devoted to you. Don't ask me why, but she is. Even after you decided to abandon her for six months, just when she needed you the most, she would still never be unfaithful. So that was your first stupidity, jumping to such a ridiculous conclusion. As for this girl in Brussels, what are you trying to tell me? That you thought you might leave everything behind here, and go to live with her? In Belgium? Are you completely stupid? How do you even know that this is what she wants? When thousands of strangers come together, from all over the world, in a strange atmosphere like that, of course stupid things are going to happen. Even now, she is probably regretting what you both did. She is probably telling herself that she did a stupid thing, and nothing like it should ever happen again. And she's right. So I'm telling you right now: forget all about her. She's not important. Your wife is important. Your child is important. Your family is important. Of course you feel unhappy now. That's because you've been stupid. But that will change. The feeling will pass.'

Thomas bowed his head, as a family of four walked by, the little children zigzagging from side to side and throwing a red plastic ball between themselves with shrill notes of instruction and excitement.

His mother's words had been agony to hear. Each use of the word 'stupid' had been like a blow to the skull. He said nothing, just let their meaning sink in, settle, find its place and its level. When he raised his head again the family had almost disappeared from view: he could just about still hear the cries of the children, bringing back a distant memory, some cloudy image of another time he had come to this place, as a young boy, with his mother and father. A picnic? Yes, they must have brought a picnic. Disorientatingly, this long-forgotten excursion, which he had not thought about for twenty or twenty-five years, probably, now felt more real and more recent than the picnic at Wijgmaal which had taken place little more than a week ago.

As if intuiting her son's train of thought, Martha Foley looked down at her lap, where she was holding the photograph Thomas had brought home for her.

'This is a nice picture,' she said. 'It was kind of you to do what I asked. I'm going to frame it and put it on the wall in the sitting room. But this buttercup field doesn't look at all how I remember it. Are you sure you went to the right place?'

He couldn't write to Anneke while he was at home. It felt all wrong, sitting at the bureau in the dining room long after Sylvia had gone to bed, staring at the sheet of Basildon Bond on which the words stubbornly refused to form, his fountain pen casting a long shadow across the page beneath the amber glow of his reading light. He wrote it at work instead, on his second day back at the Baker Street offices. The task he had been given on his return to the COI was scarcely inspiring: composing the voiceover commentary for a short film about underage drinking. He knew that he would not be able to apply himself to it until the letter was out of the way.

Even when it was finished, he was not happy with the result. How could he be? But he posted the letter anyway, on Wednesday morning at the post office in Marylebone High Street.

There was no reply for almost a month. He assumed that he was never going to get one. And then it came, delivered to his work address, garlanded with exotic Belgian stamps and franked with the official postmark of Expo 58.

Dear Mr Foley,

Thank you for your letter. It was very polite of you to write and explain your position – just what I would expect from an English gentleman.

Since this is how you feel, I am sure it would be best if we both forgot everything that happened during your time in Brussels. I would not like to cause you any pain, or any embarrassment; which I think are probably one and the same thing, in your case.

Rest assured that I will not disturb or intrude upon you in any way from this time onward.

In fact, allow me to borrow from your two friends – the mysterious men in raincoats and hats – a phrase which might prove useful to us in this respect: 'this conversation never took place.'

I remain respectfully yours

Anneke Hoskens.

Unrest

Sylvia was on her knees in front of the toilet. The Marmite on toast she had eaten for breakfast had just come back up. It was the third day in a row that something like this had happened. She gasped for breath and tore off some sheets of toilet paper, wiping her lips and wincing at the sour, rancid taste in her mouth.

Thomas was at his desk in Baker Street, feeling thoroughly depressed. Two items of news had just come his way. One was that his next assignment was to draft a pamphlet on the perils of drink-driving: it seemed that he was now first in line for any job with a connection to pubs, licensing laws or the consumption of alcohol generally. The other was that his friend and colleague, Carlton-Browne, had effectively just been promoted over his head, having been chosen for the much more prestigious task of writing the script for a big-budget public information film about the measures to be taken in the event of a nuclear attack.

'I think we're going to have another baby,' Sylvia said to him that evening, at the dinner table.

'I think it's time I looked for another job,' Thomas told her, as they lay awake in bed that night, side by side, holding hands beneath the sheets.

'I think we should move,' she told him the next morning, at the breakfast table. 'I don't like living in London. I never have liked it. I want to be close to Mum and Dad again.'

Things happened quickly. Thomas mentioned his plans to another colleague at work, Stanley Windrush. Word got around, and a few days later Carlton-Browne approached him in the canteen with some useful information.

'Chap I know knows a chap who reckons there's a firm in the Midlands looking for someone to head up their PR department. Sounds as though it could be right up your alley.'

The firm in question was a large manufacturer of car components, both for export and for the domestic market. They were based in Solihull, not far from central Birmingham and only a few miles from King's Heath, where Sylvia's parents lived. On the morning of Thursday, 16 October 1958, Thomas took the train from Euston station and arrived promptly for his interview at eleven o'clock. By eleven-fifteen, it was being made clear to him that the job was his for the taking. No references were requested. No questions were asked, in any detail, about his suitability for this particular role. The personnel manager simply told Thomas that he was 'just the sort of fellow they were looking for'.

He spent the next few hours agreeably enough, visiting the offices of local estate agents, and exploring the area on foot. Really, Birmingham was not half as grim as he had imagined. Compared to Tooting, these south-eastern suburbs appeared leafy, quiet and spacious. Walking along the wide, tree-lined streets close to the Cadbury factory in Bournville, enjoying the colours of fast-approaching autumn, he found himself easily able to imagine living here: he pictured himself escorting Gill to the school bus stop on spring mornings, the feel of her trusting hand clutched tightly within his; playing Sunday-afternoon football in the nearby recreation ground with his son (for they were both convinced that it was going to be a boy, and had already agreed that he should be named David, after Thomas's father). He was pleasantly surprised to learn that they could afford to buy a much bigger property here, and still turn a handsome profit on the sale of their house in Tooting. With the money they looked likely to make on the deal, he could easily afford to buy a family-sized car.

Thomas arrived back at New Street Station in plenty of time to catch his London train. He bought a copy of *The Times* at the station newsagents', and installed himself in an empty second-class compartment. He did not open the newspaper, though, preferring to gaze out of the window, lost in half-formed fantasies centred around the pleasures of family life, and the satisfactions of living as a solid, middle-class, respectable citizen. He did not tire of these agreeable daydreams until the train had passed Rugby: at which point the door to his compartment suddenly slid open. A young man in a British Rail steward's uniform looked down at Thomas and said: 'Mr Foley?'

'Yes?'

'Message for you.'

He handed Thomas a scrap of lined notepaper, and left without waiting for a reply. Thomas unfolded the note and read it. All it said was: 'Fancy a drink?'

Warily, he rose to his feet and, taking his copy of *The Times* with him, made his way down the corridor to the restaurant car. This, too, was empty: empty, that is, except for one table, upon which three glasses of whisky were resting. Three glasses of whisky, and a solitary packet of Smith's *Salt'n'Shake* crisps. Sitting on one side of the table, squashed together rather tightly on the banquette seat, were Mr Radford and Mr Wayne.

They looked up when they saw him, with every appearance of surprise and pleasure.

'Why, it's Mr Foley!'

'Bless my soul!'

'Here, of all places!'

'On this train, of all trains!'

'Do sit down, there's a good chap.'

'Take a pew, old man. Make yourself comfortable.'

'Whisky? We took the liberty of ordering for you.'

'Don't know why, just had a sort of feeling that you might show up.'

'Just a hunch, you understand.'

Thomas flopped down into the seat opposite them; taken aback, of course, to find that they were still following him, but more angry than anything else. These two ludicrous figures belonged to a part of his life that he'd assumed was long since over and done with.

'Good afternoon, gentlemen,' was all he said, investing the words with as much hostility as he could muster. He looked at the whisky but decided not to touch it.

'It's not poisoned, you know,' said Mr Wayne, sounding almost offended.

Thomas pushed the glass away, all the same.

'Cigarette?' said Mr Radford.

'No thanks,' said Thomas. He had given them up, and was trying to persuade Sylvia to follow suit. (Although, as a concession, he had agreed that she could smoke while she was pregnant. It was a stressful time for a woman, after all, and smoking did help her to relax.)

'So,' said Mr Radford, lighting his own cigarette with a gold-plated lighter, which he then passed on to his companion. 'Job interview went well this morning, I gather?'

'I see,' said Thomas, 'so you're still tapping my phone?'

Mr Wayne looked even more offended.

'I say, we don't go in for that sort of thing, old man.'

'You're not in the Soviet Union now, you know.'

'Well, you seem to know an awful lot about my movements.'

'Just taking a friendly interest, that's all.'

'Just finding out what you're up to.'

'After all, it's not as if you made any effort to keep in touch.'

'Not even a postcard.'

'Keep in touch?' said Thomas. 'Why should I?'

'Well, I don't know . . . Call us sentimental, but I thought we established quite a . . . rapport, out there in Brussels.'

'Did you, indeed?'

'Well, it's all water under the bridge now, anyway,' said Mr Wayne. 'The fair's almost over. This weekend, everyone will be packing up and going home.'

'I dare say there'll be something about it in the newspaper on Monday,' said Mr Radford.

Thomas made no reply.

'Of course,' Mr Radford continued, 'not everything that happened at Expo 58 was reported in the papers.'

'Far from it,' said Mr Wayne.

Mr Radford shook his head. 'That terrible business with Mr Chersky, for instance. Thank goodness *that* never got into the news.'

'Ghastly affair,' Mr Wayne agreed.

Thomas did not like the sound of this. He decided to rise to the bait.

'Mr Chersky?'

'Yes. Surely you heard what happened to him?'

'No.'

'No? That's extraordinary.'

'Well,' said Thomas, impatient now. 'What happened to him?'

'He died, of course.'

'Died?'

'Yes, poor chap. Died of a heart attack.'

'They found him,' said Mr Radford, 'in the honeymoon suite of the Astoria Hotel.'

Allowing time for this information to sink in, the two men sipped their whiskies, and then sat back, with a certain air of amused satisfaction, to wait for Thomas's response.

'But that . . .' he said at last, forming the words slowly and carefully, 'that was where Emily took him.'

'Really?'

'Is that a fact?'

'You know even more about it than we do.'

Thomas leaned forward, now, and the mounting anger could no longer be kept out of his voice. 'Come on, then. Tell me what you've got to tell me. Tell me what happened.'

'Well, I'm not entirely sure we can help you there,' said Mr Wayne. 'What do you think, Radford?'

Mr Radford shook his head.

'Shaky ground . . .'

'Thin ice . . .'

'Then again . . .'

'On the other hand . . .'

'We have already taken Mr Foley into our confidence, to a certain extent.'

'True, true.'

'He's already in possession of some of the facts.'

'Yes, you have a point.'

'Oh, shut up, the pair of you,' said Thomas. 'Was Emily involved in all of this? Has she been implicated?'

'*Involved?*' repeated Mr Radford.

'*Implicated?*' echoed Mr Wayne.

'Well, of course she's involved.'

'Naturally she's implicated.'

'You know that better than anybody.'

'You're involved too, after all.'

'And implicated, if it comes to that.'

'You had a role to play in the whole scheme.'

'And you played it very well.'

'In fact, one might almost go so far as to say that we couldn't have done it without you.'

'What *scheme?*' Thomas asked. 'Couldn't have done *what* without you?'

Mr Radford and Mr Wayne exchanged questioning glances, as if finally seeking confirmation from one another that they should let Thomas further into the secret. Now, apparently having reached agreement, they inched themselves forward, and Mr Radford began his narration in a low voice.

'Well, it all started right at the beginning of the fair. Even in the very first days, it became obvious that there was a . . . leakage of information, from the American pavilion. Certain pieces of confidential data were being passed to the Soviets. So the Americans came over and set up camp in that nice old country house you visited, and they started looking into it.'

'That was where Miss Parker came in.'

'Not her real name, you understand.'

'She was an American agent, of course.'

'But you knew that already.'

'No? Well, I would have thought it was obvious.'

'How could it be obvious?' said Thomas, in exasperation. 'You told me she was an actress from Wisconsin.'

'Oh, you don't want to take everything we say at face value.'

'That was just her cover. We assumed you'd worked that out for yourself.'

'Anyway. Before long, even though she couldn't see where the leak was coming from, she could see where the information was ending up.'

'With Mr Chersky.'

'And she could also see *where* he was receiving it.'

'At the Britannia.'

'The Britannia?'

'Yes. Your precious pub. That was the drop-off point. That was where everything was happening.'

Thomas could not restrain himself any longer: the whisky was too tempting. He picked up the glass and drained half of it in one draught. He could already feel every belief he had entertained about his time at Expo 58 tilting, being slowly inverted. A whole world of assumptions turned upside-down.

'But how?' he said. 'How was it being dropped off?'

'Ah – well, that was the beauty of it, you see.'

'That was the genius of the whole operation.'

'They had an accomplice, clearly.'

'Someone to do their dirty work.'

'And you know who it was, I imagine?'

'You can probably guess.'

But Thomas couldn't.

'Well, it was the barmaid, you see.'

He gaped back at them. 'The barmaid? Surely not!'

'Yes – Shirley Knott. Precisely.'

'You've got it in one, old boy.'

'You're beginning to cotton on, at last.'

Thomas sat back, and sipped at the whisky. Armed with this crucial new piece of the puzzle, he was starting to see the full picture take shape.

'Then the man who was passing things on to her,' he said, 'must have been that American who was always hanging around the place. Mr Longman.'

'That's right. The two of them were in cahoots.'

'In it together.'

'Up to their necks.'

'Both members of the Communist Party, as it turns out.'

'And of course, you know how they did it?'

'The beauty of the whole thing.'

'The fiendish ingenuity of it.'

'Well, Miss Parker worked it out just in the nick of time.'

'They were using these.'

Mr Radford lifted up the packet of crisps and held it aloft.

'Look,' he said, tearing the packet open. 'Inside every one of these is a little blue paper sachet, for the salt. Longman was using his position to get access to documents in the American pavilion offices, then transferring them onto microfilm, then putting them into one of these little sachets and passing them on to the barmaid . . .'

'. . . and *she* would slip them into a packet of crisps, and serve it to Mr Chersky.'

The two men shook their heads, in genuine admiration.

'Brilliant.'

'First class.'

'You have to hand it to them.'

'Then,' said Mr Radford, shaking salt onto his own crisps and offering them around, 'things finally came to a head. It happened one Friday afternoon – your last day at the Expo, as it happens.'

'Word reached Miss Parker that a new document had gone missing. A big one, this time.'

'The biggest of the lot.'

'It was a directory –'

'A list –'

'An index –'

'Of every American agent currently operating on Russian soil.'

'There were about fifty names –'

'Addresses –'

'Personal details – '

'And if this fell into the wrong hands . . .'

'. . . every one of those people was as good as dead.'

'However, by an amazing stroke of good fortune . . .'

'Not really – I mean, it was damn clever of her to work it out for herself.'

'Point taken, old man. That evening, you see, Miss Parker was having a drink with you at the Britannia, and she suddenly realized how it was being done.'

'The barmaid handed the packet over to Mr Chersky, with his beer, and she said something that made Miss Parker prick up her ears.'

'Something about a "special delivery".'

'And a "jumbo-sized" packet.'

'And that was when she saw it.'

'In a moment of inspiration.'

'In a flash.'

Thomas cast his mind back to that evening. It was true: Emily had been grabbing fistfuls of those crisps as if she couldn't get enough of them. It had amazed him at the time. And Andrey as well. They had been racing through the packet, each one trying to be the first to reach the salt sachet at the bottom.

'Well . . .' Mr Radford finished his whisky, and signalled to the steward for three more. 'Now, as you can imagine, she was in a quandary.'

'Mr Chersky had the sachet.'

'He had the sachet and the packet.'

'He had the sachet and the packet in his pocket.'

'He had the sachet and the packet in the pocket of his jacket.'

'So she couldn't afford to let him out of her sight. Not for a moment. She *had* to get it back off him, before he could pass it on to anybody else.'

'And this is where she really showed her mettle.'

'The stuff she was made of.'

'Because she took him back to the Astoria Hotel and . . .'

'Well, you can guess the rest.'

'She did the necessary thing.'

As the steward poured three more glasses of whisky, Thomas tried to recall where he had heard that phrase before, and realized, with a shiver, that it had come from Emily's lips, on the day of the picnic. That awful story she had told: about her father, the mild-mannered scientist, seizing hold of a fallen branch and using it to bludgeon a timber rattlesnake to death, driven to a frenzy of violence by the impulse to protect his own daughter's life. Had it been something like that? Had she used her own brute strength to kill a man? Or had she fired a bullet into his chest, stuck a dagger in his heart? Strangled Andrey with his own necktie? 'When it comes to safeguarding the things that are most precious to you,' she had told him, 'there can't be any limit on what you're prepared to do.'

'It was easily managed,' Mr Wayne now told him, in a tone of voice that was almost – almost – kindly and reassuring. 'She had a cyanide capsule.'

'They provide them with these things, you know. Standard issue, I believe.'

'She slipped it into his champagne glass.'

'Piece of cake, when you think about it.'

Thomas did think about it. And now, instead of picturing Emily, her face contorted with anger and revulsion, raining lethal blows down on Andrey's head, he found himself prey to another vision: a memory: a memory of Emily sitting opposite him in the bar of the Grand Auditorium, looking down into a glass of pale effervescent liquid and saying, 'I just adore champagne . . . I love to watch the way the bubbles dance in the glass.' Her eyes sparkling, her cheeks dimpled into a smile. No wonder Andrey had been distracted. No wonder he had not guessed what was coming to him . . .

'But I still don't understand,' he said, swallowing hard, 'how I got involved in any of this. You told me a pack of lies out at that house, and acting on your information – or rather, misinformation – I pro- ceeded to behave like an idiot, and . . . I don't see how that can have helped you at all.'

'My dear fellow,' said Mr Wayne, 'you underestimate yourself.'

'Your part was absolutely vital.'

'In what way?'

'Well, because there came a moment, in the whole operation, when it all looked like going wrong. The Russians were getting more and more suspicious about Miss Parker's cover story. Mr Cher- sky was getting to know her rather too well, and was beginning to wonder if she was really a naive young actress at all, or indeed really the daughter of the famous Professor Parker from Wisconsin. These people are temperamentally programmed to mistrust any- thing they are told –'

'Not such a bad idea, when you think about it.'

'And so somehow the Americans knew that they had to do some- thing to convince him. To *re*-convince him, if you like.'

'And that was when *we* offered to engage *you*.'

'Engage me?'

'Yes. Engage you to take Miss Hoskens out to dinner, at the res- taurant of the Czech pavilion, and tell her precisely what we wanted you to tell her.'

'And precisely what we wanted Mr Chersky to hear.'

'Namely, that Emily Parker was falling in love with him.'

Thomas looked from Mr Wayne, to Mr Radford, and back again, as the penny finally began to drop.

'That restaurant . . .' he said. 'That private room . . . it was bugged?'

'Of course it was.'

'And you knew it was bugged?'

'Of course we did.'

'So you knew that . . . everything I said in there . . .'

'Would go straight back to the Russians . . .'

'And straight back to Mr Chersky . . .'

'Which was just where we wanted it to go.'

'Simple,' said Mr Radford, spreading his hands.

'Easy as pie,' said Mr Wayne, shrugging his shoulders.

'And that was it? That was all you wanted from me?'

They nodded, in unison. And for the last time, another of Emily's once-mysterious utterances came back to him. The words she had spoken as they said goodbye after the concert, on the footbridge overlooking the lake in the Parc d'Osseghem: 'You've already done your duty,' she had said. And then, when he had protested at the word: 'You can consider your mission accomplished.'

He stared out of the train window for a long time. They were travelling through Buckinghamshire, one of England's most non-descript counties, but even this unremarkable landscape looked attractive at this time of year, in the late-afternoon sunshine. Thomas wished that he was out in those fields, feeling the moist and springy soil beneath his feet, breathing in the cool air instead of this foul cigarette smoke. Anything to clear his head, to give himself the time and space to think about all that he had been told.

'Anyway,' said Mr Radford, breaking the heavy silence at last. 'The point is, old man, that we're eternally grateful for your help.'

'As I said, we couldn't have done it without you.'

'Which is why we decided to do you that little favour in return.'

'What little favour?' said Thomas, turning away from the window, his eyes narrowing with suspicion.

Mr Wayne coughed. 'Well, you didn't exactly have to try very hard for that new job, did you?'

'More or less walked into it, from what I understand.'

Thomas did not answer. His silence seemed to unnerve them.

'Least we could do, really,' Mr Wayne added.

'Small token of our esteem, and all that,' said Mr Radford.

Thomas looked away again. 'I see,' he said, his voice flat with sarcasm. 'And you want nothing in return, do you? You're doing this entirely out of the kindness of your own hearts.'

'Well.' Mr Wayne coughed again. 'I'm not sure you should think of it *entirely* like that.'

'Everything comes at a price these days, as you know.'

'No such thing as a free lunch, as they say.'

'So?' He stared at them defiantly, accusingly. 'What are you after?'

'Now look, there's no need to panic . . .'

'No need to get in a flap about this . . .'

'We're reasonable men, after all . . .'

'We're not monsters, by any stretch of the imagination . . .'

'It's quite simple really. This firm you're going to be working for. They do quite a lot of business abroad. Some of it in the Eastern bloc. Poland, Hungary, Czechoslovakia in particular. Occasionally some of the management will be going over there –'

'Trade delegations, and so forth –'

'And we think there's a fair chance you'll be asked to go with them.'

'And when you do . . .'

'Well, there may be some little favours you can do for us, while you're out there.'

'Small errands you might be able to run.'

'Routine jobs that call for a reliable chap like yourself.'

'You see, Mr Foley, we like your style.'

'We like the way you operate.'

'We feel you're someone we can trust.'

'And that's pretty rare, in our line of work, I can tell you.'

Thomas smiled combatively, and shook his head. 'Well, I'm sorry to disappoint you, gentlemen, but I'm not running any more "errands" for you, or carrying out any "routine jobs". Once was quite enough, in my opinion. If you had any part to play in getting me that job, you have my heartfelt thanks, but now you can kindly leave me alone, to get on with my life.' He finished his whisky, set the glass down on the table, and started to get up. 'I trust I've made myself clear.'

For the third time in the last few minutes, Mr Wayne coughed, and then reached into a briefcase under the table. Mr Radford, meanwhile, laid a restraining hand on Thomas's arm.

'Just a minute, old man,' he said. 'Before you do anything hasty.'

Reluctantly, Thomas sat down again. He tried to see what it was that Mr Wayne was taking out of his briefcase. It appeared to be a set of black-and-white photographs – about twelve of them – but it was hard to be certain, because instead of spreading them out on the table, Mr Wayne fanned them out with their backs to Thomas, and held them jealously in front of his chest, like a bridge player with a particularly choice hand of cards.

'Now, we really didn't want to do this, Foley . . .' he began.

'But sadly you give us no choice,' Mr Radford concurred.

'You see, on the night that Miss Parker was doing her patriotic duty by dealing with the threat posed by Mr Chersky . . .'

'It seems that you had very different activities in mind.'

'You had a rendezvous with Miss Hoskens, I believe . . .'

'And took her back to the Motel Expo . . .'

'Where, by an extraordinary coincidence, our colleague Mr Wilkins . . .'

'You remember Wilkins?'

' . . . was roaming around with his camera.'

'Bit of a loose cannon, old Wilkins . . .'

'Bit of a lone wolf . . .'

'Takes a good photograph, mind you.'

'My word, Radford, have a look at that one.'

'Good lord. Doesn't leave much to the imagination.'

'Nor this.'

They both chuckled.

'I must say, Foley, you've certainly got an inventive approach in these matters.'

'And a highly versatile partner, I might add.'

'I wouldn't overdo this sort of thing, though.'

'You could put your back out if you're not careful.'

'Good grief, what on earth's that?'

'Where?'

'Here.'

Mr Wayne pointed at a detail in one of the photographs, while Mr Radford squinted more closely at it.

'That's Wilkins, I think. He's got his thumb in front of the lens.'

'Ah.' Mr Wayne put the pictures face down on the table, and said: 'Well, you get the general idea. It would be a tragedy if your wife saw any of these. A terrible tragedy. Probably send your whole marriage up the spout.'

'Of course, a puritan might argue that you should have thought of that before you got involved in any of these . . . shenanigans.'

Mr Wayne replaced all but one of the photographs in his briefcase, and then they both sat back, with their arms folded, smiling at him in the blandest, most infuriating way.

'By the way,' Mr Radford said, passing Thomas that one remaining picture, face down. 'We thought you might like to keep this one. As a souvenir.'

Thomas took the photograph, and slowly turned it over. It was a picture of Anneke, alone. It must have been the last one taken – while he was in the bathroom – just before Wilkins slipped from his perch by the skylight and tumbled down to the ground, waking her up with a thump and a bang.

He looked it at for a long time. God, she was beautiful, when you saw her like this: deep in her trusting sleep; naked; oblivious to the webs of deceit and betrayal that were being woven around her. It broke his heart to think that he had allowed her – however inadvertently – to be used in this way; and it broke his heart to think that he would never see her again; that the night they had spent together, the night that was receding faster and faster into the duplicitous shadows of memory, could never be relived.

What's gone is gone . . .

While he was looking at the photograph, Mr Wayne and Mr Radford glanced at one another, nodded their agreement, and quietly (tactfully, one might even say) rose to their feet and withdrew. By the time Thomas raised his eyes – now filmed with mist – rubbed them with his knuckle and looked around the restaurant car, the two men had disappeared.

Much later (many years later, in fact) he would find himself wondering why he had agreed to their terms, why he had let himself be cornered so easily. It would have been simpler, quicker and cleaner to tell them both to go to hell. Was his marriage really worth saving, at such a high price? Because the thing that struck him as most mysterious about his adventures at Expo 58 was not, after all, the improbable intrigue in which he had become embroiled, but the proven fragility of his loyalty to Sylvia during those weeks. As he grew older, it seemed to him more and more likely that he had done a cruel thing, not by marrying her, but by staying married to her. That was the real pity of it: that he had condemned her, through vacillation, to a lifetime of unrest.

Hollahi hollaho

On Sunday, 19 October 1958, the Brussels World's Fair came to an end. There was a final display of fireworks at ten-thirty in the evening, and the gates were closed to the public for the last time at 2 a.m. After that, from Monday morning onwards, only those with official passes could enter, and the lorries, tractors and removal vehicles arrived to begin the long task of dismantling the buildings. They were dispersed all over Belgium and, indeed, all over Europe. Some were turned into schools, some into temporary and then permanent housing. The Restaurant Praha from the Czech pavilion was taken apart and reassembled in Prague's Letna Park, where it was used first as a restaurant and then as an office building. Few structures remained on the Heysel site itself, although the Atomium continued to stand there, still open to the public but falling inexorably into neglect as the years went by.

On Monday, 20 October 1958, Thomas handed in his notice at the Central Office of Information.

On Monday, 1 December 1958, Thomas began working as Public Relations Officer for Phocas Industries Ltd in Solihull, Warwickshire. Shortly before Christmas that year, he, Sylvia and Gill moved to an address in Monument Lane, on the Lickey Hills on the outskirts of Birmingham.

In May 1959, Sylvia gave birth to a son. The boy was named David James Foley, after his two grandfathers.

On 30 June 1960, less than two years after the close of Expo 58, the Belgian Congo achieved independence. Today it is known as the Democratic Republic of Congo.

On Monday, 26 March 1962, a new pub called the Britannia opened at 41 Townwall Street in Dover, Kent, on the site of a former

Wine Lodge. According to the *East Kent Mercury* (23 March 1962), it was modelled on 'the famous pub of the same name which was specially constructed at the World's Fair in Brussels four years ago'. Included in its decor were many exhibits from the original Britannia, purchased at an auction in Birmingham some years before, one of the most prominent being the scale model of a BOAC Britannia aeroplane. It became only the second pub in the United Kingdom to serve Britannia bitter, as created by Whitbread in 1958 especially for the World's Fair.

In 1963, Thomas travelled to Bratislava in Czechoslovakia as part of a business delegation from Phocas Industries. It was the first of many trips he made to Soviet bloc countries throughout the 1960s and early 70s.

On 13 January 1967, the *East Kent Mercury* reported that the Britannia in Dover had become 'one of the most famous public houses in the world. Every year thousands of overseas visitors visit the Britannia to see the unique collection of nautical prints and models.'

In October 1970, Mr Edward Perry became the new licensee of the Britannia, inheriting the job from his father. Five years later, his own son took over as landlord. In 1980 the *Dover Express* noted that Townwall Street, the road on which the pub stood, was now 'with its dual carriageway, six times wider than its predecessor'.

On Friday, 4 May 1979, Margaret Thatcher became the first female Prime Minister of the United Kingdom.

Thomas and Sylvia's daughter Gill married in 1983, at the age of twenty-six. She had two daughters, Catharine (born 1984), and Elizabeth (born 1987).

On Thursday, 9 November 1989, the government of East Germany announced that all GDR citizens could henceforth visit West Germany and West Berlin. Crowds of East Germans started to cross the Berlin Wall, which was broken up piece by piece over the next few weeks, and destroyed for good using industrial equipment in 1990.

In 1996, David Foley and his wife Jennifer (from Melbourne, Australia) had their only child, a daughter called Amy.

By the late 1990s, the Atomium was still standing on the Heysel plateau outside Brussels, but, according to the official guidebook, 'a lack of maintenance had reduced the building to a pitiful state.'

On Tuesday, 15 May 2001, Sylvia Foley died, at the age of seventy-seven, of complications following a stroke.

On Friday, 3 October 2003, there was a launch party at the Britannia in Dover, which was under new management, to celebrate the opening of its restaurant and family bar. The new landlady said that from now on the pub would be welcoming children because 'it adds to the overall atmosphere'.

In October 2004, the Atomium was closed to the public for the first time in forty-six years, while a two-year programme of restoration took place. The main task was to replace the faded aluminium sheets on the spheres with stainless steel. The Atomium reopened on 18 February 2006, with new features including exhibition spaces, a fully restored restaurant and a futuristic dormitory for visiting schoolchildren.

On 17 November 2005, the landlady of the Britannia in Dover announced that she was planning to introduce regular pole-dancing nights in the New Year. She insisted that they would not be sleazy and told the press that 'people who would object to exotic dancing in Dover need to wake up. It exists all over Europe.' She also added that there would be no sexism because she would employ both male and female dancers. The *Dover Express* asked a number of regular customers how they felt about the plans, and found the majority had no objections. However, one local resident, aged fifty-three, argued that it was a sign of things going downhill and said, 'Where do they think we are, Thailand? This was a decent town once.'

In the spring of 2006, Thomas reluctantly moved into an annexe of his daughter Gill's family home in Oxfordshire.

On Sunday, 8 October 2006, Sylvia's younger sister Rosamond died alone at her house in Shropshire, at the age of seventy-three. The official coroner's report gave the cause of death as heart failure.

On Thursday, 30 November 2006, the Britannia in Dover opened for twenty-four-hour drinking.

In 2008, celebrations were held throughout Brussels to mark the fiftieth anniversary of Expo 58. Among other festivities, 275 Belgians born between 17 April and 19 October 1958 were invited to an evening reception at the Atomium, a series of commemorative postage stamps was issued, and a number of exhibitions and films were displayed in a new building called the 'Pavilion of Temporary Happiness'.

Also in 2008, the Britannia pub closed its doors for the last time. The premises were bought by the local council and stood unused for three years. In April 2011, the building was finally demolished. The site it once occupied currently stands empty.

On Wednesday, 4 November 2009, Thomas Foley, now aged eighty-four, was awoken at six-thirty by his radio alarm clock, tuned to the *Today* programme on Radio Four. He sat up at once, aware that he was going to do something special today, but unable – temporarily – to remember what it was.

Then he recalled that he was travelling down to London. He would connect from Paddington to King's Cross stations and then take the Eurostar to Brussels. It would be mid-afternoon by the time that he arrived. After checking into his hotel, the Marriott on Auguste Ortsstraat, he would walk to the Central Station, taking a train to Antwerpen-Berchem, then a taxi to the suburb of Kontich, where he had his dinner appointment.

It was a busy schedule, in other words. But it felt good to be doing something, for a change. He had been too much prone to idleness lately.

Gill drove him to the station, and stood with him as they waited for the London train to arrive.

'You will be careful, won't you, Dad?' she said. 'You're getting on now, you know. Not many people your age still travel by themselves.'

'Do I look like an invalid?' he said.

But Gill was right. It was a foggy day in Brussels and the streets were damp and slippery. On his way from the hotel to the Central Station, walking up Infante Isabellastraat, he had a fall. Luckily he did nothing worse than graze his elbow, and there were two young women – American tourists, as it happened – close at hand to help him up again; but still, he took it as a warning sign. He was getting very old. Too old to be travelling alone, perhaps.

Why had she chosen Antwerp, for God's sake? Why this unlovely suburb of Antwerp, in particular? She still lived in Londerzeel, he knew that, so why could they not have had dinner at the Atomium? It would have been much closer, for both of them, and of course it was the obvious location for a sentimental reunion. He'd not seen it since the restoration work was finished, and now he was going to have to make a special trip there tomorrow morning, before going back to London.

And a Chinese restaurant, too . . . Why come all the way to Belgium to eat Chinese food?

Dusk was just beginning to settle as the taxi stopped and started its way down Koningin Astridlaan. It was five-thirty and traffic was heavy. Very early to be having dinner – but again, that had been her idea, and old people, he supposed, got set in their ways and no doubt she was in the habit of eating early. Chicken chow mein, however, was the last thing he felt like right now.

The taxi driver was confused; possibly lost. He kept consulting his GPS and had already driven back and forth along the same stretch of road three times. Thomas shivered in the back of the car and wiped some condensation from his window, peering out into the blue-black light, punctuated at regular intervals by the misty amber coronas of the streetlights. Fog was beginning to gather. Finally the driver let out what Thomas assumed to be a volley of Flemish swear words, and swung the car violently off the main carriageway to the left. They had now entered a forecourt in which perhaps half a dozen cars were parked. The taxi came to a halt and Thomas clambered out, paying the driver thirty-five Euros, which included a generous tip to assuage his guilt for bringing him to this remote part of the world.

Then he stood uncertainly on the forecourt, looking at the building ahead of him, an imposing wooden structure which bore the name of the Peking Wok restaurant. Should he go inside, and wait for her there? He was a few minutes early, and it would do him good to have a calming drink before seeing her again.

Just then, however, the decision was made for him. From one of the parked cars ahead of him came an unmistakeable signal: the headlights flashed on and off, and for an eerie moment Thomas was transported back through the years, more than half a century, to an evening in the summer of 1958, the twilit street just outside Josaphat Park, when he was being manhandled by that idiot Wilkins, and the driver had been waiting for them, in that absurd little Volkswagen Beetle. The same flashing of headlights . . . The sense of déjà vu was dizzying, at first, it was enough to paralyse him and hold him to the spot. But then the car-door opened and a woman stepped out, closed the door, and began walking towards him. And there she was: quite unmistakeable, practically unchanged, even after all this time: Clara.

They kissed each other on the cheek, three times, the Belgian way, and held each other in a close, friendly hug. Both were wearing thick overcoats, so there was little sensation of bodily contact. Clara held the hug for rather longer than Thomas did. When she eased herself away, she turned and gestured towards the dark, looming building which, although only twenty yards away, was already becoming indistinct, half-shrouded in fog.

'So, what do you think?'

Thomas did not know what to say. This place seemed to hold some significance for her which he could not fathom.

'You don't recognize it? But you've been here before.'

'I have?'

'Yes.' She looked at him with that smile, that slightly too beseeching, slightly too needy smile which he remembered so well, and
said: 'Doesn't it look a little . . . *Bavarian* to you?'

Recognition dawned, and suddenly the wide, low angles of the
roof, the long balcony running the full width of the upper floor, the
amiable Germanic heaviness of the whole design, took on a stag-
gering familiarity – despite the fact that the word 'WOK' was spelled
out at the apex, in gigantic pseudo-oriental calligraphy.

'My God,' said Thomas. 'It's the Oberbayern!'

'Of course,' said Clara, her eyes sparkling with pleasure at the
surprise she had sprung upon him. 'After the Expo, they brought it
here, lock, stock and barrel, and here it's been ever since. It has had
many uses. This is only the latest. Shall we go inside?'

The lighting inside was dim, but good enough to see that the
interior bore little resemblance to the space in which, fifty-one
years ago, Clara, Tony, Anneke and Thomas had sat along a
crowded trestle table, draining German beer from quart-sized
tankards and raising a toast to 'cheer and good times' while the
orchestra pounded its way through a medley of Bavarian drinking
songs. The tables were laid mainly for four, and the decor was clean
and angular, with low ceilings, a multitude of pot plants arranged
on shelves and in alcoves, and a self-service buffet counter running
alongside one wall. They seated themselves close to this, and took
off their coats.

'It's good to see you, Thomas,' said Clara, when they were settled.

'You too.'

She had emailed him a few months earlier, having tracked him
down easily enough through an internet search engine. Her motive
for making contact had been quite simple, and in her characteristic
direct way she had made no secret of it: she wanted to know if
Thomas had stayed in touch with Tony Buttress. Did he know what
became of him? Thomas replied that he had not maintained close

contact with Tony after Expo 58, but they had sent cards to each other every Christmas until 1998. And that year, the card had been signed by Tony's wife alone, and contained a note with the news that he had died in the autumn, only a few months after a diagnosis of lung cancer. 'That is sad,' Clara had written back. 'My own husband died last year. I must admit that I was hoping your friend was still alive, and perhaps widowed. I was fond of my husband but I never forgot Tony, never for a single day. It would have been pleasant to spend my last years with him.' There had been no mention, up until this point, of Anneke. But Thomas could wait no longer to find out, and in his next email had asked if Clara knew where she was. 'Alas, she too is no longer with us,' she replied. 'She passed away five years ago. I would tell you more, but it would be easier to speak in person. Do you ever find occasion to come to Belgium? It is so easy now, to get here by train.'

So, that had been the bait with which she had drawn him towards her again. Further information about Anneke. But she seemed to be in no hurry to impart it, this evening, and in the meantime, Thomas had to admit that it was pleasant to see her again, to bathe for a while in their pool of shared memories. Clara would be in her early seventies now, he supposed, but she wore the years lightly. Of course, even in her twenties, she had never looked especially young: there was something curiously ageless about her, which had worked to her disadvantage then, and worked to her advantage now: her short, reddish-brown hair looked no different, either in colour or in styling; her figure remained robust and stocky; the few wrinkles sat easily around her unflinching brown eyes. Thomas found himself warming to her, this evening, and feeling comfortable with her, and this had never really been the case – if he were to be honest – back in 1958.

'That night, you know – the night we came . . . *here* –' (she gestured around the restaurant) '– it was so important to me. I knew that you wouldn't understand at the time, none of you, so I didn't try to explain. But you have to imagine what it was like for me and my family, after the war. We lived in Lontzen, in the East Cantons of Belgium. This part of the country has a very difficult history. Until the end of the First War, it was part of Germany. And then in 1940 the Germans took it back again. The people who lived there had very mixed feelings about this. Some of them felt more German than Belgian. At the end of the Second War, in 1945, many people from the East Cantons were accused of collaborating with the Nazis. And, of course, some of them had: but most of them hadn't. But we were made to feel ashamed of our language, ashamed of our culture. There was a movement to "de-Germanize" us. And for my own family, it was even worse when we came to live in Londerzeel. Many of the people in Flanders hated us; they ostracized us. They thought that we were the enemy. So that night at the Oberbayern . . . To see so many people gathered together, from so many different countries, having such a wonderful time, so happy together, singing German songs, eating German food . . . It felt as though the nightmare was over. It felt as though I was being accepted again. It was one of the happiest nights of my life.'

By the time that Clara had confided these things to him, their plates were empty and they had eaten their fill. Thomas poured her what was left from their bottle of Riesling and said: 'And do you remember that other time, when you cycled out from Brussels to have a picnic with us, by the side of the river, not far from Leuven?'

Clara laughed. 'How could I forget? I came with Anneke and Federico.'

'That's right. I'd forgotten his name. I wonder what became of him.'

'She married him, of course.'

There was no reason, no sensible reason, why hearing these words should strike such a blow. But even as Clara spoke them, Thomas could feel himself being weighed down by something dull, something creeping: some spreading, cancerous mass. The leaden sadness of it was overwhelming. It came from somewhere within him. He could feel it slowly rising up, in his gut.

'Really? Is that what she did?'

'Yes. They were engaged even before the Expo ended. A few months later, she had already left Belgium. She went to live with him in Bologna.'

'I didn't think . . . I didn't think she even spoke Italian.'

'She soon learned.'

'What did she do there?'

'They had two children. A girl, Delfina, and then a boy. I forget the boy's name. Anneke worked for a long time in a shop, I believe. She worked very hard. Federico was a good man, but lazy. He was always complaining about feeling ill, always taking time off work. He stopped working altogether, when he was still quite young. He became very fond of this game, this Italian game – what is it called? *Bocce*. He became very fond of it, and very good at it. It took up most of his time, playing it with his friends. He used to enter competitions, travel round the country. And Anneke would stay in Bologna, with the shop, with the children. A hard life for her, I think. Anyway, that's really all that I know. We lost touch with each other a long time ago – in the 1960s, I would say. I have a picture from that time, though – something she sent me. Here.'

She passed him a photograph, some four inches square, its colours bleached and faded. It showed Anneke sitting beside a table, inside some house – her own house, presumably – with a pretty, dark-haired, seven- or eight-year old girl on her knee. Taking it between finger and thumb, Thomas gazed at it intently. He had only ever seen one other photograph of Anneke, a very different photograph, which he had always kept in a locked drawer at home, and had only rarely trusted himself to look at in the intervening decades. To see her in this entirely different role, looking so motherly, and so happy (he had to admit it), was disorientating.

'I can make you a copy if you like,' said Clara.

Thomas nodded and, with a powerful sense of reluctance, handed the picture back to her, after giving it one more lingering glance. Then he fell into silence. It was hard to tell whether Clara could see how affected he had been by her news. There was still a note of pronounced – if forced – cheerfulness in her voice when she said: 'And that other woman who came on the picnic – Emily, the American. You must remember her.'

'Oh yes.'

'Of course you would. The thing I remember best about that day was that it made me feel . . . invisible. Emily and Anneke were so good-looking, and the three of you, you three men . . . You never really looked at me.' Her voice was matter-of-fact, almost jaunty. 'Oh yes, I was used to it, I suppose. But in another way, you never get used to it. It always hurts. Knowing that you are plain, in a world which is obsessed with beauty.' She took a long sip of her wine. 'And so, did you keep up with Emily? Do you know what happened to her?'

'No,' said Thomas, forcing out the words. 'No, she just seemed to vanish. She just seemed to vanish into thin air.'

'Ah, well. That's how it was, in those six months. People passed through, came and went.'

The mood between Thomas and Clara never quite managed to recover, after that. It was only a little after eight o'clock when she looked at her watch and announced that it was time to go. 'I want to be back before nine o'clock,' she said. 'I belong to a club. We all play cards together. Bridge. It's nothing special, but I don't like to miss it. There are always a few men there and – of course I already know most of them already, but still . . . You never know. You never know what might happen one day.'

Thomas insisted on paying for the meal. Out on the forecourt, in the yellow half-light thrown from the restaurant windows, he thanked Clara for bringing him here; and meant it. It had been good to see this place again, this vestigial reminder of that unique moment in their lives: a moment poised on the edge of the future, when past conflicts had been left behind, and anything had seemed possible.

'Yes,' she said. 'Expo 58 will never be forgotten. Not in Belgium.'

They went through the ritual again, the three kisses on the cheek, and the friendly hug, and then Clara was just about to walk to her car when she turned and said: 'I lost touch with Anneke, but I did see Federico again.'

'Really? When?'

'He came to Brussels last year, for the fiftieth-anniversary celebrations. There was a party for people who had worked at the Expo, from all the different countries. You weren't invited?'

Thomas shook his head. 'I haven't been on the mailing list of the Central Office of Information for many, many years.'

'Ah. Well, Federico came. In fact, we had quite a long conversation. And he told me quite a curious thing.' She paused, and Thomas could see the glimmer of that smile on her face again: the somewhat chilling smile she always prepared when she was about to throw a surprise at him. 'Apparently, their daughter – Delfina – was born in May, the year after the fair. Which always puzzled him. He thought it was early, much too early . . . It made him always believe that the father might have been someone else.' She avoided Thomas's eye, busied herself instead with buttoning up her overcoat. 'But he was a good man, as I said. It never made any difference, to how he treated her. She would be fifty now. The same age as your boy David.' She looked up at him again, waiting for him to speak. She waited and waited; but still Thomas did not respond. Finally, Clara said: 'I'll make you a copy of that photograph, as I promised.'

'Thank you,' said Thomas at last, his throat now tighter and drier than ever. 'I'd like that.'

'And the next time you come to Belgium,' she added, brightly, 'come in the summer, and we can go to Wijgmaal, and have a picnic together.'

'Yes,' he answered. 'Yes, that would be nice.'

'Can I give you a lift anywhere?'

'No, thank you. I think I'd like to walk.'

Clara nodded, and as she turned towards the car, Thomas heard her begin to sing a tune under her breath. A tune he had not heard for more than fifty years:

Laß sie reden, schweig fein still
Hollahi hollaho
Kann ja lieben wen ich will
Hollahi aho.

She climbed into the car, started the engine and turned on the headlights. It was a hybrid model and the engine made almost no sound. The driver's window opened smoothly and through it Clara smiled and waved at him one more time. As the car nosed its way out into the line of traffic, he heard the words again, and the lilting melody:

Laß sie reden, schweig fein still
Hollahi hollaho
Kann ja lieben wen ich will
Hollahi aho.

But now, Thomas could no longer be sure that it was Clara singing. He wasn't sure if the tune was floating back to him from her car window, through the moist and wintry air, or if it was just echoing and rebounding inside his head, from all those years ago. Was it real, or imagined, or remembered? Sometimes, these days, it could be hard to tell the difference.

Acknowledgements

My first debt of gratitude is owed to Ann Rootveld, of Belgian Radio One. It was Ann who suggested interviewing me on location at the Atomium in September 2010, thereby sparking my fascination with this extraordinary building and, soon afterwards, the whole history of Expo 58.

Lucas Vanclooster answered all my queries about Expo 58 with a promptness and thoroughness beyond the call of duty. Annelies Beck was a constant source of wisdom, advice and Flemish translations. Both of them read my manuscript with great attention to detail: their comments were invaluable.

As before, the writing of this novel was made possible by several residences at the Villa Hellebosch in Flanders, funded by the Flemish government under the Residences in Flanders scheme administered by Het Beschrijf in Brussels. I would like to express personal thanks to Alexandra Cool and Paul Buekenhout; to Ilke Froyen and Sigrid Bousset; and to my fellow residents Ida Hattemer-Higgins, Giorgio Vasta, Saša Stanišić, Ófeigur Sigurðsson, Corinne Larochelle and Rhea Germaine Denkens.

Special thanks are due to Marcela Van Hout, who generously shared with me her Expo memorabilia and her memories of what it was like to be a hostess at Expo 58.

Staff at the Koninklijke Bibliotheek van België helped me to locate surviving copies of *Sputnik* magazine, from which Honoured Worker of Science Prof. Yuri Frolov's article 'The Man of the Twenty-first Century' is extracted verbatim; Jane Harrison at the Royal Insitution in London made copies of Sir Lawrence Bragg's papers relating to the British presence at Expo 58; and Sonia Mullett at the BFI arranged screenings of archive footage.

Further help, advice and inspiration in its various forms came from Rudolph Nevi, Marc Reugebrink, Stefan Hertmans, Paul Daintry, Ian Higgins, Tony Peake, Nicholas Royle and Chiara Codeluppi.

This novel draws on many published sources, most notably: James Gardner's self-published memoir *The ARTful Designer* (1993), from which I learned the story of the replica ZETA machine; the day-by-day calendar of the fair contained in Jean-Pierre Rorive's *Expo 58 . . . ambiance!* (Tempus, 2008); Jonathan M. Woodham's excellent chapter 'Entre plusieurs mondes: le site Britannique' in *L'Architecture moderne à l'Expo 58* (Dexia, 2006); and, for many details on the espionage background, *World of Fairs: the Century-of-Progress Expositions* by Robert W. Rydell (University of Chicago Press, 1993).

My description of the Britannia's interior in the chapter 'Rum sort of cove' is taken more or less verbatim from the souvenir booklet *The Britannia Inn: Universal and International Exhibition, Brussels* (Whitbread, 1958); the story of the Britannia's successor in Dover, and its subsequent fate, was found at http://www.dover-kent.com/Britannia-Townwall-Street.html.